THE
QUANDARY

OTHER BOOKS BY
JOANNE SOUTHERN:

Yesterday's Shadows
A Walking Shadow
Nets Of Gold
Keeping Mum
Taking Stock
The Emperor's Women
The S.O,B.
Doin' It
No Smoke Without Fire
Romany Legacy
A Grievous Burden

Check out the web page at
www.joannesouthernbooks.com

THE QUANDARY

A NOVEL

JO-ANNE SOUTHERN

PRIMIX
PUBLISHING
THE WRITE CHOICE

Primix Publishing
11620 Wilshire Blvd
Suite 900, West Wilshire Center, Los Angeles, CA, 90025
www.primixpublishing.com
Phone: 1-800-538-5788

Published by Primix Publishing   10/21/2021

ISBN: 978-1-955177-37-5(sc)
ISBN: 978-1-955177-38-2(e)

Library of Congress Control Number: 2021920894

CONTENTS

"Love in a hut, with water and crust is - love, forgive me - cinders, ashes, dust; Love in a palace is perhaps at last more grievous torment than a hermit's fast."

John Keats, 1795-1821

CHAPTER ONE

Surrey, England, 1959

"You'll bring the children home?" the doctor asked as they stood by the coffin.

She nodded, unable to speak.

John was dead. Hard to believe, but he was *dead*. His death had so devastated her that, though he lay in front of her white and still, it seemed unreal. Seven days later it was still a horrible nightmare. Putting out a tentative hand, she touched his face: cold, as cold as she felt inside. Numbed with shock, she felt somehow removed from everything, as if she were in another world where sounds were muted and people only blurred shadows.

Even as she experienced bereavement, she struggled to quench the anger that rose in her, knew she should not blame it on him. Yet how could he have done this to them? She drew back from the coffin, her eyes repelled, unable to comprehend the finality of it, grasping at the vain thought it was only a nightmare, yet knowing it was real. How cruel God could be, although now she was not so sure He existed.

One moment she had everything. At the age of 36 she had no worries about the future: had a loving husband, three children, and a dream home. Then, in a split second, all her dreams crumbled into ashes. Abandoned, her mind repeated, abandoned with three children to support. Her life was without a focus, and she felt old, older than her years, shriveled up inside, like her heart had died with him. It was, she knew, going to take her a long time to come to grips with her loss. Grief consumed her, yet how could she be so selfish, think only of herself? Other people had survived worse tragedies, had gone on alone after horrendous catastrophes, yet she could not think any further ahead than the next few days.

The doctor took her elbow and steered her to a chair. As she sat dry-eyed, her brain seemed stuck, like a needle on a cracked record. Repeatedly, it wondered how John could have done this to her. Death was something beyond his control, but he could have looked after his health, could have seen a doctor now and again, could have watched his diet. She sighed, deciding introspection was useless when all she saw ahead was an uncertain and frightening future.

The children. Yes, she must call the children. From the second it happened she had wanted them with her. Then reality took over when the doctor said the authorities required a postmortem, and the effect this would have on them was not lost on her. She kept delaying that phone call, not wanting to disrupt their secure little world of academia where each day brought no shocks and many pleasant surprises.

In the past few years, the children had grown away from her, became little adults with their own personalities and foibles. Vincent, the eldest, was a verbose individual with definite tendencies to socialism: this, she supposed, in rebellion against his materialistic father. Patricia, or Trish, the "Complete Princess," believed the world owed her everything and had her own selfish ways of attaining her goals.

Robert was her love. Robby, the youngest, outgoing and cheerful, saw the good in everything and loved life. She shook her head, knowing Patricia would see things as an inconvenience that would not bother her until something she wanted was withheld. Vincent would pompously assume the role of man of the family, and little Robert would be upset.

"Would you like me to call the schools for you?" Dr. Matheson asked now, breaking into her reverie.

"No, I have to do it myself." She picked at her bitten nails, thinking John would not like to see them. He always expected perfectly manicured hands. She wrapped her hands around each other, hiding her mortification as if he could see from the coffin.

"I think I'm being selfish, Doctor." He regarded her with surprise. "If John had been more open with me, if he had shared his problems, told me what arrangements he had made in case anything happened, I might cope better. However, he never did, and now something terrible has happened, I have no idea of our financial circumstances. All I know is that a trust fund pays for the children's education."

"Hmm," he murmured.

"You know, Doctor, John was the type of man who played his cards close to his chest. He kept the bad to himself, let me live a trouble-free life, and I, fool that I am, never pushed him for details."

Dr. Matthews cleared his throat. "This is common in many families, especially here in England. The public schools of the last two generations taught many men to think, they, being the breadwinners, should shoulder the financial responsibilities. I think you told me your husband attended a public school here."

"Yes, worse luck." She could not help the scathing tone.

"Never fear, Mrs. Montgomery, things will sort themselves in time. I'm sure once you go through your husband's papers, his desk, and his files, things will become clear."

"I surely hope so, Doctor." She thought about that for a moment. They lived well, never seemed to lack for anything. As their standard of living had improved, their surroundings became plusher, until now people regarded them as an upper-class family.

Gail nodded to a neighbor who had come to pay his respects, but his gaze slid away from hers. Now she came to think about it, the people who came to the funeral parlor avoided her chair. British *sang-froid*, she supposed. She saw their figures through a haze, her mind recognizing neighbors and a few people they had entertained, and wondered why they ignored her. The doctor told her that this system of "laying out" was something comparatively new in England, that usually the body lay in state at home, or in a side chapel of a church, the lid to one side. The undertaker would close and tighten the lid once the visitation was finished. How barbaric that seemed.

Now she wanted to be alone, to go home and huddle in the large double bed: hide from this terrible nightmare, take a sleeping pill. She forced herself to smile at the doctor who stayed by her side, finding some comfort in his solid presence.

The family had moved to England from Toronto when John's company made him director of European operations. A well-educated, energetic man, John had always longed to return to the land of his birth, so the English posting held obvious attractions. Working for an American company, he told Gail, meant they could live a lifestyle far improved to that of their previous spacious, although cookie-cutter, apartment home.

His salary afforded them the best of living conditions. Starlings, the large country home they rented in Surrey, was luxurious and comfortable. Because John had attended a British school, he wanted his children to have the same opportunity, now all three attended prestigious and historical institutions.

Since they used the house to entertain for the company, the firm paid half the rental cost. Gail particularly loved the entertaining, considering it the best part of her role as John's wife, and they entertained almost weekly when he was at home. Activities filled her days, and time rarely weighed on her hands.

Now she agonized about when to fetch the children home for the funeral. She must tell them of the sudden death but feared upsetting them. No, she must wait until she could speak without hysterics. The coroner's report stated John had suffered a massive heart attack, that nobody could have helped him. Knowing she must make the phone calls, she decided to wait until the body had gone to the funeral parlor, but even then kept procrastinating. How much a coward she felt, and procrastination did not help.

Even so, she felt ambivalent about their attendance at the internment. John, she reasoned, was often away from home, sometimes for as long as six months, or in one case 18 months, so they were not close to him. School protected them, and they would, with the resilience of the young, accept his absence from their lives. No, it was the internment that bothered her. The act of burial was horrible to a young, impressionable mind. That she knew firsthand, when at the age of six, a streetcar had killed her grandmother. Gail could clearly recall her fright at the funeral, because too young to comprehend death, she thought her Gran was shut in the box, still alive.

"All right?" Dr. Matheson said as he stood. "I'll get you a cup of tea."

She nodded. Tea? The English thought tea cured everything. She focused her eyes on the room where people stood around like a tea party, speaking in murmurs, looking everywhere but at the coffin in its flower-laden alcove.

It had happened so abruptly. One minute John, smiling after a delicious supper, stood leaning against the mantelpiece, drinking a large brandy, the next, he lay dead at her feet. Sudden death was better, the doctor had said, held little pain, no forewarning, no presentiment. However, John being John, even if he'd had a twinge or a hint of something wrong with him, would never have told her.

Having not been involved in a death before, and with so much to arrange, she had not known where to begin, particularly since she was residing in a foreign country. The doctor offered his assistance.

Immediately after the doctor signed the death certificate, she telephoned the company in Chicago. Without apparent delay, they dispatched an officious young man by the name of James Watson, who arrived at the house within twelve hours. He arrived on the doorstep as she finished signing papers for the necessary autopsy. James assumed control at once, saying his responsibility was to tie up the loose ends of the business. She could barely abide his presence as she waited for the coroner to release John's body to the undertaker.

The doctor, Eric Matheson, whom she knew socially, sent an undertaker to the house. Stonelike and unfeeling, she sat as a funeral director showed her photos of coffins and explained the government red tape necessary for the internment of an alien.

Gail wanted to send the body back to Canada - until she spoke with John's few remaining English relatives. When she notified them of his passing and mentioned her plan, they insisted she bury him in the land of his birth. So here she was, in what the English called a funeral parlor, staring down at a stranger who wore John's face, wondering what she was going to do next.

CHAPTER TWO

The children arrived home to attend the funeral. Vincent's attitude to her was one of the death being her fault. He snottily informed her that he would run the family when he got his degree. Gail smiled at his naivety and said nothing. Trish, on the other hand, seemed to think a holiday was just the thing; her father's death had not yet made any impression. Robert seemed terribly upset, and Gail comforted him.

"I don't suppose you'd want to stay in England without your husband," Dr. Matheson had said. "That being so, your children will also return to Canada, without their father. Surely it is better they know about his death now; otherwise, they might assume he has deserted you and them for another woman."

"They'd never think that." His words shocked Gail, but he was right. *Children are very imaginative,* she thought, *better do as he suggests and tell them now.*

"They might like to attend the internment," he said. "This, if nothing else, will afford closure."

So while she did not agree with his last statement, he had lifted the decision from her shoulders. She telephoned the schools to request their return home.

She called 16-year-old Vincent first. He sounded offhand, his speech clipped. Talking quickly so she would not cry, she visualized him in the headmaster's study, tall and slim, his thick hair falling over his eyes as usual. He wanted to be a man, to make his mark on the world, to publicly display his abilities. His grades were always excellent.

Then she called Trish who sounded sulky. "But Mother, we're having an away game tomorrow. Do I really have to come? I'm playing centre."

"Yes, Patricia, you must come home. This is important. Your father is dead and this is his funeral." God, how blunt must she make it?

"All right but you must talk to Matron and tell her it isn't my fault." Now her tone was indolent. Gail visualized her leaning against the desk, primping her hair with those long fingers. At 14, Patricia was already a femme fatale in her own mind, aware she would marry well and into a good family. From where she got those values, Gail could not imagine. *"Princess Patricia,"* she thought, smiling grimly. How on earth could she make the girl see the gravity of the situation?

She could not speak to Robert, who was on a paper chase with his class. The headmaster said he would make sure Robert caught the correct train and would call her with his time of arrival. Poor Robert, he was so sensitive and would be heartbroken. Now nine, his intellect was of someone much older, but he was her baby, her last child, and the one she loved the most.

Peculiar that she thought that way, as Vincent, her firstborn had been her pet, until he became aware of his position in life, attended school and became a snob. Patricia - how she had longed for a daughter - was such a sweet baby until she learned to speak, from which time she definitely ruled the roost. Robert alone was uncomplicated, a normal little boy.

Gail thought no further than the funeral, the formalities of death, but Dr. Matheson was right about one thing: she could not remain in England without John's financial assistance. Life has a way of reasserting itself over grief, and the daily problems of living became glaringly apparent. She scanned the mail eagerly, hoping for a letter from the company with an enclosed insurance check. Even if the money was enough to pay for essentials, she realized she would need a job, even while convinced nobody would employ her. Although she had a university degree, she never worked in business, had no experience, considered herself lacking in practical qualifications, and was a foreigner here. No longer could she brush these thoughts out of her mind while she dwelt on her loss. She must shake off her apathy, help herself break free of depression, take charge.

Now Gail looked around the warm, cosy living room of Starlings with its overstuffed chintz-covered furniture, gazed through the latticed windows at the lush, green countryside in the distance, the closer flower garden. She saw John everywhere she looked: in his favorite chair, or outside pruning the roses, sitting by the window to read a book, or poking at the fire. She knew it would be a wrench to leave. Gail then experienced another sense of loss, of the physical anticipation of turning her back on something she loved. It had become a real home to them, so returning to Canada to live in a cramped rental apartment would be difficult.

Since their marriage they had never stayed anywhere long enough to buy a home, residing, instead, in rented houses or apartments in Canada and the States. Before the children were born, they had also lived in Beirut, Lebanon, Nassau, Jamaica, Australia, New Zealand, and many other locations to which the company assigned John.

Their longest tenure had been this English posting. Before that they leased a large four bedroom apartment in Toronto, and all their larger possessions remained in storage there. They had arrived in Surrey to live in another rented home with their clothes and little else.

The day of the funeral was warm and sunny, which made Gail feel even more despondent. She wondered why it was not raining and dismal, and did not want it to be light and summery looking. In her melancholy, she craved rain and grey gloom.

Earlier she had made Trish change clothes twice, pointing out that one wore dark colors to a funeral. "Oh mother, you are so old-fashioned." Trish snarled.

Vincent wore his best suit and a black tie. Robert was in his school uniform, hair slicked back with water, looking somber.

At the house later, John's relatives talked about how wonderful John had been, how educated, how energetic, how pleasant. They repeated improbable anecdotes about his childhood until Gail thought she would scream. John had been one of life's gentlemen, she admitted. He was elegant, slow to anger, warm to strangers, able to talk to anyone without stress. When they first met, he had great ambitions, aspired to power and prestige. Sadly, he somehow missed the greatness, though he settled for comfort and a good home life.

How they laughed in the first years of their marriage. Everything was an adventure, everything was humorous even when things went wrong. Back then the darkest of clouds hid a shining day, but now the dark clouds threatened to envelop her. Gone were the days of loving, of being together, although John was often away for months on end. The difference being that in those days, she knew he would return.

Even when alone she could not say it aloud. "John is dead." Today she watched his coffin being lowered into the grave, said her last farewell, gently talked to the children and tried to offer comfort. She did all the things expected of her, yet could hardly swallow the bitterness that escalated and threatened to overwhelm her. What had she ever done that God should punish her this way? She had been a good wife, a good mother. No, this self-abasement was a waste of time.   Throughout the past week, outwardly dispassionate, she had not yet cried. It was as if the grief sealed her tear ducts, somehow enabling her to walk dryeyed through the entire ceremony, numbed and reproachful.

The children took it well, not being close to their globetrotting father. John had regularly missed birthdays and special school celebrations. She observed their detachment with pride, although she speculated whether they realized he was really gone forever. None were too chatty, although she heard them talking to each other about how he had died, and because she could not possibly know their true feelings, she decided not to raise the subject. Talking about the finality of the situation with children seemed impossible, as she felt unable to handle any more than her own grief, so management of upset children seemed beyond her present capabilities.

Patricia, in particular, was noticeably offhand, and tossed her head as if this unfortunate death was an imposition, as if the gathered mourners were an annoyance for which she blamed her mother. Gail foresaw difficulties in dealing with Trish.

A month after their arrival in England, the older children had begun attending public schools, so naturally Gail grew apart from Patricia and Vincent. She recalled now how it upset her to see them leave, how soul-destroying to watch them go to schools that seemed institution like and cold. After a while she accepted their absence and wrote them long letters. Each month she received a duty letter from each of them and heard how well they liked their school chums, how they liked the teachers, how super it was at school. At first, this hurt her feelings, but John pointed out they were learning independence while getting a first-class education.

Gail wanted were her babies back. They had entered school as children but too quickly assimilated other personalities, as though the act of leaving home turned them into pintsized adults. She now regarded the older two as strangers, felt uncomfortable with their new personas, because their learned values were now completely alien to those they held back in Canada.

Somehow the British school system had transformed them into miniature English, upper-class snobs. She recognized their seemingly callous behavior was not really that, although in Trish she sensed a hidden enmity. It was, she thought, simply the fact that they were still too young to envision the finality of death. What a shame they had never allowed them to have pets, she thought. Pet ownership would have taught them something. After musing about this, Gail realized she probably could not explain death to them in words they would understand.

Watson, the briskly efficient company man, quickly went through John's papers, contacted the branch offices and agents, and installed himself as a tenant of the house almost before she was aware of it. They ignored each other, meeting sometimes for scanty meals, although James preferred to dine at a local restaurant. This made less work for Gail, who had not yet regained her appetite.

They held the catered funeral tea in the library. Now as she talked to John's elderly and stooped aunt, she glanced around the room and spotted James talking on the telephone that seemed so much a part of him.

In true British 1950's fashion, the GPO had installed a single telephone in the library, neglecting to provide even one extension. How annoying it was to receive dead-of-night phone calls, and quickly dash downstairs to stand cold and shivering. John had taken many such calls.

James stuck a finger in his ear and glared at a deaf, elderly couple standing close by, chattering loudly about a perennial bed in the centre of the lawn. Gail could see his annoyance, could almost read his mind, but since it was a funeral, he could do nothing. She tactfully steered the couple over to the buffet catered by a local restaurant, and James flashed her a lukewarm smile of thanks.

When the guests had depleted the buffet, finished the sherry and whisky, and the caterer cleared the table, they all decided to leave. They left en masse, as if staying longer might be impolite. Gail accepted their condolences, silently thanking God they were departing. All the stock phrases rolled off their tongues, all the platitudes. Knowing what to say at such times was difficult, she knew that, but even only half listening, she needed much patience not to appear rude. All the repetition, she thought, all the phoney words of sympathy from people she hardly knew.

Gail knew none of John's English relatives well, and, though they expressed compassion, they were hardly chatty or warm. As they were leaving, they said all the right things, but in her heart she knew their attendance was a matter of doing their duty, nothing more.

The two blacktied and pin-striped company executives, who attended for reasons of courtesy, did not stay long. They each took one cup of tea and a ham sandwich, after which they closeted themselves in the kitchen with James Watson. Without even saying "hello" to her, they sneaked out by the side door. She felt annoyed, for surely they could have spoken a few words to her, the widow. Surely diplomatic protocol demanded that at the least?

The house grew quiet.

Sent outside to amuse themselves, the children were on the lawn, screaming and laughing. A day away from boarding school was a treat, and they did not seem at all affected by the day's events. She vaguely wondered if she should go outside and ask them to be quiet, but why bother? Children were children. Gail smiled as she saw Patricia trip over a croquet hoop and land on her behind.

"Nice to see them happy and carefree," James Watson said from behind her, making her jump.

She turned back to the living room window to watch their enjoyment of life, free from the confinement of school and house. "Yes, it is," she said, knowing appearances lied. "I was worried about the effect the funeral might have on them, but they apparently seem to have weathered it well. I wish I felt as unconcerned, Mr. Watson."

"Could we have a chat, Mrs. Montgomery?" James asked in a sober voice. Gail immediately turned around, as the tone of his voice sent a cold chill down her spine. Something was decidedly wrong.

Taking a seat on the couch, she waited until he sat in the wing chair across from her.

"Mrs. Montgomery, please let me assure you the company does not wish to cause you any hardship at this sad time." He looked uncomfortable and fussed with the crease in his pants.

"But?" Gail said quietly, forming her hands into fists, sensing he was going to say something terrible.

"The company has requested me to ask you to vacate the house before the end of the month. The new director and his wife want to move in by the first." She saw James almost squirm at having to deliver this news.

"Gee, they're all heart, aren't they?" she said sarcastically. "Sorry," she apologized, "I shouldn't shoot the messenger. I know you're only following orders, but this is terrible. I must confess that I have no idea about John's finances, and I have nowhere to go in Toronto." She could hear herself gabbling but was unable to stop the flow of words. "John worked so damned hard for this company for over 20 years, and now they want to get rid of us, his family, before he's hardly cold. Why didn't those two geeks in the pinstripes say anything to me? This is preposterous! I can't get things in order so quickly. I need more time." Her mind raced in top gear, thinking of all the problems caused by this ultimatum. "Anyway, the children are in school, and I think the least the company can do is allow us to stay on until they finish the school year. Let them put the new people elsewhere until I can move out. I think it's the very least they can do for twenty years' dedicated service."

"I really don't think that's possible, Mrs. Montgomery." James moved uncomfortably in his chair. Gail knew he had his orders, had probably done this countless times before for various reasons.

He glanced around the sumptuous room. "You cannot possibly afford to stay here alone. The company will not pay half the cost as they did when John was, er…" He paused uncertain of what word to use. "er, here, and I'm sure you cannot carry the rent alone. Unless, of course, you have the means."

She stared at him blankly, knowing he had not listened to a word she said and did not care about her circumstances. He would say nothing to the head office about her situation but would evict her and the children without a qualm.

He stood and extended his hand. The interview was at an end. *Goddamn man*, she seethed, *he has no heart.*

James smiled, relieved the worst was over. "Well, I'll leave it with you, Mrs. Montgomery. I do hope we won't have any animosity. I'll be staying on to look after business until the new man arrives." He stood, walked into the library, and sat behind the desk ignoring her as he picked up papers.

She collapsed onto the sofa in the living room and wound a strand of hair around her finger, twiddling with it, unable to sit still. What could she do? She was homeless and alone. Penniless, apart from the few dollars she had sent back to Canada, which was hardly enough to pay the rent on this huge house. She felt boxed in and completely discouraged.

Night after night she had lain awake, thinking about the injustice of it, thinking how stupid she had been not to learn about their finances. How abandoned she felt, how humiliated to announce to perfect strangers that she was destitute. Suddenly, her grief fell around her like a heavy, woollen shawl, and she burst into tears. She wanted to leave the place now, wanted to get away from the memories threatening to overwhelm her. She could not tell the children of this latest catastrophe, would write to them instead. Surely they had heard enough bad news.

She heard the library door close softly. James had heard her outburst and, not wanting to get involved, had shut her out of his world. That made the tears come faster.

CHAPTER THREE

D r. Matheson prescribed pills to help her sleep at night and a sedative to calm her during the day. The pills, however, could not help her cope with the overwhelming responsibility of arranging their return to Canada, so she kept procrastinating.

"Tomorrow," she told herself, "I'll do it tomorrow. Somehow I'll be all right, somehow I'll weather this storm, somehow a savior will come to my rescue." Her loss left her so devastated that she could hardly think straight. Things had turned out all right for Scarlet O'Hara so she felt sure they could turn around for her as well.

She wandered around the huge house, wondering where to start. As was usual with couples who moved from country to country, they had accumulated many things from England and Europe. This conglomeration of souvenirs required having a company pack and ship them to Toronto, and the only place she could send them was the storage warehouse where they stored their other household goods.

A letter arrived from the company and she almost kissed it before she tore it open. This must be the insurance check.

Then she gasped with shock. The tiny amount stupefied her, she could not believe how niggardly the amount of John's insurance policy. She had expected, had hoped, she and the children would be financially secure, but this was not so. James Watson, trying to appear sympathetic, told her that if John had died on duty, the company would have doubled the amount. Nevertheless, since he had been at home, was not entertaining and, therefore, not on business, the amount was small. When Gail objected, pointing out they were residents in a foreign country, he told her that counted for nothing.

After she paid the undertaker, the caterer, and received a quotation from the exporters for shipping the packing cases to Toronto, the remainder was about enough to pay their economy airfare back to Canada.

Gail felt cheated and decided to call the head office. If only she were financially solvent, she thought, these problems would vanish. Money couldn't solve all her problems, but it could at least make life easier and less stressful.

Angry, she telephoned the head office in Pittsburgh and spoke to John's superior. He glibly, in a smooth, practiced and patronizing tone, assured her they were not liable for return air fares.

"Surely you could find yourself a place to stay in England," he said. "Didn't you tell James Watson that your children are in school?" When she said yes, he said, "Simply take the children out of their expensive schools and request a refund. Under the circumstances, they can hardly refuse. That should cover any costs you may incur." He sounded so damn imperious that she almost swore.

After much begging and arguing on her part, the answer remained the same. Yes, she must move out of the house, and yes, the insurance policy was correct, and no, they did not class John as a higher executive, though he was a director. Director was simply a name they gave their European supervisors.

More shocks awaited her. The company had demoted John when he assumed his present position, he informed her, something John never thought to impart. The company had taken away his position as divisional vice president when he lost a lucrative contract in Saudi Arabia.

Her heart plummeted. What else had John kept from her? Did she really know the man after all these years? For hours after this conversation, she cursed the company, the company that was so efficient that it took over from John almost before they buried him. Sure, big business operated that way, particularly some American corporations, but why could they not have taken her feelings and those of her children into consideration? The trouble with mega-corporations, she fumed, was that all the family feeling was gone, and they operated strictly as a profit-making concern.

The man she had married suddenly became a stranger. How much else had he not thought to share with her? His demotion might be the least of it. His failure to impart their financial situation and leave her in a position of insolvency, began to weigh heavily. She hated him, really hated him. John had ruined her life.

Gail's depression was a private thing. Refusing to allow herself to become addicted to sleeping pills, she lay for many sleepless nights thinking about her past life with John, strangely remembering the good times and few of the bad. She could almost smell his aftershave, recall how the skin of his back felt beneath her amorous fingers, and yet he was a man hidden from her. She had never really known him. They'd had good times, of course, many of them. Later she thought, strange how usually a person's death infers sainthood on them, although by no stretch of the imagination, could I call John a saint. No, I guess he was my other half, and I feel incomplete without him.

Unwilling to share her heartbreak with the children, in front of them she acted as if life was normal. They stayed outside most of the time, scouting around the grounds or wandering around the village. She cooked their usual meals, although she had no appetite.

One afternoon she talked with the doctor who had called in to see how she was. Over tea and biscuits, she unburdened herself. "I can recall our arguments over his lack of consideration for me and the children when they were small. While he was gallivanting around the world living a life of ease in plush hotels, I struggled with toddlers in a small apartment in Chicago. While he was in Australia, sunning and swimming, bar hopping and barbecuing, we shivered in sub zero weather in Juneau, Alaska. How often I cursed John and his trips to Japan or Thailand or India, when I saw the children off to school each morning. How often I told myself I would put my foot down when he got home, would insist he find a job in the States or Canada, where we could settle and become a regular family." She smiled ruefully. "But I never did insist and he never did offer."

"Still, you knew what his job entailed when you married?"

"Yes, but I was fresh from college, madly in love, and thought we would live happily ever after." She shrugged and smiled ruefully, "A normal enough daydream for a young woman in her late teens. I had not yet learned about life."

"No, I suppose we're all like that. We learn from experience because, with the wisdom of youth, we already know it all."

She nodded. "Together we were magic, a well-matched team." She chuckled. "I remember how we always resolved my outbursts in the same way. He brought me flowers and wine, and we finished up in bed while he showed me how much he really loved me."

Dr. Matheson patted her hand. "I'm afraid most men are like that, even myself, I'm sorry to say. We all like to think we're the lord and master."

"Once, he tried to force me into the type of social life I hate. That was when we lived in Saudi Arabia. I essentially became a wellkept prisoner in a residential compound. I didn't like the other wives much, and they, in turn, I suppose, thought of me as a snob. When we first arrived, I tried to get to know the other women but soon discovered we had nothing in common."

"I don't suppose such a disparate group would ever really click."

She grimaced. "John was very annoyed. "Don't you ever get together with the other wives these days?" he once asked me, "I haven't heard a word about Florence or Carol lately." I told him I didn't see them, and didn't want to either, as we had nothing in common. You know, Dr. Matheson, their petty gossiping and back stabbing annoyed me immensely. I much preferred to stay within my own four walls."

Her mind flashed back to that evening meal.

John threw down his fork. "You know what your trouble is, don't you? You have no feelings, can't relate to others, and have no personality. Nothing about you attracts other people."

"How could you say that?" she had hissed, mindful of the maid hovering as she removed empty plates.

"It's true, though. I don't know how you ever became an executive's wife. The company expects you to act the part, you know, expects you to be involved with the other wives and families. It reflects badly on me when you shut yourself away as if you were too good to mingle."

How John needled her over her lack of fellow feeling. However, that served to point out that she was also a company employee, albeit an unpaid one, but still an employee. Putting her mind to it, she became an appendage of John Montgomery, trained to smile, talk, flatter, and entertain clients, her own personality subdued to make him look good.

For the sake of her marriage, she tried hard. She learned to smile and talk with morons, tried to give the impression that John Montgomery's wife was congenial. It galled her, but eventually, she learned to do it well and smiled as if she were really enjoying every minute of pure boredom.

Now she said sadly, "Over the years I gave up so much of myself for him, yet where has it got me?" She shook her head and stirred her tea, knowing the doctor did not want to hear this litany of self-pity. *I'm here and alone,* she mused, *cast adrift in a tossing sea of adversity. I have nothing to show for the years except three children and a handful of memories.*

She looked at him. "Do all new widows feel this way?"

He nodded. "Yes, they do, and new widowers too. I know it's easy for me to say, but you must relax and stop worrying about the past. Things that happened before today are finished. You need to look to the future and, although memories may swamp you at times, look ahead, never back."

All right for you to say, she thought as she forced herself to agree. In her reminiscing she regretted much of the time they spent in petty spats and fullblown arguments. John wanted her to be kinder, more malleable, more subservient; not a separate person with her own feelings, but a part of him, always at his side to make him shine. She sighed. How well she had learned to subdue her own feelings and personality to make him happy.

What a waste of effort on her part, she thought now, simmering with anger at her own obeisance, in her abject submission to his wishes. If she had asserted herself back then, maybe he would have found a position with another company. Found a position that would enable him to spend time at home.

Gail's secure environment slowly crumbled before her eyes, each day now seeming to bring some new disaster. She felt like the loneliest woman in the world, and now this, the damned company with its heart of stone was kicking her out so quickly. How could they be so callous? John's heart attack was probably the result of overwork plus his wholehearted dedication to a company so insensitive that the corporate managers did not care what became of her and the children. As though John, having served his purpose, was now a statistic.

The doctor said his good-byes and left.

The children wandered into the room, squabbling as usual.

"Yes, you did."

Trish pushed at Vincent, who 'ouched.' "No, I didn't."

"You did, too."

"Yes, you did, Trish," Robert said, grinning.

"All right, let's sit and have our tea in peace, if you don't mind," Gail said calmly as she poured their milky tea. Tempted to scream in rage, she held herself in check.

"Are we staying home for good now?" Trish asked.

Gail shook her head. "Of course not. You return to school tomorrow."

"Told you. I said we were going back, Miss Know It All." Vincent stuck out his tongue and screwed up his eyes.

Still children, Gail thought, smiling, public schools or no.

"Dash it all, Mother, I'd like to stay at home," Trish said now. "Cynthia said I could visit her brother's stables this weekend, and I wouldn't want to miss that."

"Dear Cynthia!" Vincent sniggered. "She looks like an old nag."

"No, she does not," Trish shouted.

"All right, we can all hear you," Gail said, keeping her voice low. "Mr. Watson is trying to work."

"Oh, him!" Vincent scoffed. "He's trying to do Dad's job, isn't he? Bet Dad wouldn't have wanted an American to take over."

Gail cast a warning glance. "All right, Vincent, that's enough. Mr. Watson works for the company. He's sorting out the paperwork and getting things organized for the new man."

"Boy, they don't waste much time, do they?" Vincent slumped in the easy chair and stuck out his long legs. Tempted to tell him to sit up straight, she did not, supposing he heard enough of that at school, because his deportment was excellent.

Robert had said nothing throughout and now cleared his throat. "Mummy?"

"Yes, Robby?"

"Will Daddy ever come home again?"

She shook her head and smiled. "No, he's gone to Heaven."

Vincent sighed dramatically. "Oh, Mother, don't fill his head with rubbish, there's no such place as Heaven."

Gail's heart sank. Robert was the youngest and most vulnerable, and she had tried to shield him.

"You shouldn't tell fibs, Mother," Trish said, tossing her head. She turned to Robert. "Daddy is dead and buried. You saw them covering over the coffin. He won't be coming back because he's dead."

"Mummy?" Robert looked on the verge of tears.

Gail put out her arms. "Come here, Robby, we'll talk about it."

"Well, I'm going out," Vincent said, rising, "Coming Trish?"

"Rather!" Trish leapt to her feet. "Don't fill his head with nonsense, Mother, tell him the truth this time."

Gail told Robert in the most simple terms about death. Much to her surprise he asked few questions and did not cry at all, though he looked very sad. Maybe he was smarter than she had thought.

After she saw them off at the station, she walked home slowly. Each way she looked she could see nothing but problems. Bills were beginning to trickle in for John's new suits and handmade shoes. Then came the caterers' bills and the usual housekeeping invoices that she normally handed to John. Now it was up to her to find the money. It was no wonder that the stress had stretched her nerves to breaking the point. Self-control was difficult but seemed the most successful way of dealing with things.

She had kept herself cheerful for the sake of the children, but now that they were back at school, maybe she could sort things out better. The house seemed empty when she arrived back from the station. James was keeping out of sight, tying up the phone as he kept in touch with the head office and branch offices. He had prevailed on British Telecom to install another line and this he had installed in the library.

The living room felt cold, although it was a warm day and the odour of ashes from the fireplace smelled like sweet cider.

What will tomorrow bring, she wondered, next week, next month? The pain of her loss held her in thrall, each morning she faced yet another aimless day, and she felt as dead as John, felt she had no future and no hope.

For the first time since they moved here two years ago, the weather was hot and the sun shone brightly. John would have loved it, she thought, visualizing the barbecues to which he would have invited the neighbors. He was always lively and amusing, gregarious and charming, and, without effort, made everybody his friend. She found it peculiar that she was suddenly invisible. The neighbors did not drop in to chat as they used to, and she was reluctant to visit them.

Yet though her grief became all-consuming, she desperately wanted to savor it, keep it to herself. She wallowed in self-pity, told herself no outsider could ever understand how badly treated she felt. They would think her selfcentered. To them, John appeared charming, warm, and so efficient, but they had not known the real John.

The long nights of weeping for what once were futile. The sedative made her feel soggy and disoriented, and James Watson treated her like an interloper in the house she once called home. She went through the days, heedless of things around her, read books she did not see or remember, wrote letters to her parents, to the children, and somehow the long hours passed.

Then, much to her amazement, local people they had entertained and close neighbors came to pay sympathy visits. James rudely slammed the library door so they would not interrupt his work with their socializing.

She asked the visitors about rental housing, saying she was alone and rattling around Starlings, that she found too many memories in the place. Her day brightened considerably when, through the doctor's contacts, she found a small furnished house for rent in the village and arranged to move in at months' end.

CHAPTER FOUR

From the road it looked like an illustration in a child's book, old, probably pre-Victorian, and well settled into its location. As she arrived with her suitcases and boxes, Gail eyed it, speculating that the previous owners had probably removed the thatch to install the scalloped grey and green slates. The small windows were leaded and formed of diamond shaped panes.

To passers-by, it looked charming and inviting with walls of rosy red brick and white woodwork, with roses massed on a trellis around the front door. Flourishing perennials lined the borders of the path and a white picket fence surrounded the small garden. The space left for a lawn was the size of a tabletop, and the low golden privet hedge was neatly trimmed in scallops like the fence.

Inside the house was dinky, the interior too cramped and too dark. To Gail's Canadian eyes, the individual rooms seemed the size of walk-in closets, the ancient furniture looked drab and massive. An antiquated gas stove and a small pine table with two wooden chairs crowded the so-called kitchen. Instead of cupboards, someone had nailed shelves to one wall and these held a meager selection of dishes and cooking utensils. Off the kitchen was a small, dank scullery containing a rusted sink, and an ancient washing machine with an old-fashioned mangle.

Now Gail looked around her with dismay. The agent showed her the house on a bright sunny day and it looked pleasant: although she thought then that a good cleaning could work wonders. On that day the house seemed like the answer to her prayers. Today, when she arrived with the luggage, it looked much too dim and rainy. Now she noticed the damp patches on the ceilings and walls, the cobwebs in the corners.

To make it more cheerful, she plugged in her radio and tuned it to an easy listening station. The strains of "Everything's coming up Roses," made her switch it off. Roses? Not today, not for her. She sighed as she wrinkled her nose at smell of mice that mingled with the damp, musty odour pervading the entire house. Blocked sewers, dry rot, clogged drains? Obviously the rental agent had arrived long before she came to view and opened all the windows to air out the rooms. Another person who had deceived her, she thought, with a sense of exasperation at her gullibility.

Struggling up the crooked, uneven stairs, she dumped her cases in the largest bedroom that held a sagging double bed and a warped chest of drawers, nothing else. She looked around, irritated at herself. Why had she not noticed the lack of closets? The carter would bring her other possessions over in the week and, while she had a few small items of furniture, she had nothing resembling a wardrobe or armoire.

She must be in the centre of the room to stand upright, because the ceiling sloped with the roof. Though the windows were larger than those downstairs, the small panes and deep overhang kept the room dim. An unshaded light bulb dangled from a single cord in the middle of the room, and she flicked the ancient turn-switch only to discover a burned out bulb. Sighing with annoyance, she made a mental note to call at the local ironmongers to buy one before nightfall.

Gail checked the smaller bedroom the kids would have to share when they came home for their holidays. She could put up a blanket as a screen for Trish, and maybe Robert or Vincent would agree to sleep on the couch. Meanwhile, she would decide whether to keep them here at school, or take them back to Canada.

The back room looked small, gloomy and dirty. Pushed against one wall stood two single beds, so she would need to buy a third. It looked like the previous tenant had used this as a sewing room because scraps of thread and bits of cuts-offs lay on the unvarnished wood floor. In one corner, an enterprising mouse had built a home from scraps. Two bright eyes peered out when she stooped, thinking to toss it in the garbage. She jumped back in fright, then laughed at herself. A tiny mouse was not much of a threat.

It was a small house, so within two days she had cleaned everything. Spending money on rubber gloves and cleaning materials soon depleted her on-hand money. She desperately needed money, and from a public call box, she made an appointment with the bank manager for the following day. John's financial affairs remained a complete mystery and she had not yet found his will. Of course, she knew he would have left everything to her and the family, which was a small consolation, but the will would probably have to be probated in Canada. The bank manager informed her that he required the death certificate to sign over John's account, suggesting she contact a solicitor to help smooth the way.

She found it most peculiar when no one displayed any sense of haste, obviously assuming her as financially self-sufficient. Maybe it was her own fault that, in front of these professional people, she showed no distress or urgency, appeared calm and serene. If so, she thought, I must be a good actress, because all I feel is panic.

Each month, since their arrival in England, she had transferred as much as she could spare to her Toronto bank account, and this awaited her return. It was not much, but the interest must have been accumulating, and she figured she had about five thousand dollars. However, to take money from it meant miles of red tape and the completion of reams of forms. The British made everything so complicated, and then too, maybe Canada would want taxes paid on the money before the bank could transfer the money to England.

Access to John's account would be of tremendous financial help and she wondered whether she would ever find his Canadian bank book. Still, she felt sure he must have savings in a local bank. Maybe she should write to the Toronto branch, ask how much he had transferred there, or if, in fact, that was where his salary had been directed?

She had spoken to James and asked him to search the files and desk for any papers regarding John's banking. He told her he had found n nothing personal and must have kept them elsewhere, maybe in his dresser drawers? She had emptied his drawers to find nothing but clothing.

Constantly she reflected on her mistakes. How imprudent not to insist John show her the insurance papers, his will, his bank books, and explained any legal problems she might have in case of his death. How stupid she was to think he would live forever. Now she was suffering the consequence of her own carelessness. Never in her wildest dreams could she foresee his dropping dead at 41. No matter what, she still blamed him and felt guilty even as she did so, for how could he possibly know when he was going to die?

Looking back, she realized John's penchant taste for good food and good wine had made him a prime candidate for a heart attack. John enjoyed the charcoal blackened fat on steaks, crackling from roast pork, gravy, butter, rich desserts smothered in cream, chocolate doughnuts, ice cream sundaes, good brandy, vintage wines, and straight scotch. The only exercise he normally took was the odd round of golf for business purposes, or a leisurely stroll around the garden.

Of course, she should assume some blame, as too late she realized her failure to change his eating habits. Yet she had not bothered, knowing that whenever he stayed at a hotel, he would indulge himself at the company's expense. Gail admitted to herself she also liked the good life he provided and had not nagged him unduly. Now, with the wisdom of hindsight, she wished she had.

The solicitor urged her to return to Toronto to check John's safety deposit box for his will, and to check the goods in storage. He could do nothing in England that could be of any help, he said, as he smilingly presented her with his bill.

The bank manager, however, completely understood her problems and said he would undertake to release the funds on receipt of the death certificate and her identification papers. She left the bank feeling better and treated herself to tea and a chocolate eclair at the local tea room.

The euphoria she felt at knowing she could have access to the money in John's account soon dissipated when she received the bank statement. His account held little money so she was, to all intents and purposes, destitute. Her heart sank as she read the statement for the tenth time.

What on earth had John done with his money, with his substantial salary? At her request, the local bank managed telephoned the Royal Bank in Canada where John held an account and she talked to the manager whom she knew well. A search of the records revealed only $225 in the account.

So shocked by this turn of events was she, that she almost fainted. John earned a huge salary, and the company was paying half the rent of the house. So what had he done with the money? She knew he paid the children's school fees out of a trust fund set up years ago by his father. His trips were at company expense, and she knew full well he sometimes padded his expense accounts, adding personal receipts and putting them through as company expenses. This practice sometimes nearly doubled his monthly salary. He often bragged about his "fiddle sheets." Maybe, she thought ruefully, that could be one reason for his demotion.

Dr. Matheson, she decided, could possibly advise her where to start her search as professional people usually charged a fee for their services. Eric Matheson listened to her tale of woe and made appropriate muttering noises, but professed his inability to help.

"I think a private detective could find something for you," he said, wanting to say something. He fiddled with files, seemed nervous.

"Do you really think so?" Gail asked, feeling a surge of hope.

"It surely couldn't hurt, Mrs. Montgomery. Why don't you contact our legal aid association in town and see if they can help? Our social services are good. Put your mind at ease," He looked up and smiled warmly. "You will not lack for a roof over your head, or a meal, in this country. We have a good social safety net here and someone will always rally around. You did say you had money for the return fares to Canada? I suppose as a last resort you could return home to your family or relatives. Or is that out of the question?"

"At the moment, yes."

She didn't like the way the conversation ended, for no matter how she looked at it, going to see Social Services was demeaning and meant accepting charity. Yet what else could she do? Swallowing her pride, she made an appointment.

The legal aid association people were pleasant. They promised to contact a local investigation agency and have them make inquiries. Then they asked her to complete four long complicated forms - a means test - and return them as quickly as possible. Meanwhile, would she like a food voucher to use at the supermarket?

The idea of being publicly thought destitute horrified Gail and she refused the voucher. How horribly embarrassing to be observed handing over a food voucher in front of people who knew she had lived in luxury at Starlings.

Gail dejectedly sat on the bus, despondent and pessimistic. *John Montgomery, you have a lot to answer for. If only I had talked to you more about our finances, if only, if only...* Tears flooded her eyes and, not wanting anyone to see, she turned her head to stare out the window at a blurred landscape.

That night, after a lonely supper of boiled eggs and toast, she decisively resolved she must snap out of her depression. No more feeling sorry for herself. Life could not continue in this manner and did not achieve anything. From now on she must find her own way, must make her own life. Taking a lined pad out of the drawer, she sat at the unsteady kitchen table to draw up a plan of action.

Drawing a line down the middle of the sheet, she wrote Assets on one side, Liabilities on the other. In a short time she established her assets were few, but her liabilities were many, and included the welfare of three children. She must obviously find herself a job, one that paid enough to keep a roof over her head until the children finished school. Bringing them home would be selfish. She saw no reason they should not finish the education for which John had already paid. With a snort of disgust, she tossed the pad back in the drawer and morosely went early to bed to cry over the injustice of her life.

Each day she searched the newspapers for any position that might accept her limited capabilities. Because of the rural location, the local paper never listed much, but she pursued any avenue that might unearth a prospect. She even got to know the local postmistress, a positive walking encyclopedia of trivia and gossip, and, through her, found a job.

A week before she started work, she received a letter from Social Services asking her to visit the office. While there, a manager interviewed her, asking whether she could support herself, or did she require assistance? The effusive woman said while they could not put her on the permanent welfare rolls as she was not British, she could receive monetary assistance to tide her over until she left the country. Furious at such a demeaning conversation, she told the well-meaning woman to find someone else who needed help because she had found herself a job that would pay the rent and her living expenses. She even waved away the bus fare. No, she could stand on her own two feet, she could beat this and come out of the experience with more confidence.

The job was as a table server at a nearby inn. Modeled on the lines of an American fast food franchise, the inn sold beer, wine and boasted a varied menu. Connor's Inn was situated on a major highway far from the village and frequented by lorry drivers and travelers. Far enough away, she hoped, for local villagers not to see her. Why that bothered her, she could not say, for she knew none of them by name, apart from the postmistress. She supposed the thought of being seen working as a menial after lording it over the higher class neighbors for all those years in the grand house with a gardener and cleaning lady, would be cause for malicious gossip that might come to the children's ears.

In the village shop she distinctly heard someone say, "How the mighty are fallen," as the shop keeper served her with a quarter pound of cheese. Gail flushed hotly and walked out, without raising her head to see who had spoken.

The investigator discovered nothing she did not already know. On meeting him to explain her problem, Gail thought he might turn out to be as ineffectual as he looked. His performance proved her right.

The mystery of the whereabouts of John's money remained, and each time she opened her purse, she wondered how John had managed to hide it so well. When she wrote requesting information, the company informed her that John's pay was current, apart from any expenses not yet submitted. Yes, and obviously could not now submit, she thought angrily as she had no idea what he would have claimed. They had transferred his pay automatically from their bank to his and what he did with it then was none of their concern.

In the box of papers from the desk at Starlings she found a slip for a bank in the next village. However, on talking to the manager she discovered the company never transferred any money into this account, although John had cashed cheques there from time to time. Maybe, the manager suggested, he held an account at another bank.

Gail left the bank in a raging hurry and went to Starlings to see James Watson, still ensconced as he helped the new man learn the ropes.

"Mrs. Montgomery," James said unctuously as a neat maid in a uniform showed her into the library. A uniformed maid? "What can I help you with today?"

Gail noticed they had moved the furniture around. The desk now stood in the bay window.

"I wanted to ask a question, Mr. Watson. What bank does the company use, and how can I find out to which bank they transferred John's salary?" He looked amazed and she felt silly because she did not know. "John being typically British," she said, "was secretive about our financial affairs."

James regarded her with a small smile, a pitying smile. "Well, I do know the company uses the Toronto-Dominion Bank in Canada, but have no idea what bank your husband used. Don't *you* know?"

She looked away, embarrassed at her confession. "No, Mr. Watson, I do not. My husband apparently never thought it necessary to tell me and always gave me the housekeeping money in cash. While I have my own small account back in Canada, I don't know which bank John used for his pay, or where they deposited his pay check. To be honest, I never thought I'd need to know. Foolish of me, wasn't it?"

"Are you having financial difficulties, Mrs. Montgomery?" he asked, eyebrows raised.

"Yes, I am," she said firmly. To heck with keeping up appearances. "Can you help me?" Although painful, she said it loud and straight, wondering how he would reply.

He looked out the window, plainly disconcerted. "Well, not personally, no, I can't help you. My salary is back in Chicago. This is a temporary posting for me, as you know, and I'll shortly be heading back. I will warn you, though, that the company won't be very helpful since John is no longer an employee."

"So what's new?" Gail said caustically. "I didn't expect the company to be of any help. I simply need to know what bank they used. However, I do know it wasn't the account John used when we lived in Toronto." She rose and went to the door, putting her hand up to halt him. "Don't bother. I can show myself out, Mr. Watson. Thank you for your time."

Going through the hall, Gail nosily stuck her head around the living room archway. It looked the same, but again they had moved the furniture. Darn it all, she thought, my entire rented cottage could fit in this one room.

The elderly maid said, "Can I help you, madam?" which startled her and she shook her head, blushing guiltily at being caught. She rushed to let herself out the front door.

Back at the cottage, she went through John's personal phone book, found the number for the TorontoDominion Bank branch in Toronto. She went to the nearest phone box and dialed the number. A clip toned woman said they could not give such information over the telephone, but said they had no branches in the UK. She suggested the possibility of a transfer to a UK bank, a branch of Barclays or

NatWest. Annoyed but curious, she took the bus to Guildford, an hour's ride, and asked to see the manager of the NatWest Bank.

Her request seemingly perplexed him. *Well, so it should puzzle him,* she thought, *how many other women are in my situation? Not many, I can bet.*

"Well now, Mrs. Montgomery, this is a most unusual request, however, your identification is in order. I do hope I can be of assistance. If you could wait for a few moments, I'll check our records."

In five minutes, he returned from checking the accounts.

He shook his head. "Mrs. Montgomery, I'm afraid your husband did not hold an account here, neither did we receive funds from Canada to transfer to an account at another bank. Could it be that your husband dealt through a London branch? Surely his company can tell you what bank he used?"

Still at a dead end, and annoyed at the wasted time, she decided to telephone the head office, and this time *demand* the information.

"Mrs. Montgomery! How are you today?" The personnel office voice gushed along the transatlantic cable.

"Fine." She could not afford senseless chat. "Could you help me, please? To which bank was my husband's pay transferred?"

"I can't give that information over the telephone," the smiling voice gushed. "It's against company policy. You should write to us. Sorry."

Gail blew her top. "Not half as sorry as I am, young lady. I'm calling from a public call box in England, and you give me an answer like that?" Gail slammed the phone down and burst into tears.

What a shirty lot they were, and to think John lived and breathed that company for so many years. In fact, he thought more about his blasted company than he did about me or the kids. Damn them and their rules. She felt cheated, experiencing a feeling of hatred for John she knew was unwarranted, but found hard to erase. How could he have done this to me? She asked herself for the millionth time.

The doctor, always ready to listen and offer a shoulder, told her the Bank of Canada should have the information. The transfer of funds out of any country demanded the account holder inform the country's main bank to simplify an audit on due taxes. He also thought the income tax department would also have the information and advised her to contact both as soon as possible.

Gail started her job at the inn and enjoyed meeting the people. She found the work easy as she simply carried the meals to the table, set tables with condiments and napkins, served hot rolls, tea and coffee and fetched drinks from the bar. For this they paid her a nominal amount, but people left tips from which she made extra untaxed money. The fact she was now out in the world earning her own living, gave her confidence. *So I can do it,* she thought, *and I'm proving it.*

Yet she worked with a peculiar group of people. None were much interested in the job, and few tried to be courteous. They slammed plates down in front of the wrong people, and completely ignored requests for cutlery or sauces. Most of them were young people who possessed neither manners nor education, working to kill time and collect money for doing as little as possible.

Two other women of her age worked as supervisors and did more work than their staff. Nobody in management seemed worried about the young sloppy staff's attitude so Gail figured it must be the norm. Too, the older employees found it difficult to interface with the youngsters, who spoke a type of slang sounding like a foreign language. Gail applied herself to her own area and, since she did not work slipshod, soon discovered she had regular customers who preferred to sit at her station and tipped well. The manageress also noticed the favoritism and moved her around.

A month later she met Geoffrey Haslett, a professional man, a barrister, who dropped in once or twice a month for lunch. Each time he lunched, she spent a couple of minutes passing the time of day, and it was not long before he invited her to attend the opening of a new play at the Haymaker Theatre in London. Thrilled with the invitation, she eagerly accepted, starved as she was for a social life.

CHAPTER FIVE

Geoffrey was good company. They went out several times. Gail discovered him a brilliant, witty conversationalist, and a debonair sophisticated escort. She thoroughly enjoyed her evenings with him. The theatre, new movies, good restaurants, social and charity events he attended often required a female companion and he came to rely on her company. Going out with him was a pleasure for they never talked about anything of any consequence, their conversation always easy and relaxed. Never did she think of their outings as a date, but more of a social occasion shared between friends.

Thanks to John, she always looked smart and cosmopolitan. He always insisted she purchase good clothes, some of which were designer labels. Since his death, she had lost weight and some of the older clothes now fit her again. However, the people she met at Geoffrey's social occasions, dressed down rather than up, wearing clothes shiny, or so worn that apparently they were never cleaned. To Gail's eyes, the gowns were years out of date, although the wearer's air of arrogance and old-fashioned jewelry helped draw attention away from the garments.

Gail found it hard not to laugh when she noticed a dowager sporting an extremely dirty diamond tiara also wore a hand-knit cardigan with a large hole in the elbow over her crumpled evening gown. She looked straight at Gail and from the way she looked Gail up and down Gail could almost hear her saying *"nouveau riche."* She smiled, recalling the youngsters she saw on the streets, who were into punk and walked around with Day-Glo spiked hair and wore tatty Salvation Army castoffs.

Most of Gail's clothing came from foreign venues and were timeless styles, so she had something to suit every occasion. *Thank goodness I dress well*, she thought again, smiling wryly as she examined her reflection in the lobby mirrors. Then it occurred to her, that was the first positive thought she'd had about John since his death. Her grief was diminishing.

Geoffrey admired her clothes. He often remarked on how well they suited her, how stylish. Tonight she wore a dark blue satin Chanel evening gown with her mink stole. No woman standing near them dressed half as well, she noted, preening. She looked about twenty-five in the outfit, she thought, slim and trim. Two weeks later at the intermission of Agatha Christie's "The Mouse Trap," it occurred to her that she was beginning to feel feminine. For months she had felt invisible, a nonentity. Yet that this transformation had happened so quickly, surprised her.

"Would you like a quick drink before we go back to our seats?" Geoffrey asked her as he took her elbow.

"Yes, please," she said, as they headed to the lobby bar where he ordered two champagne cocktails.

Ah yes, this is the life, she thought, sipping the drink. Then it occurred to her she had begun to look on Geoffrey as a prospective husband and felt a jolt of shock. John been dead for less than six months, yet here she was looking with interest at another man. She had thought that part of her life over, had not even contemplated looking around for another partner. *Mind you*, she told herself as she looked at him over the rim of her glass, *Geoffrey is good looking, well dressed, extremely wealthy and eligible and has even invited me home to meet his mother next Sunday for tea. Should I interpret that to mean he is romantically interested in me?*

"But moth… er!" Patricia whined long distance. "I *have* to have it." She was in tears or close to them. Gail could hear it in her voice.

Patricia had written her a letter, not asking, but demanding a hundred and twenty pounds for a new riding outfit, saying she had been selected to ride for the school in the county gymkhana. Having outgrown her riding togs, (apparently she had shot up nearly three inches in the past six months), the new gear was apparently a matter of life and death.

Gail dreaded having to tell her it was impossible. Having no telephone at the cottage, she now stood in the call box at the intersection of the main road. Huge earth shaking, articulated lorries roared past, while on Main Street irate motorists tooted their horns at pedestrians who strolled slowly across the road as if time did not matter.

She took a deep breath of diesel laden air. "I'm so sorry, sweety, I don't have the money. It's hard for me to suggest this, but can't you borrow from one of your school chums?"

Patricia screamed loudly. "Moth… er! How can you even *think* such a thing? Borrow clothes? It isn't done at this school. All the girls got new riding gear this year, everyone except me, that is. You'll *have* to send the money. It isn't fair, not fair at all."

No, Trish, it isn't fair. Life isn't fair. Gail wanted to say it wasn't fair that she had to work as a table server, that she lived in a damp dark cottage, that she was solitary and lonely. Children didn't want to hear the realities and would not believe them, anyway. So she held her tongue and vainly tried to find some way around the problem, something to placate her daughter.

"…so you *have* to send the money, Mother, you *have* to. I can't stand it when the girls snigger about me in my old gear." Patricia was now well into her whining stage. "The jodhpurs are too tight around the bum and my knees stick out. Please send the money. You wouldn't want me to look like I didn't fit in, would you? I know Daddy wouldn't have wanted that. Mother? Mother? Mummy? Mum…meee?"

Trish calling her Mummy was usually a last resort and Gail knew she was beaten because Trish would write letter after letter.

She sighed. "All right, Trish, I'll see what I can do. I'll call you in a day or so, but don't count on it, sweetheart. You know I have no income now."

"Come off it, Mother!" Patricia's tone scalded her ear. "You and Daddy had pots of dosh. You must still have *heaps* of money. Look at Starlings. You can sell it, can't you? It must be worth positively millions." Gail had to smile at her daughter's naivete. "You sent me to this school and I know it costs a lot, and it probably costs more for Vincent and Robert, so we are not *that* poor. Daddy had a good job and made piles of money. Anyway, what have you done with Daddy's insurance money?"

If Gail could have gotten her hands on Trish, she would have shaken her until her teeth came loose, but realized the girl could not possibly know what she was suffering through. Let's face it, she told herself, I'm doing the children no favors by trying to protect them from the harsh facts. No more than John did me any favors. Too bad that over the past few years they've grown accustomed to asking for something and immediately getting it. It's all my own fault. No, it's our fault, John and mine. We've spoiled them for the real world.

"Yes, Trish," Gail said in small voice, "Your Daddy did earn a lot of money, but unfortunately he didn't tell me what he did with it. As for Starlings, we were only tenants. You know very well that I moved to Wisteria Cottage." Gail wanted to cry for her comfortable lost life.

"You really are stupid, Mother," Patricia said heatedly, her tone inferring old people were sometimes so dense. "You *have* to find the money. I need clothes and I'm going to need other stuff, too. I'll look myself when I come home. You obviously don't know what you're doing. Call the police, they'll find it," Patricia said in a patient voice. Gail knew Trish realized she would get her new togs and was humoring her senile doddering old mother. "Call Scotland Yard. We saw a program on television about how they can find anything, anywhere, anytime."

Gail chuckled. "It's not that simple, Trish. The police don't handle this kind of personal matter." She sighed. "Anyway, to set your mind at ease, I'm having a private investigator do some research. Don't worry, dear, we'll manage somehow."

Gail prayed she would soon find John's money. She decided she could use part of the precious air fare money, unwilling to borrow money to outfit Trish with riding clothes that, darn it all, she would not wear once the school year ended, or if she continued to grow.

That was another thing she must do, contact the lawyer in Toronto who looked after the children's trust fund. Maybe he could let her have money to buy the new clothes and school supplies. Another problem she must solve.

"Listen, Mummy, let me tell you what Judith told me." Trish was all sweetness and light now,thinking she had managed to get her own way.

Wondering how she could cut down on her own expenses to replace the money she took from the bank, she left the phone box. Her job paid her enough - thank God for tips - to cover her rent and day to day living expenses, but it left little or nothing for extras.

Gail trudged back to the cottage wondering how much new riding gear would cost this year. Her own needs would have to wait. Buying herself good sturdy shoes for work was necessary, but so far she had not saved enough. To dip into their air fare money was dangerous since she had little chance of replacing it, unless she found John's savings.

She thought then about Trish, whose complete self absorption was wonderful to behold. In a way she admired her daughter's headstrong attitude, her confidence that inevitably she would get her own way. Whatever subject they talked about contained herself as the leading character. If someone in Trish's class became sick, it was a major disaster because she might have caught the disease, and why did they let sick people stay in class when they felt ill? She showed little compassion for the sick girl.

That her mother had to find the money was not so Gail could provide a decent roof over their heads, or live in the style to which she was accustomed, it was so Trish could have her new clothes and other luxuries. As she considered the outcome if she could not find the money, Gail became discouraged. Catching her reflection in a shop window, she realized her stance was that of an old woman, head down, almost shuffling, her back rounded.

This will never do. Mentally shaking herself, she drew herself up, put back her shoulders and strode out along the street, head high, a smile on her face. "Show the world a confident grin," her mother often told her, "and people will admire you."

A car horn honked and honked again. Gail, curious, looked round to see who was in trouble for jaywalking or parking in someone's spot, and noticed Geoffrey waving at her from his Bentley.

Her heart jumped at the sight of him. He was always so nattily dapper, "bandbox sharp," as John would have described it, straight out of a tailor shop window with each detail meticulously impeccable. His straight brown hair always neat with never a hair out of place, his small military mustache perfectly trimmed. Did this denote a certain amount of prissiness, she wondered? Would being with a man who aligned his cutlery exactly square with his plate be annoying to the point of exasperation?

Crossing the road after a large lorry full of industrial machinery passed, she met with him as he locked the car door.

He straightened up, putting his keys in his pocket, and beamed at her. "Good afternoon, Gail. How pleasant to bump into you like this. Would you like a cup of tea?"

"That would be pleasant, Geoffrey," she said, pleased to see him so unexpectedly. "Tell me, what are you doing in this neck of the woods?"

He crooked his arm and she slipped her hand though. "I was passing through on my way to Woking and spotted you walking down the street."

She gave him a dazzling smile. To think he might have seen me slouching along like a zombie.

Arriving at the tea room door, he held it open for her to enter. A real English gentleman, Gail thought, the small courtesy pleasing her.

They sat and companionably chatted about nothing until the

pot of tea arrived, accompanied by fresh scones and jam. Geoffrey polished the spoon on his handkerchief before he stirred his tea.

"Which is your cottage?" he asked, "Is it at the end of the main street?"

Geoffrey never picked her up in daylight and she realized in daylight he might not recognize the small, damp cottage of which she felt so ashamed.

"Yes, that's the place," she said, hoping he would not ask to visit. He didn't.

"It's so very charming. All those rambling roses, and the garden looks nice."

"Yes," Gail said, deciding to change the subject. "Did you manage to get tickets for the Royal Ballet?" Gail did not much like ballet. She admired the athleticism, but disliked the phoney posturing and hard to follow involved plots.

Geoffrey tapped his forehead with the palm of his hand. "Sorry, I thought I told you. I managed to get tickets for early November. Ah, tempus fugit. It's catching up with me, I'm afraid. I have to make notes of anything important these days or I completely forget." He sipped his tea and twinkled his eyes at her over top of the cup. As he put down the cup, he prissily patted his lips with the napkin.

The tea room was well patronized and parties of hatted ladies gossiped over cakes. Gail always found this something of a puzzle since they all lived in the village and could drink tea at home at their leisure. Why pay someone to make it? Unless, of course, their homes were like hers, though she somehow doubted that.

She turned her attention back to Geoffrey who was talking about the London Philharmonic. Her eyes wandered to his attire: well-tailored country tweeds today. His patrician tones were soothing and she liked to hear him talk. Yes, she liked him and much admired his mother, a lady from the tips of her toes to the top of her head.

Their visit to the house at Walton-on-Thames for Sunday tea had been a success and she thought Mrs. Haslett, or Jill as Mrs. Haslett asked her to call her, a refined though a warm and easy conversationalist.

Jill Haslett was one of the old school of well-bred females raised to be upper class social butterflies and socially skilled wives. This meant her conversation, though on diverse subjects, inclined toward the wispy. She steered well away from subjects too graphic or too masculine, and never openly criticized anything. Her remarks held hidden meanings, sometimes too subtle for Gail's ears, and many innocent remarks held veiled hints of displeasure. While she never came right out and said anything deleterious, neither did she say anything one could interpret as tolerant. A most peculiar trait that often left Gail wondering what she meant by her last remark.

Holding up her end of the conversation was difficult for Gail, yet she felt Jill was good hearted enough to make allowances for her son's new friend who came from "The Colonies," as she called Canada.

Then, too, both Jill and Geoffrey had a habit of taking over a conversation. Whatever the topic, they chewed it to death and neither would stop until they exhausted the subject to their own satisfaction. Geoffrey always took the masculine point of view, of course, and Jill the feminine. As they interrupted the initiator of the subject, they skillfully homed in on the topic from their own point of view and continued to worry at it until they had the last word. Gail found them fascinating as they argued back and forth on some insignificant item in the newspaper. It was obvious they got along well, were indisputably fond of each other, and she thought Geoffrey's concern for his mother showed his love for her.

Responding to Jill was difficult at first as Jill's diction was of the Queen's English and she spoke as though instructed by the same elocution teacher as Elizabeth II. On meeting Jill for the first time Gail's Canadian ear could not sometimes understand her meaning, as Jill clearly enunciated each ending 'g', crossed each 't'. Her ending r's became h's so 'dear' became 'de-ah'.

Geoffrey was also correct in his speech, but not as hard to understand. Gail wondered, amused at an article she read in some magazine, how Jill might sound if woken from a sound sleep. Would she still say 'orf' for 'off', 'may dee-ah' for 'my dear', 'gorn' for gone?

The family called their ancient manor house 'River's End,' situated as it was on the bank of the River Thames. It lay back from the main roads, concealed by ancient oaks and beeches, on the outskirts of Walton-on-Thames near Windsor Castle. Although Geoffrey always said his mother was alone when he worked in London, she lived with four cats, two golden Labrador retrievers, and a loquacious parrot. Also, two love birds lived in a huge brass cage near the fireplace in the lounge. Gail gathered she also had tropical birds in the enormous Victorian conservatory built onto the side of the house.

"Since Geoffrey has taken a flat in London for his weekday practice, I am usually alone," Jill informed Gail.

Because Gail had met the housekeeper, one of the two maids and saw three gardeners and a chauffeur, she guessed the help was not considered fit company for a lady, and animals obviously did not count.

Widowed for twenty years, Jill seemed sensitive and sympathetic. She was a tall, svelte woman, who wore classically and impeccably tailored clothes with flair and a regal air. The conversation inevitably came around to Gail's recent bereavement. Not something Gail wanted to discuss, but Jill displayed great sensitivity and insight, something that endeared her to Gail who sorely lacked for female input to her problems.

Geoffrey did not have much to say on the subject of John's death or her dependent children, seeming aloof and dispassionate. She was relieved in a way, yet somehow saddened at his disinterest. *Never mind*, she told herself, *he takes me out, wines and dines me and that's a heck of a lot. Still, it rankles.*

Now Geoffrey sat back in his chair, legs crossed at the ankles, a tea cup poised over his saucer. "Mother sends you her best and reminded me yesterday to be sure to remind you that you are welcome to drop in anytime. She rattles around in that big old house on her own, but alas, " he sighed petulantly, "I cannot talk her into moving. Not that I would since the estate has been in her family for generations, back to pre-Elizabethan times. She was born there, you know, she's a Hoare you know, and quite convinced she will die in the same bed."

Gail almost choked when he said his mother was a Hoare, she thought he said 'whore.'

"The Hares are a famous family in Surrey," he continued, "they sailed with Raleigh, went on the Crusades with King Richard and have always been active in politics until this generation. The blood of Kings runs through our veins. Much diluted, of course."

Gail nodded, the family was well established, she already knew, but this bit about having blue blood made her smile. She wondered how long he had tried to work that into their conversation.

She thanked him for the message, feeling pleased at the invitation. However, because of her job and lack of transportation she could hardly accept. Then, of course, Geoffrey thought she worked only occasionally, and she had not said otherwise.

Today was her first day off in a month as normally she worked six days a week. If she opted to work Saturday evenings, they paid her double time. However, the management frowned on this practice, contending a sixday week was adequate, that double shifts could cause undue stress and hardship for families. The staff believed the real reason was because they objected to paying double time to full-time staff when they could bring in part time helpers who received a lower hourly wage.

"What do you say, Gail?"

Darn it all, now she had to say something. "I'd love to drop in and see her, Geoffrey, but you know I don't have a car. The house is so far away from the bus stop in the village." Gail could have bitten her tongue. Always the perfect gentleman, he might now feel obliged.

"My dear, that presents no problem," he said immediately. "Let me know when you'd like to visit and I'll take you. Never let anyone say that a gentleman would refuse to squire a fair lady. Mother really has taken a shine to you, you know, and I worry about her being alone so much. My work doesn't leave much time for sitting around chatting to Mummy, and now I have my London flat, I don't get home so often."

"Thank you, Geoffrey. I'll let you know," Gail said, wishing she had not committed herself. Now he would discover she was a common working woman and not the higher class person she acted when with him. *It is silly, this pretense,* she thought, *why don't I tell him before I get too accustomed to his attentions? After all, royal blood flows through their veins and here's me, a lowly destitute commoner.*

While he was aware she worked at the inn, she had led him to believe it was something she did for pin money. This he believed readily enough when he saw her good clothes and jewelry. *I wish now I had been up front with him,* she thought, *and told him the truth about my life. How can I bring up the subject of my lack of funds? Yet then again, how could I possibly have known the relationship was going to go any farther than one visit to the theatre?*

That night as she lay in bed, she thought about him. She found him ever more attractive, but if she subtracted his London flat, his mother's obvious wealth, his profession and his blue blood, would she feel the same way? Would she like him better if he were a bricklayer or navvy, if he were not as educated, if he were ugly? Stupid thoughts, she told herself. Geoffrey is Geoffrey. He can't change himself into anything else, so I should accept his largesse and enjoy it while I can. I don't exactly have a line up of males knocking at my door. Anyway, does he have the same thoughts about me, or is my acting enough to lead him to believe I am more than I appear?

Tossing in the uncomfortable bed, trying to find a spot where loose springs did not dig into her back, she decided to tell him the truth about her financial situation and let the chips fall where they may.

CHAPTER SIX

After wiring money to the school for Trish, Gail returned to the inn.

A tour company had scheduled four motor coaches of American tourists for lunch today and she hoped to make lots of tips. Americans were good tippers. The British were stingy and somehow assumed the inn included the tip in the price of the meal. Canadians left 10 percent and Europeans were so pernickety as to leave the exact pennies, as though to a mathematical formula issued by their travel agent.

She chatted with the staff about everyday things. The birth of Prince Andrew to Elizabeth and Philip, the first baby born to a reigning monarch since 1857. The marriage of Princess Margaret to Anthony Armstrong-Jones, the death of Aneurin Began, a British politician, the election of John F. Kennedy as President of the US. All topics that meant little to her personally, but she felt she must try to fit in with her coworkers. Her mind went back to when she read four morning papers cover to cover in order to be an informed conversationalist at dinner parties. While she had little in common with her work mates, she tried not to mention Canada or her travels in case they thought she was denigrating Britain. Sticking to trivial topics, she managed to make a niche for herself.

Because the work was not difficult so much as tiring, when

she took money from the bank for Trish, she took extra to buy appropriate work shoes. Usually by the time she finished work, her feet were swollen and sore. Yet today had been a bonanza because the Americans tipped lavishly.

At home, a card shoved through her letter box advised her a registered letter awaited her signature at the Post Office. Excited, hoping it was good news from Canada about John's money, she walked quickly before they shut the shop at six.

The Post Office occupied a corner of the newsagent's shop and a was popular place. Chattering senior citizens, whose only exercise consisted of the trip to pick up their pensions or tobacco, normally occupied the four chairs backed against the Post Office rear wall. Gail made her way through the racks of paperback books and magazines to the rear corner where a small counter sold cups of tea and coffee with biscuits to the customers and retirees.

The young woman hired to deal with the tea orders, passed a toasted tea cake to an old lady whose face was so wizened it resembled the "apple granny" Gail once made for Trish. She smiled as she saw the old lady dip the toasted scone in her tea, noticing she had no teeth. Poor thing, she thought, hoping she never got to that stage.

She passed the notification card across the counter through the space under the grill, watched carefully by four elderly but exceedingly bright eyes. The postmistress passed her the book to sign and they chatted about the weather. While waiting for the woman to find her letter, she smiled at the two oldsters who watched every move and memorized her clothing so they could talk about her when she left. A registered letter was probably the most exciting thing to happen today.

She smiled as she saw the letter came from John's company. After investing in a solicitor, he, at her request, wrote to demand information about the bank to which the company transferred John's money. This must be the reply. Putting it in her purse, she headed for the door, eager to get home to open it in private. The old people looked disappointed. *Too bad*, she thought, giving them a small smile, *find something else to amuse yourselves.*

The company gave the address of a bank in Woking, the Barclay

Bank on High Street. A wave of relief swept over her and she felt like crying. All the bones in her body seemed to melt as an utterly peaceful feeling came over her. Good old John, he had come through for her. Too bad everything was shut for the day, but she would take time off in the morning to see the bank manager. Quickly she assembled all the paperwork required: her passport, the copy of the solicitor's letter, the company reply, John's death certificate, and a few other bits.

That night she slept exceedingly well.

The bank manager, Mr. Fairbright, was a pleasant man who had come up through the ranks by dint of hard work and dedication. He listened gravely to each word she uttered with evident concern and interest.

Smoothing back his hair, he made a few notes. *At last,* she thought, *someone with brains and manners.*

He stood. "Let me check our records, Mrs. Montgomery. I'm sure we can deal with this in short order." He left her in his office drinking tea, and went into the bank.

She felt confident soon she would have John's funds. The thought that maybe she could quit work warmed her, and she wriggled in the chair, wishing Mr. Fairbright would hurry.

Gail looked up expectantly as he came back into the office reading a ledger card. "Well now, everything is in order. We'll soon have this sorted out, Mrs. Montgomery."

As he dug in his desk drawer to find the right form, Gail vainly tried to read the ledger card upside down. The British system of pounds, shillings and pence foiled her efforts, then he put two forms down on top, concealing everything.

"This will only take a few minutes, Mrs. Montgomery, if you will bear with me." He grinned ruefully, "Government red tape, you know." He started completing the forms. "One thing does surprise me, though," he said as he wrote, "Why on earth didn't the Canadian Embassy look after this for you?"

Gail felt sick to her stomach. Of course! Obviously she should have called them immediately, yet all this time had elapsed. She never gave them a thought, and she had thought herself intelligent. Still, grief did awful things to one's mind.

She started to feel her anger rise. *That solicitor is going to get a piece of my mind, and I'll demand a refund of the money I paid him. He should have advised me to contact the Embassy, or done it himself. I'm an idiot. Never mind, it's all worked out all right, and this nice man is sorting out everything.*

"Here we go," Fairbright pushed a form across the desk to her, handing her a pen with the other hand. "If you would sign here, and there, and initial here."

Gail did as he said and sat back, waiting for him to complete the remaining form. Soon she would be out of here and with money in the bank. She felt so much easier in her mind and relaxed in the chair as she sipped the tea.

He turned the form around. "Right, here we go. Sign where I've put the crosses and we're all finished."

He chatted politely about Toronto as she signed and signed. "I've always had a yen to go to the United States," he said, "I'd love to see the Grand Canyon, but I've never been outside Britain apart from the Isle of Man. That still belongs to us, or it did last time I heard," he said chuckling as he put the forms in a folder. "This is a new check book. I'll fetch you a current statement of account and you'll be all set."

He hummed as he went to get the statement and Gail sat looking at the pristine check book. At last she would have money on hand and could replace the air fare money.

"Here we are," he said as he passed her the statement sealed in a window envelope. She saw that instead of an address it said "To be Picked Up. Do not Mail." So that explained why she had never seen a bank statement. Still, what had John done with the statements after he picked them up? Destroyed them?

She opened the envelope with shaking hands and unfolded it.

"This cannot possibly be right," she said when she saw the balance was only one hundred and seventy pounds. Her brow was suddenly damp with perspiration and she felt a cold chill. The figures blurred and ran into each other. "What happened to his last pay transfer?

Are you sure he doesn't have a savings account here?" Again John had baffled and defeated her.

Taking the statement, he glanced at it. "Mrs. Montgomery, if you check the statement, you'll see the company transferred more than a twelve hundred pounds into this account, but your husband withdrew nine hundred and fifty-five the following day. It appears that was his normal way of operating."

He held it toward her with an expression that looked much like pity. Gail snatched it back and could hardly see the figures because she felt so angry. What the bloody hell had her ever loving husband been doing? What *had* he done with the money?

Realizing Mr. Fairbright could no longer be of any help, she picked up her purse, thanked him, and left with her head held high. Self-control, she found, was becoming easier. She'd had lots of practice by this time.

Later today she would contact the Embassy. How foolish of her not to have done so in the first place. Somehow she was going to find the money. Eager to learn anything that might be of help, she called the embassy from a phone box on the High Street. The Canadian Embassy was supportive, but not sure they could do anything under the circumstances.

"We would have to ask every bank in the area to disclose information," a suave aide told her, "That could take a long time. They have to cooperate with us, but they don't usually do it right away. It is not an urgent matter to them unfortunately, though they get around to it eventually."

After asking him to do anything he could to help, she went home dejectedly, tired to the bone. One minute she had high hopes and the next she was again in the doldrums. It was debilitating.

CHAPTER SEVEN

On the long bus ride home she thought about her life, thought about all the years she had yearned for independence. She married John after she attained her degree and shared her life with him. Now she had finally gotten the independence she craved, but at what cost? Gail had never known what it was like to be completely alone. Until her marriage, she lived with her parents. Never had she experienced a separate life as a single person because, eager to marry and live with the man she loved, they married within four months of meeting.

What would it be like, she had often wondered in the past years, to be accountable for herself alone? Well, now she had independence because John was gone, but now she was responsible, not only for herself but for three children. Without first considering them, doing what she wanted was impossible.

While they are away at school I can live my daily life to my own routine, although it's not at all what I envisioned. Without funds to make my life easier, I don't have enough income to splurge on little things for myself. To be able to walk into a store and buy something silly because I feel like it, would be wonderful.

The bus wound its way through streets of terraced houses, others of small stores, past a market place with wooden roofed stalls, a park and a small lake. Parts of England were beautiful though the streets were so narrow and traffic considerable. Housewives walked home with their shopping bags, mothers pushed strollers and prams, small children ran with their chums, some pushed bicycles as they talked. How wonderful it would be to be one of these citizens, born and bred on this small island, with a little house and friendly neighbors. Then she shook her head, no this was not for her, her world was elsewhere she felt sure.

She considered her present state worse than being married. At least then she had a breadwinner who supported her and removed the worry of finding the rent or money for food. *No, she sighed, it was not at all as I pictured, to be my own woman, not an appendage of John Montgomery, was always my dream though now it has happened, I'm a woman of no consequence. Is this what I wanted?*

Gail spent many hours combing through each scrap of paper she brought from Starlings. Nothing gave her a clue about his banking, or how he had disposed of the money. The teller at the bank told her John often drew out most of the deposited money within two weeks or less. What *had* he done with it? She felt more embittered and angrier as the days passed. Her sense of self worth was suffering. Surely she must have more intelligence than this situation denoted. Darn it all, she had put herself into this predicament and now she would have to suffer.

John's clothes were still packed in the boxes she had brought from the house, and presently sat on the second bedroom floor. Although she originally decided to give them to the Salvation Army, she reconsidered, deciding that Vincent, who was filling out across the shoulders, could surely wear some of the jackets. He was growing fast and would soon be almost as tall as his father. John paid a lot for his clothes, and to give them away when his son might find use for them seemed a waste of money and incredibly foolish.

With a feeling of trepidation, she changed into old clothes and went to sort out the boxes. Further procrastination seemed futile.

Taking each item out of cases and boxes, she laid them on a sheet on the floor. The shirts she put to one side, knowing Vincent could always use shirts. She laid the suits on one bed, trying to erase the pictures that flashed into her mind.

John wore this navy blue pin stripe when we attended a Canada House reception, she remembered. *He wore the tweed hacking jacket when we spent the weekend with the agent in Orly.* His evening clothes with the satin lapels brought hot tears to her eyes: John looked so handsome in black tie. She buried her face in it and inhaled his smell, the expensive cologne still clinging to the satin lapels.

Angrily she wiped away the tears with her sleeve. This would never do. Better to get it finished, better to rid him from her life completely than live with residual memories that made her sad and so terribly angry.

After she sorted out the better jackets and shirts, she hung them on the door. None of them were much worn. John had so many clothes and Vincent could get years of wear out of the jackets.

Gail started going through pockets, finding odd pound notes, some loose change. Then in the breast pocket of a suit she discovered a safety deposit box key. Her heart soared. Maybe this was the answer to her financial problems, once she discovered the bank to which it belonged. She should have made this search earlier, she told herself, feeling suddenly much better.

In an inside jacket pocket she found a bank statement from a bank in London. It showed a balance of more than fifty-four hundred pounds. Hurray! Gail cheered aloud as her heart thumped rapidly. Today she had solved another part of the mystery.

At the bottom of the pile and in the last suit jacket, she discovered a small photograph inside an old wallet, one she thought he had thrown away. The picture showed a dark haired woman holding a small baby. Who could it be? It was no one she had ever met. Why had John hidden it away in a suit he had not worn for at least ten years?

She slept little that night as thoughts of John having an affair threaded through her thoughts. Always at the back of her mind she instinctively sensed he was probably not faithful but then she, ostrich like, had not really wanted to know.

Tomorrow she would ask for more time off so she could travel to the London bank to check the account.

Leaving work two hours early, she caught an express train to London. Full of expectation, she wondered if she were again letting herself in for a disappointment, She tried to look more on the positive side, knowing another failure would be too much.

After taking two buses and the underground, she found the bank, a small suburban branch of Barclays that looked shabby and needed a paint job. She wondered why on earth John would open an account here in this backwater, on the back street of a district that would hardly appeal to his sensibilities.

As she waited to see the manager, she took the necessary papers from her purse. The patrons of this bank were seedy looking, she thought, as she watched them lining up to pay in or withdraw. All down at heel, lower class, unkempt and unwashed looking. Mentally she chastised herself for thinking such things, knowing they were all regular people.

The manager, Sid Greenbank, a roly-poly man, reminded her of Humpty Dumpty with his three chins and balding head. His face broke into a broad smile as he saw who waited to see him. Wanting to keep up appearances, and maybe make an impression, she had worn her best coat and her alligator shoes and purse.

"Mrs. Montgomery?"

Gail stood, extending her hand. "Yes. Good morning."

"Won't you come into my office?" he asked as he gestured with his right hand to the corner of the building.

"Are you an American?" he asked.

"Canadian."

He smiled and nodded as he said, "How can I be of assistance to you, Mrs. Montgomery?" He pushed shut the door.

Gail told him her sad tale and passed him her identification papers, and a copy of the death certificate.

"Let me see. Would you like a cup of tea, Mrs. Montgomery? I'm afraid I'll have to check our records and that might take a little time."

Gail sipped the stewed and acidic tea as she waited. The bank statement dated over a year earlier showed a hefty balance, and maybe John had deposited more. Please God, let that be the case, she prayed as she waited for Mr. Greenbank's return.

Sid Greenbank waited patiently as a teller rummaged through the files. Eventually the woman found John Montgomery's account. It showed a balance of nine pounds twelve shillings. Someone had made a large withdrawal the previous month.

"Do you recall who withdrew this money?" he pointed at the ledger entry.

"Oh yeah," she said, popping her gum, "That was his missus. She allus comes in once a month to get her housekeeping money. She's ever such a nice lady, got two little kids. Both screaming their heads off, they was, 'cause she didn't have enough to buy them an ice cream and the truck was right outside the bank playing his bells. Her hubby hadn't put any money in and she wasn't half mad. That's why I remember it, Mr. Greenbank."

Sid found himself perspiring although it was chilly in the faux marble clad office. If Mrs. Montgomery was sitting in his office and this other woman had withdrawn money claiming *she* was Mrs. Montgomery, it meant the man was a bigamist. He stood chewing his lip, staring sightlessly at the ledger card. Maybe the best idea was to tell her and let her take it from there. After all, he was only a bank manager.

As he entered the office, Gail looked up expectantly. When he cleared his throat two or three times, she felt her heart sink. Same old story, no money, she guessed, but after he told her the bad news, worse news than she expected, Gail sat straight backed in the chair, shocked.

"Where does she live, this Mrs. Montgomery?" She finally asked. Maybe it was a relative, though she doubted it.

Sid blushed. He had seen the address on the ledger and not thought to take note.

"The ledger card states the statement will be picked up." Sure, Gail thought spitefully, John was a master at hiding his trail. "However, I'm sure we have an address on file, if you'll excuse me for a moment."

It was as though someone had hit her over the head with a two-by-four It felt staggering. She never thought John would have a mistress, not really. One night stands she could cope with, but a mistress? John's penchant for the good life often brought him into contact with beautiful women, and men are men. That she accepted. Still, a mistress, and why here in this run down a neighborhood? This was not his type of place.

John Montgomery, you have a great deal to answer for, she fumed, *yet somehow you managed to get away with it until after your death.* Strangely she felt no heartbreak, only blind rage. How naive she had been all these years, how blind to what was going on around her, how stupid in her ignorance.

"Here we are, Mrs. Montgomery." Mr. Greenbank passed her a small piece of paper on which he had written the address. "14 Hoggs Lane." It sounded unsavory.

"Thank you for your time, Mr. Greenbank," Her voice sounded exceedingly calm as she fought to control the scream of despair she felt building up behind her smile. "I might have the money transferred to my Woking account, but meanwhile we might as well leave things as they stand. This might be a relative of my husband. I'll let you know."

Gail stood outside the bank and considered her plan of action. First thing to do was find 14 Hoggs Lane and see the woman purporting to be Mrs. Montgomery. The nine pounds were not of much use to her, or the other Mrs. Montgomery.

She found Hoggs Lane, a narrow cul-de-sac with sixteen terraced houses on either side. A brick wall twenty feet high formed the end of the street and was chalk marked with goal posts. On the other side of this wall were the railway lines and, as she looked, a locomotive passed with much huffing and puffing of sooty smoke.

All the front doors opened directly onto the cobblestone street, a relic of the Victorian era, she thought. If what she saw was the norm, the landlords had neither upgraded nor maintained them. A gang of kids, ragged and extremely dirty, noisily played football on the road.

Number 14 was, like its neighbors, run down and poverty stricken. The cracked and ancient paint on the front door was almost colorless, a nondescript grey-brown. Scabrous layers peeled around the dirty window in its centre. Surely John would never have stayed here?

She loudly banged a brown painted knocker and the kids stopped their game to stare at her, a stranger here on their street. Two or three of the boys sidled over and leaned on the front window ledge, cheekily waiting to see what she wanted.

Gail heard footsteps in the hall and the door opened on a slatternly woman holding a squalling baby.

"What'd yer want?" she asked screwing up her eyes in suspicion, looking Gail over from head to foot.

"Mrs. Montgomery?"

"Yers," She patted the baby's back, but it only screeched louder.

"Could I come in for a moment?" Gail asked, taking a step back when a gust of vomit laden air gushed from the hall.

"What you after, then?" she asked, suspicious, rocking the baby violently. It increased the volume.

"May I please talk to you for a moment, away from the street?" She gestured at the boys who were now standing next to her, listening to every word.

"Get away with you, you lot. Go on home," the other Mrs. Montgomery shouted savagely. The boys turned and ran. "Little hooligans." She nodded at Gail, "All right, you can come in, not for long, mind. I've gotta get Arfur's tea ready."

Turning away, she shuffled in broken down heels along the narrow linoleumed hall and through a door at the end.

As Gail closed the door, she decided to breathe through her mouth. The house smelled of unwashed diapers, vomit and garbage. In the hall it seemed clean enough, but who knew what the living quarters were like?

At the end of the dark narrow hall they turned into the kitchen where the woman started changing the baby's diaper on the table already laid for a meal with knives and forks and plates. A dish of crumb-covered butter sat with a knife stuck in it, while sauce bottles, sugar, jam and a dish of pickled onions sat alongside a bread board with half a cob loaf. With only one narrow window, it was dim and someone had painted the walls dark blue. Not midnight, but more like navy. Who, she wondered, would paint a small room such a color, and why?

Mrs. Montgomery stuck in the last nappy pin. "Now, whatchew want?"

Gail bluntly asked, "Are you married to John Montgomery?" She had no idea what to say, but had to let the woman know John was dead. On the other hand, her John would never have had anything to do with such a slattern. He was always so fastidious, hated anything soiled or unclean. Surely he had never been romantically involved with this woman?

The woman picked up the baby and put it over her shoulder, patting its back. It started wailing loudly. "Shurrup! Yes, I said I was Mrs. Montgomery, din't I? What's it to you, then?"

"I also married John Montgomery," Gail said.

This statement did not seem to bother the woman who shrugged and said, "So, he must of divorced you then, eh?"

"No, he didn't."

"Go on with you!" The woman grinned gap-toothed, not at all upset.

"Sorry, but if you were married to John, then he must have been a bigamist. When did you marry him?"

The woman scratched her backside with her free hand. "Can't say for sure. About eight years ago, I reckon." She put the baby on the table while she stirred something in a saucepan on the stove. Gail cringed and hoped the child would not roll over and fall to the floor. It lay like a rag doll and waved one tiny hand.

A small boy came dashing into the house through the back door and came to a sudden stop when he saw Gail, who looked at him closely. "Is this your son?" she asked.

"Yes. That's our Johnny boy, in't it?" The woman picked up the baby and roughly ruffled Johnny's hair. He put his arms around her thighs and peeped shyly at Gail from behind her torn wraparound apron.

Gail strained her eyes, trying to see any resemblance to John in him. "How old is he?"

"Our Johnny? Well, less'see, must be at least eight now, eh?" She pushed at him and he giggled.

"Silly bugger. I'm nearly seven now, Ma."

Thank God, she thought. "He's not John's son?"

"Nah. This little tyke," She picked up the baby who had fallen asleep with its hand in the butter. "This is Stevie. He's not John's, neither. He's a Lowe, he is. John didn't have no kiddies by me. He weren't a touchy-feely man, you know." She rocked the baby who started to whimper. "Now, what you want then? John did something bad then?"

"John is dead."

"Well, blimey, stone the perishing crows! Yer only now found out about that, did you? I knew that already." The woman flopped into a chair. "That's why we didn't get no money in the bank this month or last."

Gail stood erect, knowing she had to tell the woman. "John Montgomery was *my* husband and I want to know when he married you, and *why* he married you."

The woman narrowed her eyes. They flashed over Gail's attire, at her expensive shoes. She nodded. "Orl right. What's in it for me?"

Somehow she looks shrewd, but I know John never married this uneducated woman.

"Why should there be anything be in it for you?" she asked, "You couldn't possibly be his wife. I don't think John would ever have married you, no matter what you say. You're not his type."

"Ha-ha-ha," she laughed mirthlessly, "I see, and you are, eh?"

"May I see your marriage lines?"

"I dunno know where they are and anyway I gotta get Arfur's tea ready. Can't see why John married you, too much of a toffee nose, if you arsk me. You'd better talk to my Arfur about that, or come back some other time." Gail noticed she looked decidedly shifty. What was going on here?

"I'll stay, if you don't mind, and talk to Arthur. Maybe *he* will be more forthcoming."

The woman moved toward her, her attitude threatening. "You can clear off. I don't want you here. This is my house, so get out."

Gail decided to leave things as they were for the time being. Never in a million years had John married this woman and the children were not his, that much she admitted. So why was she calling herself Mrs. Montgomery, and why was John putting money in the bank for her? Whatever the reason, the woman was obviously not going to tell her anything.

Hurriedly she left and, as she walked quickly down the street, she saw a red faced, burly man turn into the house where the woman stood watching from the doorstep. Arthur Lowe did not look like an understanding person.

She sat on the train staring sightlessly at the passing scenery and thought about her morning. Why would John have been paying money into an account for that woman? She did not know this new John who lived another life about which she knew nothing. He was becoming ever more a stranger.

When she arrived home, she found two letters on the door mat. One was from Vincent, the other from her mother in Vancouver.

Gail's parents had moved to Vancouver on her father's retirement from the civil service. The mild heart attack he suffered when shoveling snow decided for them. Always thrifty, he retired with a huge pension and a large stock portfolio. Her parents liked Vancouver for its cosmopolitan atmosphere and its lovely, though rainy, climate and since they were reluctant to venture back to the colder wintered eastern provinces, Gail rarely saw them.

She had never lived easily with her father who was so pedantic and rigid in his thinking that he treated her as a mental midget. Because he thought single women incapable of living alone, he insisted she lived at home even when she begged to have her own apartment while attending university. Unfortunately since her mother sided with her father, she had to stay home, or suffer the consequences.

Marriage really had been Gail's only way out. Since her marriage she saw her father as little as possible because he still treated her like a child. Once a month or so she received a short letter from her mother. This was her only means of contact. Today's letter asked about the children and enclosed a money order for Robert's birthday.

"We hope the children are coping with the loss of their father and your life is getting back to normal," she wrote.

Sure, Mom, as normal as it will ever be. Nothing will ever be right again. She still smarted from the letter her father sent after John's death that essentially pointed out that since she rarely saw her globe trotting husband, she would soon get over his loss. He also said this was the time for her to return home.

Gail could never have contemplated living with them. While her father was correct in that she would get over her loss, she realized she had always loved John, even if he often abandoned her when traveling on business. Anyway, they spent more time together since his transfer to England. She accompanied him on many European trips, the children being safely at school, and shared the driving across the continent. They had grown closer in the past two years.

The letter from Vincent was the usual school duty letter and said nothing about anything. His handwriting was large and undisciplined, probably on purpose, so one paragraph filled an entire page. Gail was aware that school rules insisted on each pupil writing one page a month. Vincent seemed happy with his school life and his chums. Yes, she thought now, he had always been a solitary boy when at home, remembering how he preferred his own company to that of his siblings.

After supper, Gail wrote to Vincent and then to Robert. She would enclose a money order with Robert's tenth birthday card, knowing he would waste it on sweets and comics, as usual.

CHAPTER EIGHT

The next day Geoffrey came into the inn for lunch and sat at one of her window tables. He was pleased to see her and passed her a stiff envelope she thought must contain an invitation to some social event.

"Do say you can come, Gail. I know you'll enjoy it. I would like to introduce you to some very nice people. They're originally from Toronto so you should have much in common."

She read the invitation. It was for a charity auction held by Sotheby's at the Savoy Hotel in London: cocktails before the auction, dinner and dancing later. She agreed to accompany him and went to get his lunch, pleased at the way his eyes lingered on her face. The way he looked her up and down as if committing her to memory, she found most flattering.

"Mother would like to know if supper on Saturday would be agreeable with you? She would so like to see you again," he said as she placed the soup in front of him.

"Well, let me see," she paused, fingers on her temple, as if trying to remember her other important social appointments, then smiled and said, "That would be lovely, Geoffrey. Tell her I would be delighted."

"Nice," he said, looking at her breasts in the fitted uniform vest she wore. At least she thought he was looking.

Gail stood near the counter and watched him fastidiously eat his lunch. She wondered, as she always did when he looked at her that way, if he were getting serious about their relationship. Geoffrey could be the answer to all her problems. Surreptitiously she observed him. He patted his mouth with his napkin after each bite; he shook the food on his fork to ensure nothing would drop onto his tie; or maybe make sure it was dead. Geoffrey seemed such a fussbudget so she wondered if she could she stand watching that for the rest of her life. She didn't know, but she was willing to try it if he asked her. If it did not work out, divorce was acceptable these days, even to the stiff British upper crust. Even the royals were 'giving it a go,' as they said over here.

That Saturday evening she sat at the elegant Queen Anne table in the huge dining room gazing with pleasure at the splendor of the silver and crystal. The elegance of the room lulled her and soothed her tired soul. Jill did not lack for any of the creature comforts, Gail mused as she sipped vintage wine, and Geoffrey was the only heir. She blushed as she realized how mercenary she was being, but surely that was John's fault, dying at such a young age? Him and his secrets.

"Do you find it warm in here, my dear?" Jill asked noticing Gail's flushed cheeks.

"Oh no. I was remembering something embarrassing." She smiled, "Please don't ask me about it."

"Since we were not the cause of your embarrassment, we won't," Geoffrey said smiling as he poured his mother more of the burgundy.

"How are your children progressing at school?" Jill asked changing the subject with typical hauteur. "You have two sons and a daughter, if I remember correctly."

"They're fine," Gail said sipping the delicious wine. It was like oiled cream, smooth to the tongue, sun kissed. "Robert turns ten this week. My mother sent him a money order that will be spent on candy and comics, as well it should be."

Geoffrey laughed. "I recall when I was at Eton. I must have spent all of my pocket money on food. We ate well, for a school, but not the kind of food a young lad craves. You know, sticky buns and sweeties, ice cream and chocolate cakes. Mother, bless her heart, sent me tuck boxes, but my chum and I devoured those the moment they arrived, otherwise the other chaps would scoff the lot the minute I turned my back. Young lads crave sweets and have so much excess energy."

Jill regarded him with affection. "I thought that was what sports were for, Geoffrey, to run off the excess before you channeled it into other areas."

"All I know is that my sons eat like horses when they come home," Gail said. "It's like shoveling food into a bottomless pit. It doesn't even touch the sides of their mouths." Gail grinned then laughed, realizing that finding something amusing was enjoyable. She had not had many laughs lately.

"You'll find they've probably shot up like bean poles when they come home for summer holidays. New wardrobes all round, eh?" Geoffrey laughed, recalling his own school days.

Gail smiled, but inside her heart sank as she suddenly realized they would need new wardrobes for the autumn term. The few pounds she had left from John's account would be gone in short order if she had to outfit the boys, and heaven only knew what Trish might demand.

And too, she had not yet written to the trust fund lawyer about getting more money for the children. Procrastination was her forte these days.

She had not broached the subject of her financial problems with Geoffrey, being horribly embarrassed to have misled him in the first place. If she could talk to Jill alone, she thought, she might find the courage to bring it into the open. Gail had never talked to Jill alone because Geoffrey was always there, always helpful and supportive of his mother.

Suddenly she decided to come out with it. "I really hope they haven't grown too much. I simply can't afford new outfits for them." She had said it.

Both Hasletts regarded her with astonishment. Jill put down her knife and fork, patted her mouth with her napkin, but said nothing. Geoffrey looked positively sheepish.

Gail sighed, she had better spit it out, even if it did make her look stupid. "I have depleted my funds, and I can't find my husband's bank account. I know it sounds absurd, but John never let me know about his financial situation, and foolishly I didn't ask. After all, I didn't expect him to drop dead," Gail said forcibly as though to justify herself.

"Mm, yes," Geoffrey murmured, obviously ill at ease.

"You mean you are without savings or investments?" Jill asked, sitting back in her chair, putting her hands on the arms, posing regally.

Gail nodded, it was easier now she had said it aloud. "That's right. I've been unable to find John's savings, investment certificates, stock portfolio, any financial paperwork at all. Not even his will."

"I must say that makes it awkward, doesn't it?" Jill said patting Gail's hand compassionately. "Why on earth didn't you have a copy of his will? Don't you have a solicitor?"

Gail heard herself making excuses for her stupidity. "We traveled so much that the only legal man we ever had lives in Toronto, and I know John would never ask him to write his will. I'm afraid John regarded all lawyers as shysters." Geoffrey's face went red, and Jill gasped. "Sorry about that, but that was his opinion, not mine. Many of our things are in storage in Toronto, so he might have left it with our household effects. The will part is not that bad as I am obviously next of kin, but his financial affairs are a mystery to me. It makes things very awkward, in fact, more than awkward."

Gail suddenly wanted to make it appear as serious as possible. Yet even now she was ashamed to admit her gullibility. "I've been able to trace the salary they paid into his account from Canada, but then for some reason John withdrew most of it and I'm unable to find the account into which it was transferred. He must have moved it somewhere else because we were never short of money. The Canadian Embassy is asking all the local banks to search their records in the hope of finding something, but, as it stands right now, all I have is my pay from the inn." She looked hard at Geoffrey who suddenly found his vegetables interesting.

"Oh my dear, what an awful time for you," Jill said. Were those tears in her eyes? "You must let us help you over this difficult spot." Gail regarded her with admiration and thought Jill Haslett wonderful. "Don't you worry, my dear, surely they will find your husband's investments and savings. Did you find anything at all?"

"No," she said sadly, feeling duped and more than ingenuous now she confessed. "I wrote to the bank in Toronto to see if they could check in his safety deposit box, but it can't be done unless I go over with the other key, or I send a legal representative with my authorization. Either way, I understand they can drill the box out without the key, although it's a difficult thing to arrange and something they don't do often. I also wrote to an insurance company John used to deal with, but so far have had no reply." Had she gone too far? "Never mind. I'm sure everything will sort itself out eventually."

Gail started back pedaling, somehow feeling guilty at dumping this on Jill who was so sensitive and understanding. Nevertheless, she appreciated knowing Jill had offered assistance. "Once I return to Canada things will be fine."

"You're thinking of leaving us?" Jill sounded alarmed.

Geoffrey pushed his food around, saying nothing. At that particular minute Gail did not much like him. A word of empathy from him would not have gone amiss.

"I don't think I have any choice."

After the silence hovered for a second too long, Jill started talking about the upcoming fete. The community would hold it on the village green, and it would undoubtedly spill over into the nearby school grounds. Almost visibly, Geoffrey relaxed his shoulders and started talking quickly about his role as coordinator for the fair grounds.

Gail saw him with new eyes. He was not a very nice man, she decided, he did not have much compassion.

CHAPTER NINE

When Geoffrey did not come to the inn for lunch for two weeks, Gail wondered whether she had seen the last of him, and cursed her big mouth. He withdrew his open manner immediately after she dropped her bombshell. The fact she was practically penniless should not present a problem to him because he was a wealthy man, a professional, and she was still the same person, with or without money. Why should her lack of funds make any difference? He never expected her to go Dutch, nor did she ever offer. Pondering on his disappearance, she realized he had dumped her. How humiliating: another indignity in a string of degradations.

Her self-esteem slumped as the days dragged by, her life losing meaning. With no outside interests, she spent her spare time pulling weeds in the tiny garden and dead heading the flowers. The owner of the cottage sent a man around once a month to trim the hedges and mow the tiny lawn, but he did not weed. She was grateful for the landlord's courtesy, particularly since he also had the windows washed, no mean feat since the tiny panes were so time consuming.

She got many books from the local library and went in the evenings to read the daily paper, one thing on which she need not spend money. All of it was bad news and very depressing. The royals were always in the news, of course. The queen would visit India, Pakistan, Persia,

Cyprus and Ghana and the papers constantly rehashed this news. Edward Heath, Lord Privy Seal, was negotiating for Britain's entry into the Common Market. The film of West Side Story was making big headlines in the US and she wished she could afford to see it.

Then disaster struck yet again. She received a letter from the insurance company in Toronto where she knew John held a policy, stating they had canceled it four years earlier. The company let it lapse when John did not pay the premiums. They had informed Mr. Montgomery and he replied by letter, which was on file, stating that he did not wish to reactivate. They enclosed a copy of John's letter.

Why would he have done that? Surely he would have wanted his family to have some protection? Another avenue was now closed, unless, of course, he had taken out a policy with another company. Immediately she wrote to all the other insurance companies in the Toronto area.

She wrote duty letters to her parents and made it sound as if things were fine. How often had her father insisted she return to Canada now, and how often had she vowed never to stay under the same roof? Well, she had outgrown her father and had little time for her mother. Now she wrote about the weather, her job, the cottage, anything but the truth.

Next week the children were coming home for the summer holidays and she was dreading the expression on their faces when they saw the tiny home she had made for them. Because her pay allowed no frills, she again dug into the few pounds left from John's savings account and bought brightly patterned sheets for the children's beds, and purchased a second-hand single bed.

Determined to put a cheerful face on things, she placed an order with the bakery for a welcome home cake. She regretted spending the money, but, by experimentation, she discovered the old cooker useless for baking cakes. She tried three times, but it appeared something was wrong with the thermostat. Trial and error showed it might take months of waste before anything came out as it was supposed to, and she simply could not afford more costly mistakes.

Today an American tourist left her a tenpound note. Sure it was a mistake, she looked around for him and saw it was too late to give it back. Tears came to her eyes as she realized how much ten measly pounds meant to her. Time was when ten pounds to John was a tip for a waiter. Now it meant the difference between a pint of real milk and a carton of peculiar tasting long-life milk. It meant she could have a small piece of meat this weekend instead of sardines or beans on toast for her Sunday supper. It meant so darned much.

Each night as she lay in the sagging bed, she dreamed of the day when she had solved all her problems. Independence was all right, she discovered, but only if one had the money to make the road navigable.

One of these days she would find a decent man who would love her passionately. No - that was wrong because John loved her passionately at the start but, as happened with all torrid love affairs, his passion slowly waned. Their last few years were spent as intimate friends, the original intensity merely a glowing ember. They cared for each other, deferred to each other, worried about each other, but they had few moments of sexual intimacy Even so, over their years together, she had often wondered if John's roving eye landed on many other women while he was out of the country on business. Always faithful and tied down with small children, she never even looked at another man. Nevertheless, if he did sleep with other women, she really didn't want to know. It came to mind that her anger had erased much of the antipathy she felt toward John. She could think of him now without animosity, without feeling betrayed.

The days drifted by as slowly as if watching a snail race. Since Geoffrey gave her the cold shoulder, she had nothing to look forward to and that vexed her. Still, she thought, if he took umbrage so quickly, maybe she did not want to know him better. Then on reaching home one evening, it startled her to find Geoffrey's car in front of the house. Her heart gave a jump and she found herself smiling. Strangely nervous about seeing him again after his withdrawal, she childishly put her hands in her pockets and crossed her fingers.

Geoffrey got out of the car, having seen her in his side mirror.

"Hello, Geoffrey. To what do I owe this singular pleasure?" She heard the sarcasm in her voice and did not care.

He reached into the back seat and took out a huge spray of roses wrapped in rustling cellophane paper that he placed in her arms.

"I'm so sorry, Gail. I treated you abominably. Please forgive me." He blinked nervously from under his brows. She smiled, having seen the look a million times on her both sons' faces when they had done something naughty.

Gail looked at the lavish floral offering and then up at him. If he were not so darned good looking she would have told him to get lost, but still he was so attractive and rich with it, darn it all. She weakened in her resolve.

"I forgive you," she said, smiling. "Would you like to come in for a cup of tea?" She thanked her lucky stars she had cleaned the place ready for the children's homecoming. At least she would not embarrass herself too badly, apart from the cramped quarters in which she lived.

Geoffrey looked around with obvious distaste, although he said nothing. Gingerly he sat on the small couch, scrunching himself as though contact was bound to ruin his clothes. *Not laying his handkerchief down before he sits must be killing him*, she thought as she hid a smile.

She made a pot of tea and opened a packet of precious chocolate digestive biscuits she was saving for the children. Using an old tray, she carried things through to the living room.

"Here we are. Sorry I don't have any fine china, only the stuff that came with the cottage, I'm afraid." She set the tray down on a rickety small table that had a match book under one leg to stop it wobbling. "Anyway, why am I apologizing for my circumstances?" she said too brightly as she poured him a cup of tea.

Geoffrey took the proffered cup and saucer and balanced it on his knee.

"Cookie?"

"Biscuit," he said, taking one.

"Yes, of course, biscuit." Gail sat back on the couch and sipped tea, content to let him carry the conversation. She could not imagine why he was here, other than to deliver his excessive floral apology. Did he have anything to add?

"I must express how sorry I am about my attitude the other evening," he said as if it were only two days ago rather than two weeks. "It was unfeeling and callous of me, considering the situation is not of your own making. Mother gave me a good talking to and I appreciate now that I have been very selfish." He turned to look her in the eye.

Gail found victory in his words, as if she had won an argument. She smiled. "I wouldn't say selfish, Geoffrey but, yes, you were unfeeling. I was beginning to wonder what kind of man you were, to turn your back on me like that."

Yet Gail knew what kind of man he was. He was self-centered, self-involved and did not want anything to disturb the status quo.

He agreed with her, which surprised Gail. "Yes, yes, you are perfectly correct. The situation took me aback, you see. Why did you lie to me, Gail? I didn't like you lying, particularly since I was under the impression you were comfortably fixed and everything was fine. Your three children were at public school and…,"

"Yes, Geoffrey," she interrupted, "I suppose I should have come clean about everything." She saw how he inclined his body away from her. *Scared of what I have to say?* "Don't you realize how hard it was for me to tell you about my problems? I've always lived a good life in fine houses with the best of everything, and now, because of my own self-deception, I'm alone and penniless. All my life people have protected me. First my parents, then John, so facing the present circumstances on my own was difficult enough, but to tell other people, well…," Gail shivered, "Anyway, did you really *want* to hear my tale of woe? I hardly knew you when we first went out, and after that it became harder to tell you. You looked at me as self-sufficient and I didn't want to disillusion you. I thought it made me look like an idiot, and I felt like one. Do you understand?"

He nodded and placed his cup on the table. "I think so, but it does make me feel like a heel, my not helping you out in times of trouble. Mother was most upset and asked me to fetch you over for supper this evening. That's why I came today." He grinned boyishly. "I think Mother and I have worked something out which will suit admirably."

He sat back with a smug little smile and Gail felt like slapping him. *So now he has solved all my problems? Well, I'll see about that: after the free supper, of course.*

They were sipping fine old Napoleon brandy in the lounge after a delicious meal when Jill broached the subject. Neither said anything about the "perfect solution" throughout supper, nor had they mentioned it earlier as they drank aperitifs in the conservatory. Gail was beginning to wonder if Geoffrey were mistaken.

"Gail, please do not think that I intend to interfere in your private affairs," Jill said quietly, "And I know Geoffrey would not dream of intruding." She shot a warning glance at her son who was about to say something, and raised a stilling hand. "I have given this much thought, my dear, and think I have found the perfect solution. I think it is a highly acceptable resolution to your problems, one you should consider carefully."

Gail gave Jill her full attention. Her nerve endings tingled as she heard Jill say, "You and Geoffrey should marry. It would be the right move for him at this point in his career. You are quite presentable, my dear, and dress well considering you are not British."

Gail was thunderstruck. What was the woman saying? "You have good manners," Jill continued, "and are modern in your outlook. You have a decent figure, keep yourself well groomed, and never wear too much make up."

Gee, thanks a lot, lady, Gail said to herself, you sound as though you've taken inventory.

Jill leaned toward her and lowered her voice, although Geoffrey could easily hear every word. "Many noble British families have married into Colonial families to strengthen the family tree. Inbreeding has much against it, my dear, and unfortunately so many of our British families have too often interbred. No, it is time we brought new blood into the line."

Gail could say nothing. What was she? A brood mare?

Jill extended a perfectly manicured white hand and touched Gail's as it lay on the table, nerveless. "I will tell you at the start, Gail, and in complete confidence, that Geoffrey is impotent and cannot have children. Therefore, on your marriage your children would become his heirs."

Wow! The children would inherit all this? flashed through her mind.

"It therefore goes without saying that you will have no fear of sharing a marriage bed or physical intimacy. You will live your own life, even have lovers if you wish. However, discretion is the watchword." Jill sat back and posed again, her attitude one of having solved the world's problems. "All in all it is a perfect match and one which would suit you both admirably." She smiled at her son and looked again at Gail. "It is time for Geoffrey to marry, although I must tell you Geoffrey has never been inclined to the female sex, apart from a decoration on his arm. I think, no, I *know*, I spoiled him for other women." She again smiled fondly at Geoffrey who wore a face like thunder.

Gail gasped and stared at her incredulously. Her heart was thumping solidly, such was her surprise. "Well! I don't know what to say." The outright nerve of the woman, and she had thought Jill so refined. "I hope you don't consider me an opportunist. I'm not exactly a gold digger, you know. I admit that right now my future looks bleak, but I'm certain it will improve."

Jill looked at her over her crystal balloon glass and sighed. "Oh, my dear, please think about it very carefully. I have never considered you a gold digger, whatever that might be in the English language, nor an opportunist. However, this alliance not only assures your future and that of your children, but also that of the house of Haslett."

Gail wondered whether Jill was right in the head. Coming out with such an offer was something peculiar, and not quite sane. The house of Haslett? She decided to humor her.

"Do I have to answer right away?"

"No, of course not, my dear, but I do hope you are agreeable. I'd like to have you as a daughter-in-law and would love to meet your children. You must bring them to visit when they come home on holidays. If they are anything like their mother, they must be very nice indeed."

Gail felt proud of herself for giving such a good impression, but felt a need to talk to Geoffrey. He had let his mother talk for him, while surely he could have proposed to her this evening at the house? It was obvious he knew what his mother was about to suggest, and earlier disclosure could have avoided this embarrassing scene. She glared at him and he slid his gaze away from hers.

Gail sat silently as he drove her home, waiting for him to say something. What an ineffectual wimp he is, she thought. Could he not stand up for himself? Imagine any man letting his mother propose for him, tell a prospective wife he was impotent and he did not care for women very much. What a moron!

"Well? Say something, even if its goodbye!" she eventually snapped at him, not turning to face him, but staring out the windscreen at the pouring rain.

"Well, I really don't know what to say." She had him flustered and he was obviously upset.

"So you *can* speak when you want to," she retorted with a voice full of contempt.

"Please Gail, let's not argue. It was horrible sitting there, having Mummy talk as though I wasn't even in the room. She completely mortified me. I was so ashamed of her coming out with it so callously, saying those horrible things. Mummy usually has such finesse." His voice sounded strained.

Gail noticed that when he reverted into his little boy image of himself, Jill was always his Mummy. When he was a man, she was his mother. Geoffrey had problems with his masculinity. No wonder he was impotent. Anyway, what real man would tell his mother such a thing, for how else could she know?

"She told it like it was, Geoffrey," she said brusquely. "I suppose if she had waited for you to say anything, I would already be back in Canada."

"Oh, I say!" he gasped.

Gail shrugged. "Well, let's face it, Geoffrey, you could have proposed to me earlier this evening when you sat in my living room drinking tea. If you had spoken out then, your mother would have had no need to say anything to humiliate you. You had the perfect opportunity."

She glanced at him, saw his clenched jaw and white face. *At least I'm getting through to him, he's angry and that's something.* She sighed deeply as they turned onto the main road.

"What would your answer have been?" he petulantly asked, "If I had asked you to marry me?"

"To be quite honest, I really don't know, but if *you* had proposed, I'm sure you wouldn't have given me the sordid details about your lack of interest in women and your impotence. I would have still thought you were an attractive man with a good future."

Geoffrey wheeled over to the curb and parked. "I do not wish to argue about this, Gail. The subject is closed to discussion. Mother said it all." She smiled, so he's back to being a man again. "However, I would point out that I *am* a nice person, at least I hope so and have always tried to be a gentleman. My mother loves me, I love her, and it is in my favor that I have a good future. I came into my inheritance from my grandfather at the age of twentyfive, and am sole heir to mother's entire estate, which is considerable. As a future husband who is willing to take on your children and treat them as my own, I'm what they call "a good catch" in your parlance." Geoffrey spoke quietly and calmly with no emotion whatever in his voice.

Gail turned to look at him as he spoke. Darn the man, he was so good looking, and to be honest with herself she thought he really *was* a good catch. It amazed her that he had escaped the clutches of a fortune hunter to this point, but then she supposed these women would at least have wanted a physical relationship. Mummy, of course, would have final approval. Yet could she live with it? That was the million-dollar question.

CHAPTER TEN

Gail made a final check before she left the house. The children were arriving today. She would meet them at Woking station at two-thirty and so had taken a day off work so she could finish any last minute cleaning.

Stepping outside, she closed the front door, then shut her eyes. Opening the door again, she looked at the place as if seeing it for the first time. Ugh! It seemed so gloomy and cramped. Nothing like the children's first glimpse of Starlings where the marble tiled hall was larger than this living room.

In an attempt to make the front room cheerful, she had purchased some gaily colored cloth and covered the throw cushions that sat on chair and sofa. She pulled a face, knowing it had been a mistake because their gaiety only pointed out how dismal the place really looked. Undecided, she took them off the furniture and looked at the room again. No, maybe it was better if she left them.

Gail worried about whether the children would like the cottage. Of course she expected tantrums from Trish, who eagerly grabbed any opportunity to vent her spleen, and from Vincent who was becoming such a prig. She knew Robert would love any place where he could be with her, but Trish and Vincent were seniors and saw things through older eyes. This was hardly the style to which they were accustomed and, to placate the expected vehement opposition, she rented a small television, but no radio or record player. They were not going to be pleased.

At Starlings Trish and Vincent usually played their records as loudly as possible: primarily to annoy her, and secondly to exclude her. Trish used it to block out anything that did not interest her, particularly her mother's voice. Their music, if you could call it that, made Gail's flesh crawl. Both were aware it irritated her and she, in turn, tried not to show it because that gave them a certain power over her, one she was unwilling to grant. After a huge screaming match, which she won, they played their music in their rooms as she preferred. It was no use telling them they would go deaf.

"If you're not already," she had said spitefully, "You never hear a word I say."

All those possessions were now back in Toronto and she had no intention of buying anything new.

She had rationalized that if she requested more money from the trust lawyer, she would be spending money they might possibly need for further education. Maybe it was better that they learned that things did not always come to them just for the asking, that maybe they might have to earn things, consider her, and their own circumstances, before reaching out for some costly item without which they could manage Too bad that they were learning their view of the world through the eyes of those wealthy schoolmates

Sadly her children were children no more, they had grown away from her and she would never get them back. Maybe in years to come they would turn to her, but right now they were set against anything she suggested. The very mention of "for your own good" sent them into a rage She learned not to make direct suggestions, instead putting her thoughts into words that eventually they mentioned as being their own idea. She was not a good mother, and that upset her. No matter how she tried to offer her love, they pushed her away.

Yet Robert was still as sweet, loved her unconditionally and championed her with his elder siblings. A changeling, she thought, a child who was the epitome of the child of her dreams.

To Patricia and Vincent, she was too old to be of interest to them. She was the adult who catered to their needs, who housed and fed them, and that was all they thought of her. What had happened to those sweet little children who clung to her and told her they loved her? Now they thought they knew it all, as all children did when they reached that certain age, and although Gail understood that, it still hurt. Robert was still a child, but Trish and Vincent, at least in their own minds, were adults.

They showed no interest in her, eyed her with scepticism, their manner contemptuous and derisive, they rolled their eyes to heaven if she gave an opinion on anything. Scornful and full of disdain, they let her know her ideas were hardly worth listening to, were archaic, senseless. Their peevish attitude was deplorable and she did not know how to handle it, other than steel herself against their jibes, treat them as if they were still her loving babies.

The rotten thing was that she didn't know what they were thinking these days. She knew, from her own adolescence, that they kept lots of things bottled up inside, as she herself had done. What did they perceive as their own private problem? She was sure it could not be the loss of their father, as Trish showed not one scrap of remorse and only used him as ammunition to toss in Gail's face if she did not get her desire. Vincent brushed off John's death as nothing that affected him much since he had hardly been close to his father.

Gail realized she held no control over them, and she needed that control, if nothing else, to give her life some meaning. They were a problem she did not relish, because she had no way of reaching them. In a way she was glad when they were away at school, but they were not going to accept coming home to this tiny cottage gracefully. Well, at least, she thought smiling, she would have musical peace and quiet.

Anyway, why was she worrying about what three children were going to think? It was not as if they had any choice in the matter, though neither did she. They were resilient and she hoped they would adapt. Quickly she tossed the cushions back into place and left the house, locking the door behind her.

The train was, for once, on time, and as the doors slammed open and shut, she scanned those alighting. As Geoffrey had forecast, Vincent had shot up and seemed all gangly legs and arms. Robert was still his sweet self, though at least an inch taller. Patricia, who had also grown, was pouting because Vincent was making her carry her own case. She had to smile, that daughter of hers expected everyone to treat her like royalty. They clattered along the platform as she walked to greet them, arguing among themselves, not even looking for her.

"Welcome home, my darlings," Gail said, as she swept a stiff embarrassed Patricia into her arms and hugged her. She kissed Vincent on his cheek. He angrily looked around to see if anyone noticed, and sullenly wiped his face with his sleeve. Robert stood still and let her fuss over him saying, "Hello, Mummy." Throwing his arms around her, he patted her back.

She shepherded them through the underground tunnel to the street and, taking the small case from Robert, said brightly, "Come along now, the bus is due in five minutes and we have to get along sharply."

"Where's the car?" Vincent asked loudly.

"Yes, why are we not going home in the car?" Patricia asked nastily, accusing her with her tone and expression.

Gail stopped, looked at them and told the truth. "The car was on hire to the company, so the agency took it back. We must use the bus."

Vincent and Patricia looked at each other with raised eyebrows.

Rebellion came from an unforeseen source. "I don't want to go on a bus, Mummy, I feel sick and the bus smells rotten. I know it does," Robert said, pulling at her sleeve.

"Oh Robert, love, what's the matter?" Gail asked as she stooped to look into his pale face and feel his forehead.

"Do leave off, Robby. You've been eating too much junk again," Patricia said, indifferent to her brother's white face and listlessness. She raised her voice as a truck trundled past. "Honestly, Mother, you should see how much stuff he put away. He got off at a station and bought chocolate and liquorice whips from the kiosk. It was embarrassing when he started eating like a pig and his face was all sticky and smeared. Then some woman on the train gave him a revolting sandwich full of red meat with gobs of sauce. Little porker that he is, he was staring at her as though he hadn't eaten a decent meal in months. She felt sorry for him, I expect. We pretended he wasn't with us, didn't we, Vincent? Anyway, he polished it off in about two seconds flat. The woman was going to give him more, but Vincent wouldn't let her. She probably made it of road kill or something, *and* it was probably poisoned. A dirty woman who looked like a gypsy and not very clean." She sniffed disapproval and Gail glared at her.

People passing moved aside with looks of disgust as Robert bent over and suddenly vomited into the middle of the pavement. Gail held his head, and, when he finished, wiped his face with her handkerchief.

"Do you feel better now, Robby?" she asked, concerned he might be really ill with some disease rather than sick from a red meat sandwich.

He smiled up her at her, wiping his eyes with his thumbs. "Yes, Mummy, I don't feel so sick but my stomach aches something rotten. I 'spect I will be better after my tea. I do feel hungry, Mummy."

Gail smiled. From being deathly ill to being hungry took about two seconds. She took his hand and they walked to the bus stop accompanied by the gripes of the two eldest who still demanded to ride in a car. Why, they asked, had she not ordered a taxi?

They made it with seconds to spare and she bundled them onto the bus. Vincent and Patricia went upstairs and she sat below with Robert, whom she hugged against her. He was still her baby, even if he were beginning to lose his chubby face and baby fat. Robert snuggled closer and immediately fell asleep.

Vincent and Patricia came clattering down the stairs arguing about who should carry the largest case that the conductor had shoved under the stairs. Gail realized they thought they were going to get off at the nearest stop to Starlings, which was a distance from the village.

"Come and sit here, please," she said, patting the long seat at the other side of her. "We get off in the village now."

"The village?" Patricia seemed astounded. "We're going to live in the village?" Her voice rose on the last syllable with incredulity.

"Yes, we are. I have a lovely little cottage. You know that, Trish. I wrote and told all of you about it. It's the right size for us and I'm sure you'll like it. We're close to the shops, and you'll all like that, won't you? You're bound to meet some local children and will soon find new chums." Her voice was too jolly, too sweet, and Gail knew they would hate it, but sitting on a bus surrounded by gawking locals, who resentfully eyed the public school uniforms, was not the time to go into detail.

They got off when the bus pulled into Rycroft. The bus stop was a hundred yards from the house and Gail, dreading the quarrel to come, chattered brightly as they slumped along with their cases. She carried the heaviest and Robert, unencumbered and refreshed from his nap, ran ahead and came back to report what he had seen in a garden or house. At times he stood gazing at the dashboards of cars parked at the side of the road. Robert was presently going through a love affair with the automobile.

They arrived at the cottage and Gail felt relieved the sun was shining brightly. It made the cottage look lovely from the outside, and though the interior was grotty, she hoped the sun would brighten it.

"Is this it?" Patricia said incredulously, eyeing the frontage. "It's so dinky. We can't all live here, surely. It's not even as big as the potting shed at Starlings. I can't possibly live in such a tiny place."

"Yes, we can live in this tiny place, my dears, and we will." Gail pushed open the rickety white gate and shepherded them along the path. As she put the key into the lock, Vincent leaned against the rose-covered trellis and a section snapped loudly.

"Now look what you've done, clumsy clogs," Patricia said, shoving him. "Mother, this place is literally falling apart. It is all probably rotten. It might have death watch beetles or bugs. Are you sure I have to live here?"

"Huh! What about me?" Vincent asked, curtly. "I mean to say, it's the look of the place, isn't it? What *will* people say?"

"Oh, shut up, you!" Trish spat, tossing her case into the hedge and hitting him across the chest with her arm.

"Now, now," Gail did not want to listen to Trish and Vincent fighting for hours as they usually did. At Starlings they had lots of room, room to get away from each other, whereas here the small space might make them feel claustrophobic. Childish bickering was the last thing she needed.

"Pick up that case, Trish and let's get inside and have some tea. I have a lovely cake to welcome you home. Here we go." She stood aside to let them enter the two-foot square hall that held only a board on the wall with pegs for their coats. "That's right, hang up your coats."

Robert looked around with interest. "This is nice, Mummy. So cosy and…"

"What do *you* know, small fry?" Patricia spat in a sulky voice, pushing at him. "You have to be kidding, Mother. We can't possibly live in this hovel. What *will* my friends say?"

Vincent stood gawping as if not sure this wasn't a bad joke. "Honestly, Mother, this is pretty gross. Why can't we live at Starlings?" He flopped onto the small ancient couch and looked around disgustedly.

Gail looked at her thoroughly spoiled children and felt like crying. She decided to let them stew, and went into the kitchen to make tea. Robert, now completely back to normal and hungry, followed her like a shadow and hung onto her sleeve.

"I like it, Mummy," he whispered, "Never mind those two. We'll be all right. You can count on me."

Gail smiled through sudden tears and hugged him. "Thank you for your vote of confidence, my man. Look at the nice cake I bought."

As they sat morosely eating the cake, which Patricia thought was repulsive because it had vicious poison green icing saying, "Welcome Home." Her actual pronouncement being it was "pitiful and tasted like sawdust." With a sinking heart Gail wondered how she would manage six weeks of sulking and argument. Robert alone was happy to be with his mother and sat by her side, touching her occasionally to make sure she was really there.

CHAPTER ELEVEN

When, later, they saw the bedroom with the strung across blanket, Vincent gasped. "Oh, I say, I have larger quarters at school, and more privacy."

Patricia looked around her with disdain and said: "I cannot possibly sleep in a room with two males, even if they *are* my brothers! I'll share your room, mother."

She dragged the closest bed into the other bedroom, where it blocked access to everything, and sat on it pouting.

Robert sat on his small bed and smiled. "This is super, Mummy," he announced, turning his head to look out the small window at his side. "I can watch the birds in that big tree early in the mornings. Look! See that bird's nest up there? I'll climb up it tomorrow and look at the baby birds."

"They don't have baby birds at this time of year," Vincent said showing his superior knowledge. "They've already flown." He sat on his bed and stared around him, bewildered. "Where will we put our clothes? No wardrobe or closet?"

"You'll have to hang them here, I'm afraid," Gail said pointing to the arrangement she'd put up which consisted of two brackets with a broom handle for the rail.

"Oh, I say, Mother," Vincent looked at her as though she were mad. "They'll get dusty and spiders will sleep on them. Moths, too, I should imagine."

"It's all you've got, Vincent, so make the best of it. The things on the back of the door were your father's. I saved them for you as they're hardly worn and good quality."

"Oh good grief! How could you think I would want them?" Gail watched his face. How wrong she had been about his indifference. Maybe Vincent really had loved his father, and now she had wounded him. He washed away her guilt when he said. "How can you expect me to wear second-hand clothes? Those are so old-fashioned and everyone will laugh at me." Speechless, Gail left and went into her bedroom to see what Princess Patricia was doing.

Patricia stood as she entered and went to close the door, discovering it would not shut because the wood was damp and swollen.

"Mother, I *cannot* stay here. I invited my best friend to come for two weeks and this place is a positive *pigsty*. I shall have absolutely no privacy. I'll be the laughing stock of the entire school if anyone finds out I live *here*." She stood, hands on hips, sticking out her lower lip as she had at the age of three.

Gail considered what to say. Best, she decided, to tell her the plain unvarnished truth or Trish will carry on like this for the entire six weeks. "I'm sorry, Trish, but you'll have to write and tell her she can't come. First, I can't afford to have her here, and second, we have no bedroom for her. Surely you realize we can't live the way we used to? When your father died, we lost everything and I couldn't afford to keep Starlings. It was a rented house and the company needed it for your father's replacement." Gail sat on her bed and looked at her spoiled daughter who was fast learning about the real world. She felt such pity for her, knowing it was difficult for a child brought up with luxury to find it snatched away, replaced by poverty. For poverty it was, even to Gail.

"I *won't* live here. I *won't*." Patricia shouted, stamping her foot in anger. "I'll telephone Cynthia and ask if I can stay with her for the hols. I can say you've gone abroad and couldn't take me. I can think of *something*." Patricia, turned to face the small window talking to herself now, planning her lie to make it sound plausible. "You were going to visit the lepers in somewhere or other and didn't want to take me in case of infection. No, that's too gross. You're going to see some dying relative and you don't want me to see her." She swung around to face Gail. "How could my own mother even *expect* me to live here?"

Gail felt like crying but swallowed the lump in her throat. She was the adult. She was the one in charge. "Plot and plan all you like, Patricia, but you *are* going to stay here with the rest of us. Time for you to learn what life is all about, and you might as well have it all in one big dose rather than in little spoonfuls."

"Honestly, you talk like a Victorian parson's wife. Why can't we move to somewhere nice, somewhere modern?"

"This is where we live right now, and you'll have to get used to it, like I did."

"It's all right for you, Mother, you don't mix with the right people like I do. They all have huge houses and some even have titles. What do you think living here means to me, knowing I live in such a dump? You might like it, but I don't."

"Look, Trish, I don't like it any more than you, and do you really think it's easy for me? Do you think I want to live here? Do you think I like working as a waitress all day long to earn enough money for this *hovel* as you call it?" Patricia stared stonily at a point over Gail's head, her mind on her own martyrdom. "If I didn't work, we wouldn't even have this roof over our head. Are you even listening to me?"

Trish nodded sulkily but did not look at her mother. "Do you think I like coming home after a hard day's work to a toasted sandwich because I can't afford to buy meat?" Gail put an arm around Trish's shoulders, but she shrugged it off. "Thank God you have a mother who cares about you and a place to live. Rest assured, Trish, life is not all luxury and ease. It's a cruel world and grim reality is alien to you. You're a young woman now and have to learn about life as it really is, and not as you would like it to be."

Gail moved to leave the room as Trish threw herself on Gail's bed and pounded her fists into the pillow. She burst into savage tears. "I *won't* stay here. You can't *make* me. I won't, I won't." Her legs flailed and the bed springs creaked and clanged.

Gail smiled grimly. "That's right Trish, get it all out of your system. We'll be downstairs waiting for you when you've dried your eyes."

"I *hate* you, you horrible woman, I *hate* you!" Patricia screamed, raising her blotched face and red eyes. "I'd hate to be like you. All you think about is yourself. I never want to *see* you again. I want my *Daddy*. He wouldn't let you treat me this way."

Gail looked at her and left the room. Better let her get on with it, she thought, she'll have to learn to accept it. Patricia's words had cut her to the quick, but she realized the child had said them in anger. Poignantly recalling the time when she too yelled at her own mother and said she hated her, she smiled. History does repeat itself.

Robert was sitting at the open front door on the step, eating yet another hacked off piece of the welcome home cake. He turned as he heard her footsteps.

"I say! This is super cake, Mummy. It's too bad there's only one tiny bit left. Can you hide it somewhere so I can eat it before bed with my glass of milk?"

She smiled fondly at her resilient child. The one she worried about most was taking it in his stride and glad to be with her. "I'll hide it right now, Robby."

Robert shot to his feet as he saw a shiny red car drive past. "May I go look at that Jag, Mummy? The man is parking it up the street. May I go, Mummy?"

"Of course, but be careful and watch the traffic." He scampered off, slamming the rickety gate so hard it almost came off its hinges.

She went into the scullery and started loading the old washing machine with Robert's dirty clothes. Vincent sauntered in from the living room, his previous acrimony dissipated, his voice strangely pleasant. "This is a real comedown, isn't it, Mother?"

Gail said nothing, but glanced at him.

He sighed as he slouched, hands in pockets. "I really don't think I can invite any of the chaps here. I was going to ask Freddy, but think it's out of the question now I've seen the place." He nonchalantly leaned against the door frame, a young prince full of self-confidence and scholarship, and watched her. "You know, you really should have written to say it was so cramped. You only said you had moved to a cottage and I imagined something like Starlings, maybe smaller. Mother, this is grotesque. It might be all right for you, but not for us."

"Grotesque it might be, Vincent, but it is all we have." Gail was angry, first Trish and now Vincent. What had happened to family values where everyone pulled together and supported each other through times of upheaval? "All the British public school system has taught you and Trish is how to be snobs." He looked surprised, and she nodded. "That's the word for it. You are Class A snobs. I'm your mother and, while your father and I raised you to appreciate the finer things in life, that school has brainwashed you into thinking you are now better than me. I'm beginning to think we made a huge mistake with your education." She felt a certain amount of satisfaction at his expression. Good, something can get through his air of patronization. "You aren't any better than I am, Vincent, and neither is your sister. Both of you must learn, as I told her, that life is not fair."

His huge sigh of irritation did not stop her, nor did his movement to the door as this time Gail decided to have her say.

"Excuse me, but I have not finished, Vincent. Please do me the favor of hearing me out for once." He stopped and turned to face her, his expression one of utter boredom. "This is for your own good, son." As she uttered the dreaded words, she saw his expression harden. "You surely realize that you have to make your own happiness, accept life as it comes. Don't expect the world to hand possessions and money to you without any effort on your part."

She noticed he had the grace to look shamefaced. "For a start you might consider finding yourself a summer job to help with the rent for this place." He looked at her as if she were quite mad. "Now, have you any things that need washing?"

Vincent turned on his heel and went out the front door. She heard Patricia calling to him, then the sound of eager feet racing down the stairs and the front door slammed loudly.

Relaxing in the welcome quiet, she put on the kettle. Tea might not solve her problems, but it would comfort her.

The Embassy's letter arrived yesterday and she reread it as she drank her tea. It informed her no trace had been found of any bank account in John James Montgomery's name in the county. Did she want them to check further afield, London maybe? She pondered on it. Was it worth it? How much money had John hidden? Whatever, it could not hurt and she quickly wrote a short note requesting them to continue their investigation.

Robert came slamming in fetching a small skinny black child who wore a tattered hand knit sweater. Too long for him, the ragged hem dangled below his knees. "This is Alf, Mummy," he said, proud of his new chum. "May we please have some pop?"

Gail looked down at Robert and Alf, glad one of her brood had made a new friend. Alf was all eyes, so dark he was purple-black, curly headed, and frail looking.

Taking down a bottle of lemonade, she poured them each a glass. Opening a tin, she found the remains of the chocolate biscuits and gave them one each.

"Cor," Alf said, eyes like saucers. "Choccy biccy." *You'd have thought I'd handed him a new bicycle,* she thought, a lump in her throat. He carefully put it in his pocket, making sure it did not break. "I'll save it for afters," he said, regarding her with love.

Gail wondered if he ever got such treats at home, wherever that may be. His cockney accent was of the London slums and a complete contrast to Robert's cultured diction. Thank God Robert wasn't a snob, she thought, he liked everyone and accepted them at face value.

Alf and Robert sat in the living room in front of the fireplace, sipping lemonade and making small boy talk. From what she could hear as she tended the ancient washing machine and wrung out the clothes, they were discussing Robert's current passion, cars. He read everything he could on the subject and listening to his dissertation on the workings of the internal combustion engine, astonished her with his knowledge. Alf put his two pennyworth in now and again, but as his conversation was mostly slang and his accent atrocious, she hardly understood him. Robert had no such trouble and rattled on excitedly.

It was nearly nine o'clock and neither Vincent nor Patricia had returned. After she tucked Robert in bed, Gail, worried that something had happened to them, kept going to the front door and looking down the street. Then finally deciding they were trying to worry her for spite, settled down with a book. After ten minutes she became uneasy, the words making no sense. Turning on the television, she listened to a talk show, constantly glancing at the old-fashioned mantel clock that sat on the bookcase.

Had they gone to stay with their school chums, she wondered? Should she call their schools? Should she contact the police? To whom could she turn for help? Eric Matheson, Jill Haslett and Geoffrey came to mind. All would think her an inept mother if she could not control her children, and surely Trish and Vincent were old enough to take care of themselves. Patricia was nearly fourteen and Vincent almost seventeen.

Sighing at her inadequacy, she decided to go to the call box and contact Eric Matheson, who advised her to call the police.

"What time did they leave, Mrs. Montgomery?" The police sergeant asked.

After she told him her pitiful tale, he pointed out they were not so small and probably could look after themselves. Public school children, he said, were self-confident He felt sure they'd soon return home. A typical prank, he said, not to worry, but to call him if they hadn't come back within four hours.

As she trudged through the darkened streets back to the cottage, Gail seethed with rage. She would beat the pair of them once she got her hands on them, she promised herself. How could they do this to her? Deciding to go to bed, she undressed and lay reading her book by the light of a small reading lamp she had bought at a boot sale.

When suddenly someone knocked loudly on the front door, she

grabbed her housecoat and stumbled down the stairs. They were back! Blasted stupid kids, they were going to get a piece of her mind for sure.

A strange man stood on the step. "Mrs. Montgomery?"

Gail stared at him. Was he a police officer? She saw the large black car parked at the curb.

"I think I have your children in my car," he said gesturing to the road. Her hands flew to her mouth, relief suddenly displaced by anger, blasted kids! She could see the outlines of them sitting in the back, a woman sitting in the front. "May I come in for a moment, do you think?"

Gail stood aside and he went into the living room. "I really should introduce myself." He stuck out a beefy hand. "I'm Harry Donahue. I took over from your husband. Your children came to the house and wanted to stay. I did try to explain to them that they couldn't, and asked where they now lived. It took my wife and me all this time to pry it out of them. They didn't seem to want to come home, but I knew you'd be worried. I tried to call, but the GPO said you didn't have a phone."

"Yes, thank you very much. I was worried out of my mind and already called the police. Maybe you could call the station for me, let them know they have returned?" Gail felt mortified. Did he think she was a cruel mother, cruelty being the reason for their flight? What had they said to him, she wondered?

"I think those two young reprobates should be in bed. Shall we get them inside?"

Harry went to the car. As he and his wife brought the delinquents into the house, Gail noticing Harry held firmly onto Vincent and his wife hung onto Patricia. Did they think the kids were going to make a run for it again? What a rotten mother she must appear in their eyes.

The Donahues left hastily, for which she was grateful. She would have to write them a proper 'thank you' note tomorrow.

Patricia glared defiantly at Gail and in the dim light of the sixty watt bulb hanging in the centre of the room, she looked much older and somehow haggard. Vincent slouched on the couch arm, his hands in his pockets, sulky and morose.

"So what do you two have to say for yourselves?" Gail asked quietly. She was in no mood for loud arguments.

"We don't want to stay here, Mother. It's too small, dirty and much too horrible. We always lived at Starlings, but that man said we couldn't," Patricia said in a voice filled with resentment, "Isn't that right, Vincent?"

"Yes," was all he said.

Gail regarded them, seeing the ill-concealed disdain, knowing they blamed her for everything. "I don't want to live here, either, but where else could I go? Well, since both of you share my feelings, and you must have discussed it, please give me your suggestions." Frustrated, she looked at both of them, indolent and spoiled.

Silence. Gail waited and waited. They glanced at each other, made small shrugs of impotence, stared at the floor or the embers of the fire. Eventually she said, "Well, I'm going to bed and I suggest you do the same. Come along, Trish, I don't want you stumbling around in the dark while I'm trying to sleep." She turned to look at her son. "And Vincent, don't wake Robert. He needs his sleep. I'm sure after you have both slept on it, you'll come up with the right solution for all of us." She stopped herself from saying "After all, you have the education."

She gestured for Patricia to go up the stairs ahead of her, and waited until Vincent managed to drag himself up from the depths of the couch, before heading upstairs herself.

"Turn off the light please, Vincent."

"I suppose we soon probably cannot afford that, either," he said spitefully as he glared up at her. "Are you buying candles, or will we have oil lamps?"

"That's right, son," she called cheerily as she went into the bedroom.

Time for him to grow up.

CHAPTER TWELVE

Some days later, Gail received a surprise visit by Geoffrey. Though shocked, she had no alternative but to invite him inside. Robert came racing home when he saw the car in front of their house. Vincent and Patricia were outside in the back garden but came in to inspect the visitor when Robert told them about the posh car.

"I'll make us some tea, Geoffrey. I'm sorry that I don't have anything tasty to make small sandwiches but the children eat like horses."

Geoffrey sat on the couch and relaxed as much as he was able. "Don't go to any trouble, Gail, this is just a social call."

Composed and smiling, Geoffrey sat in the cramped living room as the older children stared at him rudely. It was as if they had never seen a man before. They insolently looked him up and down, lips curled. Robert sat up straight so he could look through the window at Geoffrey's car

"How are you liking school?" Geoffrey asked Vincent. Their steady and rude scrutiny made him feel uncomfortable.

"It's all right, I suppose," Vincent said gloomily.

"I'm having rugby next term," Robert said, his voice filled with enthusiasm. "Mummy is going to buy me the gear next week."

"You? Play rugby?" Vincent scoffed. "You're too much of a shrimp to get into scrums, tiddler. They'll tear you limb from limb. Take my advice, old man, go in for tennis or cricket."

"No, I shall play rugby." Robert said firmly. "We learn sportsmanship at our school. It's not like your rotten old school where they're all like you, vulgar cads and rough with it." Robert always stood his ground with Vincent. He did not much like his older brother, who was a know-it-all.

Vincent laughed scornfully. "Too bad, tadpole. Mother will be really furious when they fetch you home in a paper bag."

Vincent turned his attention back to Geoffrey and eyed his handmade shoes. "You had those shoes made for you, didn't you?" he said rudely. "How much did they cost?"

"Vincent!" Gail said, shocked, as she came in with the tea tray. "Don't be so impolite. Don't they teach manners at that school of yours?"

"Told you," Robert said, grinning.

For over a week, the four had lived in bristling silence as a resentment charged the atmosphere in the tiny house. Robert, as cheery and outgoing as ever, sailed through all of it without a care, not noticing his siblings' silences and mopes. Not that he stayed in the house much as he spent his days running wild with Alf and two or three other lads. They were a cosmopolitan group, Gail realized when she first saw them, black, white and brown, but they were good boys and enjoyed each other's company.

Of course, neither Trish nor Vincent could come up with any wonderful ideas on how to improve their lot in life. So much for higher education, she thought. Both declined to take a summer job in the village, or elsewhere, as they had no transportation, and refused to mix with the local 'village idiots,' as Vincent called them. They had, however, finally stopped their constant bickering with each other, united in their hatred of the cottage and the mother who expected them to like it or lump it.

One day when she came home from work tired and discouraged, they were screaming at each other about who should have taken the ashes out of the fireplace. It went on for nearly half an hour during which time they completely ignored her. Unable to stand it for another second, she took the knife she used to slice bread and whistled for time out.

"Right. I don't want to come into this house and find you two going at it hammer and tongs. I've had it with you two and if you can't get along, I don't see why I should suffer. Here's the bread knife. I don't want to see more than one of you coming out of this room. Sort it out between yourselves." She went back into the kitchen, slammed the door and left them staring after her in horror.

Since then they lived in hostile enmity, but silently. They no longer spoke to each other when she was around. Both glared and glowered at her, even when they thought she was not looking, and she wondered if she had done the right thing. What kind of scar would this leave on them, she wondered? Oh well, it won't be visible, that's all that mattered. She never raised her hand to them, no matter how much they vexed her, always talked sensibly about their plight and tried to make light of it.

"Tea, Geoffrey," she said brightly as she passed him a cup.

"Thank you, my dear." He flashed her a smile. "Mother would like you and the children to come for Sunday tea. You could also stay over for supper, if you wished. Mother is so looking forward to meeting the children."

"We are not *children*. I'll be soon be eighteen," Vincent, stretching a point and wounded to the quick, spoke acidly.

"Yes, yes, of course you are," Geoffrey said in an even voice, "but in comparison to me you are still a child. I am sure from your perspective that I am quite ancient, but I can assure you I have a long way to go before they can call me old."

"So exactly how old *are* you?"

"Trish!" Gail said. "Where are your manners? Do neither of you have any gentility? We brought you up to know better."

"Oh, don't worry, Gail," Geoffrey laughed. "I understand what these two are doing. They're trying to see how far they can go before I take umbrage. I must admit I did it myself when I was their age." He put down his cup and looked at them. "Well, it is not going to work, my dears. So, if you're as adult as you like to think you are, shall we have an adult conversation?"

Both seemed impressed that he spoke to them in that manner.

Maybe they need a man around to keep them in line, Gail thought, as they chatted about Geoffrey's car for Robert's benefit. Later they discussed Vincent's ambitions to enter law.

Meanwhile, Gail noticed, Trish sat quietly, mentally totaling the cost of Geoffrey's clothes and accessories, Gail could almost see her mental cash register ringing. The afternoon ended with polite goodbyes from Patricia and Vincent, and after an excited Robert sat in Geoffrey's Bentley and appreciatively touched the dashboard gauges with many an exclamation of delight.

As Gail waved Geoffrey goodbye, she sighed with pleasure that it had gone so smoothly, having wondered what the eldest two would think about her having a male friend. They seemed to have taken it well. Robert was over the moon that he could ride in the Bentley on Sunday, and already chattering about Geoffrey's mother's vintage Rolls Royce. Geoffrey had told him all about it.

Patricia and Vincent, having inspected and appraised Geoffrey, apparently found him satisfactory, so it did not surprise Gail when Vincent mentioned how much he looked forward to the planned Sunday tea. Of course, she knew both were curious to see Geoffrey's home. The covetous way both assessed Geoffrey's clothes and jewelry revealed that. *Never mind, Vincent my boy*, she said to herself, *it will impress you enormously.*

Then, with a definite sinking feeling, it dawned on her that once Vincent and Patricia saw the estate and met Geoffrey's mother, living with them would be absolutely impossible as it would make the cottage look even tinier and less attractive. Thinking it over, she wondered if she should have refused the invitation. *Too late now*, she told herself, *I'll have to live with it. That's all I seem to do these days, learn to live with it. Nevertheless, I'm surviving. We're getting by, and that's all that matters.*

Each day she arrived home to find both Vincent and Patricia languidly draped over some piece of furniture, idle and bored. With their carefully cultivated accents, they would never have lowered themselves to speak to locally educated children. They said as much, when after their first walk of exploration, they spoke scathingly of the dilapidated and crumbling village school in patronizing tones, talked of speaking to a local boy who they said spoke only in grunts.

Gail felt for them, yet resolved not to show her feelings, either way. Both sighed deeply and often, lamenting their lost life of luxury while lying around listlessly, getting on her nerves. At least the fact their education was secure made them feel better, although Patricia wrote countless letters to school friends and to her grandparents in Canada. She never told Gail what the weekly missives contained and Gail assumed that to her school chums she would pretend things were unchanged, while to her grandparents it would have been moans and complaints about her current living conditions.

Yet when Gail's parents wrote they never mentioned anything, although they mentioned both Vincent and Patricia had written. Gail clamped her mouth shut, determined not to ask her ungrateful offspring anything.

One day when she lost her temper and told them both off for not helping around the house, they looked at her as though she had lost her mind. Them? Their attitudes said, help with housework? With their education? Surely she jested? These days she worked a six-day week as the extra money was useful with three children to feed. Refusal to help being the gist of their snobbish replies, she slammed out of the house and took Robert to the tea shop for supper. Let them starve, she thought, viciously. Their lack of sensitivity appalled her: they thought only of themselves.

Yet what kind of mother was she that she could walk out on her children? Still, how did they think she felt on coming home after a hard day's work to find them still lolling around in their pyjamas, leaving the dirty breakfast dishes, empty pop bottles and the remains of their lunch sandwiches everywhere? They could not even pick up their dirty clothes, but left them lying around for her, the maid. While, as a mother, she did most things cheerfully and without complaint, she considered the eldest two adult enough to help around the house. So, maybe a touch of deprivation might get through to them.

CHAPTER THIRTEEN

The next day when she returned home they were again lolling around, hungry and disheveled, so she told them in simple language what she expected. They retaliated by giving her the silent treatment, moved not a muscle. No matter how their treatment hurt, she dared not let them see it.

Robert was her only source of joy, being bright as a new penny. Scouting around the district with Alf, he founded a gang of his own and went around dirty and bare footed as though he always lived that way. Each day she sent him off clean and tidy, but each evening on her return he appeared filthy and tattered from the day's adventures. He talked nonstop, using slang words picked up from Alf, foreign words from the others, told outrageously unfunny school boy jokes, and she loved each silly minute.

The two snobs ignored him, aiming looks of loathing, especially when he told her some silly joke and went into fits of giggles. Considering him an imbecile, they often told him so which sent him into hysterical laughter. Robert's way of dealing with them had much to offer, although she would never laugh at them like he did.

Today was Saturday. Patricia spent the time freshening up the dress she would wear for the tea party. She had almost thrown it at Gail as Gail was leaving for work the day before.

"You'll *have* to wash and iron this for Sunday, Mother. I have *nothing* else to wear."

"Pardon me?" Gail said icily, noticing Trish had the decency to look abashed. "You know where the washing machine is, Trish, and you've seen me use it enough times. Wash it yourself, you've got all day and I have to go to work." She smiled as she recalled Trish's shocked face.

Nevertheless, Trish washed the dress and, Gail supposed, attempted to iron it because the iron and ironing board stood in the middle of the small room. Poor Trish, she only succeeded in making the dress look as though she had worn it to bed. Gail examined it as it hung from the picture rail, determined, no matter what, she *was not* going to fix it, as she was sure Trish expected.

"My, you did a good job there, Trish," she said gesturing with her head to the dress. Patricia scowled at her from the chair and went back to her book. Gail pointedly put away the board and iron.

After Saturday supper, Trish again got out the ironing board and started to press the dress with much grumbling and groaning. Gail watched her for nearly ten minutes, her hands itching to do it, but decided to let her struggle. For an intelligent young woman who had watched her mother for hours while she ironed, Trish seemed to have absolutely no idea. When she went up to bed early, Gail knew she thought her mother would iron the dress, but she was wrong. Gail had no intention of mollycoddling her any longer.

"You'll never learn if everything is done for you," she said in an attempt to justify her decision. Tempted to iron the dress, and yet reluctant to do so, she took her tea out to the tiny back garden and sat listening to the crickets.

Early Sunday morning Vincent, eager to go, talked volubly. Geoffrey was to call for them at three-thirty, and he watched the clock and checked his watch, constantly fidgeting. Did going to someone's home mean that much to him?

Trish's face fell when she saw the dress still hanging from the picture rail, untouched, unironed. She sobbed and sighed as she attempted to get the creases out, pressing it doubled instead of belling the skirt over the board. Eventually, unable to keep silent, Gail told her how to do it, gave her a bottle of water to damp it, and received thanks in a look of hatred.

At three o'clock Trish and Vincent were hopping from foot to foot and dashing to the door each time they heard a car on the road. Robert went outside to sit on the gate, where he waited impatiently. Their antics amused Gail, who shuddered as she imagined what values Vincent and Patricia nursed in their now upper class minds. Robert, filled with excitement, only anticipated riding in a car.

Geoffrey arrived on the dot. Vincent and Patricia were in the back seat of the car almost before he had time to switch off the engine. He walked up the path and knocked on the door as Gail opened it.

"Right on time as usual," she said, looking over his shoulder to where Robert was sitting behind the wheel making driving motions. "Looks like young Stirling Moss is going to leave without us."

Geoffrey laughed as they walked down the short path. "I must say that young lad of yours is a delight. Talk about a chatterbox. You should have heard what he told me in the space of two seconds. You'll never have a secret with him around." She agreed, knowing Robert was completely honest in everything.

They drove to Walton-on-Thames in a bright sunshine that made the countryside look picture perfect. *Gee, this is exactly what I need,* Gail thought wryly, *perfect weather will make the estate and its large formal gardens look even better. I would have preferred grey overcast with threatening rain.*

Jill waiting stood on the terrace as Geoffrey wheeled the car around the circular red gravel drive. As Gail glanced over her shoulder, she noticed the grandeur of the old mansion with its twisted Elizabethan chimneys and huge conservatory had suitably impressed both Vincent and Patricia.

"Look, Mummy, they've got inside trees." Robert said pointing to the conservatory, his eyes like saucers.

Sure enough, the grounds were perfect. Apparently the gardeners had spent hours making sure each blade of grass was in place.

Floribunda roses wafted their heavenly scent, and Gail's heart dropped when she thought of tomorrow and dreary little Wisteria Cottage.

Jill's mood was sunny. She was so warm and gracious that Patricia immediately took to her, as Vincent gazed at her with undisguised admiration. Gail had to admit Jill looked the part of the chatelaine in her smart silk tea gown and a three-strand pearl necklace. A lorgnette would not have been out of place, she thought cattily.

"Gail, my dear, how have you been?" she said as she kissed the air at the side of Gail's face and wafted expensive perfume to her nostrils. "It has been far too long since you visited. You know I told you to consider this house your home away from home."

Thanks a lot, Jill, Gail thought as she saw a look of joy transform Patricia's face, *that's all I need right now.*

"Hello, Jill. I appreciate your invitation and thank you." Gail feigned charm and delight.

They went into the conservatory where a small table was set with lemonade for the children, and sherry waited for the adults. Here the air was warm and moist, huge palms and tropical trees shaded the interior and flowering tropical plants surrounded a small pond complete with a tinkling fountain.

"Mummy, Mummy, come and see. They've got little colored fishes in here," Robert called delightedly, his voice echoing. He squatted to see them better.

"Here we are. Why don't you feed them for me?" Geoffrey said as he took a small round box from under the table and took it to Robert. "Let me show you how much to give them. You don't want to over feed them or they'll grow too big for their pond."

"How big will they grow, sir?" Robert asked and Gail's heart swelled with pride in her young son. He knew his manners, and yet as easily he could run around ragged with a gang of ruffians.

As Geoffrey and Robert enjoyed themselves feeding the fish, Gail sat listening to Patricia giving her impression of a well brought up young lady. Her diction was faultless, her manners perfection, her deportment impeccable. Sitting erect in the chair, she held her head high as to the manner born. To look at her, she was a perfect example of upper crust girlhood. Her haughty demeanor made Gail smile with something akin to pity.

Too, she felt angry that this spoiled child, who lounged around all day in her pyjamas, could sit mincing and posturing like a duchess. She decided to ignore her, and went to see what the fish lovers were doing as Vincent walked around the conservatory reading the name tags on the flora.

Gail had to admit it was an impressive space, almost like a glass cathedral with its soaring ceiling and huge width. An ancestor had enclosed one section in fine wire mesh and in this enclosure with the plants, lived many beautiful butterflies. In the central portion of the conservatory, another section was an aviary where brilliantly colored tropical birds filled the echoing space with song and whistles.

Robert seemed impressed as Geoffrey showed him how to feed the birds. Then they went into the house so Robert could meet the dogs and the parrots in the living room with Vincent tagging along. Everything awed Robert and Gail saw how indulgent Geoffrey was with him.

Patricia continued to sit with Jill and talked about her school term, something she never ever did with Gail. Not that Gail had not continually asked, it was that Patricia simply refused to volunteer anything to her mother. Yet here she was, chattering away in a plummy accent new to Gail, and obviously copied from some upper class school mate. Poised and confident, she spoke with great aplomb to an almost perfect stranger about her teachers and school chums. It was almost as though Jill were her dearest friend. Gail experienced a pang of jealousy, tinged with relief that Patricia had, for once, decided to behave.

The maid served tea in the dining room rather than the lounge. Gail smiled with pride when Robert used the correct dessert knife instead of his hands as he did at home. Robert was the most intelligent of the lot, she decided, as she listened to him talk about cars with Geoffrey.

Patricia, her back not touching the chair, head held high, drank her tea with a little finger crooked and raised. Where the heck did she learn that affectation? Gail asked herself, smothering a chuckle. She would have to talk to Patricia about it as it looked silly, blatantly contrived and phoney. It was all she could do not to mention it.

Vincent acted the perfect young gentleman. He did not lounge about, he minded his manners, always calling Geoffrey, "Sir" and Jill, "Mrs. Haslett," and taking a cue from both of them, used his napkin constantly to wipe his mouth. If he were only so well behaved at home, she thought, wryly.

After tea, they strolled around the grounds. They admired the fruit in the large greenhouse where Geoffrey held Robert up so he could pick a peach from a tree. Geoffrey and Gail wandered off to one side and left Jill to entertain the children, although she need do nothing more than show them the wonders of her estate. That would keep them quiet for ages. Gail felt a pang of guilt for thinking that way about her children, but they really were mercenary. Money was their prime objective and Jill possessed lots.

"Have you given thought to our proposition?" Geoffrey asked as he took her hand. How smooth his hands were, almost as if he treated them with hand cream after each washing.

"Of course I have," she said, wanting to add, "it's not every day a woman proposes to me for her son who sat there silently and let it happen." Words failed her as she watched untold wealthy woo her children.

When she saw the expression Geoffrey's face assumed, she wondered if she had been too blunt.

Then he smiled at her. "Have you decided?" he asked looking at her hopefully.

Gail's mind raced madly. She knew Geoffrey liked Robert. He kept his distance from Vincent who was too old to have any respect for a second father, while Patricia was obviously of no interest to him whatsoever. Nevertheless, Robert, darling Robert, was an angel compared with the other two, and Geoffrey had fallen for his winning ways like a ton of bricks.

She sighed. "Not yet, Geoffrey. It's such a big step to take and I must consider the children. I promise I'll give you an answer next week. Is that all right?" Gail was not at all sure his wealth was the answer to everything, though she had to consider her children's future.

After their walk about, Patricia and Vincent played tennis on the clay court as the others watched from a pair of benches set under the trees. A maid brought out the tea trolley with refreshments. Gail watched as her two eldest laughed and joked about being in street shoes and everyday clothes, and acted almost as though they liked each other. This comradeship astounded Gail who wondered how they had become two completely different people here.

Nevertheless, she mused, she also was two different people: more than that if she counted how she was at Geoffrey's home. At work she was jolly and well liked, always wore a smile, no matter how irritable or out of sorts she felt, going out of her way to be helpful and courteous. At home, glances at her face in the mirror over the sink showed her looking depressed, and usually angry with the kids. With Geoffrey she was the charming social butterfly. Here at River's End she was a lady in her every action, hypocritically wanting to impress Jill. So how could she fault her children, who after all were just that, children?

Robert, bored with inactivity for very long, raced around with the dogs and had a wonderful time. Gail relaxed for the first time since they came home from school. She smiled fondly at Jill as she again urged them to stay for supper.

"Well, why not? We'd be delighted to accept," she said. Geoffrey also pleased, smiled widely and called to Robert to come see the mounted butterflies he had collected while he was at school.

That night Gail slept deeply and well for the first time since John's death. Patricia had been pleasant and helpful when they arrived home and even helped make the bedtime cocoa.

CHAPTER FOURTEEN

Gail looked at the bank statement with dismay. While it was not much to start with, she was now down to the dregs. She blew out a purse-lipped breath and reflected on the remaining pittance. No, not enough to purchase school clothes for each child, and since Robert's arms and legs had lengthened, he desperately needed new clothes. Public schools insisted the children wear their own particular uniforms and any of Vincent's clothes she had kept, hoping to pass down to Robert, were of no use other than as play clothes.

The only solution was to use the air fare money she had been dipping into, always promising herself she would replace it from her pay. Each time the withdrawal seemed like such a small amount, but these small amounts soon snowballed into a huge total, and for all her good intentions, she had not managed to replace any of it. As it stood, she had not enough to pay a single air fare.

Thankfully, she still had five thousand dollars back in Canada that she could transfer over when it was time for them to fly back. The Toronto account was her only recourse.

She paused and stood looking at the tiny garden. Was she going back, though? Suppose she married Geoffrey? All her monetary problems would vanish like mist. The kids were mad about him, which was a plus. Gail privately thought they were mad about his money, guiltily pushing the thought aside, as she admitted to herself that she also liked him for his money.

The children also liked Geoffrey's mother and begged to go during the day to visit while Gail was at work. She refused permission, making the excuse it was too far to travel on the bus. Then Patricia told her Jill said they should telephone and she would send the car.

"Oh, and she said you could come along," Trish added as an afterthought.

The little madam, Gail thought, *making out I was there on sufferance while Jill had personally invited her.* Insulted, she refused to let them go. She could be as childish as they.

Geoffrey came into the inn for lunch twice, not on his usual days either, and sent her a huge potted azalea, so large that she had to put it outside in the garden. He seemed eager for an answer, and Gail spent sleepless nights worrying over the problem. Jill mailed a short sweet note saying how pleasant the children were and suggesting that Gail bring them over at the weekend.

"Why not let them stay over for a few days?" she wrote, "They would have the run of the estate. They make the old place come alive again." She wrote in perfect script. "The sound of young voices calling to each other in the woods and the delight they have in everything, makes me feel youthful. How lucky you are, dear Gail, to have been so blessed."

This remark amused Gail. Imagine being considered blessed with the indolent and sloppy Patricia who lived only for her own selfish pleasure, and the snobbish Vincent who thought everyone beneath him. Jill had overdone the sentiments, she thought, putting the note in her purse in case the children got their hands on it.

"Mummy. Mummy, do come and look at what we've found," Robert called from the back garden. She went through the scullery into the small garden where Alf and Robert were holding a huge shaggy dog by a short frayed piece of rope. The dog had obviously chewed through its tether and run away from home. As it was the size of a small pony, it almost pulled the boys off their feet as they tried to prevent it from getting away.

"Where on earth did you find it?" Gail asked, noting its matted hair and a strong smell of manure.

"He was following a man and the man kicked at him. He was very sad, Mummy," Robert said, looking downcast.

"I wouldn't like someone kicking me, either," Gail said racking her brains for some way to get rid of the beast without upsetting Robert, who had a very soft heart where animals were concerned. Never allowed to have a pet, he was dog crazy. "I know. Let's take him up to the constable and see if he knows who he belongs to, shall we?"

Robert's face fell. "Oh, Mummy, can't we keep him? He's a good guard dog, aren't you, boy?" Already he was beginning to love the animal.

"I'm afraid not, Robby. He's far too big for our house and he's an outdoor-sy dog. Keeping him at this house would be cruel, don't you see? He needs a lot of space to run, and we don't have enough."

Robert sighed and put his arm around the dog's middle while he thought it over, burying his face in the matted filthy hair. "You're right, Mummy. He needs lots of space." His face lit up, "You know what? We can keep him at Mrs. Haslett's. She's got lots and lots of room."

Gail laughed, picturing Jill's face if she saw this huge mongrel. "No, Robert. Mrs. Haslett already has dogs and all kinds of other animals. She's not running a boarding kennel, you know. We'll go down to see the constable as I suggested in the first place."

They tagged along as the dog towed Gail along the street. She talked to Robert, trying to make him understand that maybe the dog belonged to another boy like himself who was upset at losing his pet. Begrudgingly, Robert admitted he would be upset if he lost such an absolutely super dog, and watched as the constable put it in the walled back yard until he notified the owner, who apparently owned a large farm on the outskirts.

"Excuse me, sir, but does this man have a little boy?" Robert asked politely.

Constable Brown rubbed at his chin while he thought about it, catching on as he saw Gail vigorously nodding her head from behind Robert, miming 'yes.'

"Yes, I think he does, now you mention it."

"Oh, that's all right, then," Robert said, his mood changing to one of having done his good deed for the day. He turned to Alf, completely forgetting his mad passion for the huge, shaggy beast. "Come on then, Alf, let's go to the woods and see if we can spy on any kissy couples."

"Robert!" Gail said, but they were already haring away. She had to laugh.

"Boys will be boys, Ma'am," Constable Brownlee said and laughed along with her.

CHAPTER FIFTEEN

Gail worried that Geoffrey might show up at the house looking for an answer, and prayed he would not. She could not decide. Being completely truthful with herself, she knew she liked Geoffrey for his perfect manners, his life style and the social position he held. He would never be any bother, she thought, but could she live a lie? She would be nothing but a well fed and well-housed nun. Then again, she had to consider his mother, because obviously Jill ran her son's life. What other mother would propose for a man of thirtynine?

She vacillated from one minute to the next. Suddenly she would think, yes, I will; it will give me breathing space to care for the kids. Time to settle down and start a thorough search for John's money. At other times, she realized she should never think of putting herself into a silken prison, no matter how comfortable. Then she read an article on the Royals and discovered most of their marriages were of convenience. Sure, it looked as though they were madly in love at their weddings, but inevitably the press caught them having affairs with Grenadier officers, stable managers, or other people's spouses. Yet if they managed to live a good life with money, and without love, so surely she could do it, too. They were only human beings like herself.

On the other hand, if she turned Geoffrey down, what would she do? She had little money left, apart from the money back in Canada:

had a job that paid her approximately enough for one person to exist in any kind of comfort. After the next term the school would be looking for payment for the current school extras. Extras applied mainly to Trish, who opted for everything. Gail knew the trust fund would supply the school money, but, then again, was unsure if she even wanted them to continue their education in England as she did not much like the way they had changed.

Earlier in the month she had written to the lawyer who handled the trust fund and asked for a statement, advising him of John's death and enclosing a copy of his death certificate. She had not yet received an answer. The statement would show her exactly how she stood as far as the children's education was concerned, which was the paramount problem.

The following day she received a reply from the Canadian lawyer and, while making a cup of tea, found herself praying the news was good. Much to her delight the trust fund, due to good investment management, was enormous, leaving Gail to wonder how John, through astute investment, had amassed so much money in the few short years since its inception. So much he had not told her, she thought, with a sigh, glad things were all right on the education front.

Now it was up to the children, she told herself, everything hinged on whether they wanted to go back to Canada, or remain in England. The fund could provide money enough for public school for all of them and for universities. She would, of course, have to find money to outfit them. This news resulted in a lowering of her stress. It lifted such a load off her mind, that for once she felt happy. Now, if only she could decide about Geoffrey.

He arrived at the house in time for supper and, as they ate, she sat taking stock. How completely paradoxical were her cramped accommodations and luxurious River's End. They ate sitting in the living room, balancing plates on their knees. Her kitchen was far too small for five people, whereas even the kitchen was gracious and enormous at *River's End.*

Patricia and Vincent were so chummy with Geoffrey that she found their avariciousness nauseating. Robert remained his own sweet self, chattering knowledgeably about the internal workings of the carburetors and fuel pumps. Then he was telling Geoffrey about the lost dog and how much he had wanted to keep him.

"A young boy should have his own dog," Geoffrey said, looking at her. "Don't you think so, Gail?"

"Of course they should." Gail looked around at the small room. "However, where, pray tell, would we keep such a dog, and who would take it for walks?"

"I'll look after him, Mummy, honest I will. Please may I have a dog?" Robert begged looking like a Botticelli angel, a hint of tears in his eyes.

"Have you decided what type of dog you'd like?" Geoffrey asked while Gail was still glaring at Robert, trying to get him to realize the answer was going to be no, as it always was.

"I would prefer a big dog, a shaggy one. An old English sheepdog perhaps, or a standard poodle, a tall one with long hair."

"So the dog will live in here and where will we live?" Gail said laughing, hoping to jolly him off the subject. "Honestly, Robert, we have no room for a dog. You'll be away at school, and I'll be at work. The poor dog will die of boredom. You are *not* having a dog."

"I should think so, too." Vincent, who was following this conversation with interest, suddenly said, for once on his mother's side. "I *always* wanted a dog and I could never have one. Dad always said if we had a house of our own in the country we could get one. He lied to me, though. I mean, we could have had one when we were at Starlings, but he refused. I used to take the gardener's dog for walks, remember? You'll have to get along with borrowed dogs, old man, like I did."

"I don't want a dog," Patricia announced, in her upper crust accent. "I want a horse."

Gail laughed and then sobered when she saw Trish's look. "A horse? I doubt you can have a horse for the same reason. Where would we put it?" she said sweetly, embarrassed that they were acting like spoiled brats in front of Geoffrey. Their bad manners reflected on her, though part of the blame was the high-priced public schools that had taught them to be acquisitive. It was not their fault, she realized, because the type of child they consorted with came from families whose wealth had been in the family for generations. It was too bad that her children soaked up all the wrong standards, seemingly retaining nothing of the good old-fashioned honor-thy-father-and-mother values.

"You have to be joking, Mother," Patricia said, tossing her head snippily. "You always say that when you don't want to talk about things. We're going to get nothing for Christmas this year, I know it. You keep going on and on about having no money, so you must have spent it all on something. Where's all my father's money gone? What have you done with it?"

"Trish," Gail said in warning, her heart sinking with the knowledge she could not silence her daughter.

"I want to know what you did with it, Mother. I need new shoes *and* a new long gown for the dance we're having this fall term. You'll have to take me to London to buy one. I know what I want. I cut the picture out of a magazine." She turned to Geoffrey, "Cynthia is getting hers in Paris, you know. Her mother is taking her to choose something from Dior or Chanel."

"Good for Cynthia," Gail said, red in the face and extremely annoyed.

"I'm sure you will look lovely, no matter what you wear, Patricia," Geoffrey said, hoping to disperse the tension. "You're so pretty that a flock of young men will surround you and you'll dance all night."

"I should be so lucky," Patricia said morosely as she glared at Gail.

"Take your plates to the kitchen, please," Gail said as she stood and took Geoffrey's plate.

Tonight they had eaten a store bought meat pies with mashed potatoes, peas and gravy, a regular meal for them. She had not expected Geoffrey and felt embarrassed serving him such a plebeian meal. Never mind she told herself, he was so used to eating in the finest restaurants, or at his mother's table with fine china, crystal and silverware, that she imagined eating off his knees in a cramped room would be an adventure for him. He ate every scrap and said not a word.

Vincent and Patricia morosely ambled outside to the back garden with cups of tea. Robert swigged down his milk and ran out the front door, yelling to Alf who loitered outside the front gate.

"You know why I came tonight," Geoffrey remarked as he stood and rested his arm along the mantelpiece. I wish he wouldn't do that, she thought, looking away. John stood like that and look what happened.

"Yes, of course," Gail said, wondering how she was going to answer.

"Well, what is it to be, Gail?" he asked, standing erect, putting both hands behind his back, looking down his nose like Prince Philip. "I would like us to marry. You and your children will never lack for anything. I promise you that."

Gail could not look at him. She studied his shoes, hand made on his own private last by the finest cobbler in the land. His trousers were well-tailored cavalry twill, for messing about in, he said when she mentioned them, admiring the cut. To him they were work clothes, things one would wear to perform a dirty job. It occurred to her that he had worn them so he could sit on her furniture with ease, no worry about soiling his tailor-made suit. That somehow irritated her and she shook her head. She knew John could never have afforded to buy a tie in the shops Geoffrey frequented. What to do, what to do?

He was trying to talk her into it; she could tell by his tone of voice. "Your children would have a secure future, Gail. They would inherit a great deal of land and a profitable stock portfolio. You could dress like a queen, even take Patricia over to Paris to purchase a dress for the school dance."

"Are you trying to buy me?" Gail asked him, staring at his aristocratic features. "I'm not for sale, Geoffrey."

"My goodness, Gail. Never think that." He looked shocked. "I was simply trying to help you decide. Mother told me I should point out these things. She is an intelligent lady, my mother, who fully understands what her estate can do for the children. Look at the manor where you will live, then look at this place. The children will have horses and room to run around, tennis courts, swimming, can fetch their school chums home to visit. They will benefit greatly from an alliance, my dear."

"An alliance?" So this was strictly a business deal. "Your mother told you to tell me that? I gather I will have to live with you and your mother. She seemingly expects me to take orders from her, as you do. I cannot do it, Geoffrey. Already she is trying to run my life and, if I married you, she would run it completely. I know, I know," She put her hand up to stop his interruption. "You love your mother, and so you should. I personally like her very much. However, I am not willing to be her puppet. If I did marry you, I would want a house of my own. I will not live with your mother, and my children don't need palatial surroundings. They've lived without luxury before, and they can do it again."

Geoffrey went pale as she delivered this ultimatum, amazement in his eyes. She knew why. She always kept her mouth firmly shut on any ideas she may have held that did not suit his way of thinking, yet here she was telling him as it was.

"On the other hand, I understand completely the way you feel, Geoffrey. I wouldn't expect you to feel otherwise."

He smiled. Taking her hand, he squeezed it sympathetically. "My dear, I agree. We will buy a house of our own. However, if we can stay with mother until we find a suitable residence, I'm sure you can manage."

Gail wondered about his agreement. He had given in too quickly. "Then we'll look around for a suitable house right away, Geoffrey. If I say yes, that is."

He smiled widely, happy at her words "I think the answer is yes, Gail, or you wouldn't even make such a suggestion. Oh, my dear, you have made me very happy."

Geoffrey pulled her to her feet and putting his arms around her, hugged her gently. "We'll be very comfortable together, you and I." He kissed the top of her head.

Gail stood within his embrace, inhaled the expensive cologne, felt the soft beaten tweed of his jacket, and wondered if she really could go through with it. The life of ease he offered appealed to her enormously, and the fact money would no longer be a worry obviously helped her make up her mind, but he assumed too much. She had not said 'yes'.

"What you think and what I want may be two different things, Geoffrey," she said pulling back to look at him stonily. "I haven't yet given you an answer."

"Oh, for God's sake, Mother, marry the man," Patricia said impatiently from her position at the kitchen door. She strode over and kissed Geoffrey on the cheek. "Welcome to the family, Geoffie boy. Could you take me to Paris for a frock?"

"Patricia!" Gail, her face flaming with embarrassment, stood apart from Geoffrey and faced her daughter. "How long were you out there?"

"Long enough, Mumsy," she smiled sweetly, all dimples and joy now she saw something in the alliance for herself. "Why don't you marry him and get it over with? We don't mind at all, do we, Vincent?" she called over her shoulder to Vincent, who sheepishly stumbled through the doorway from the kitchen where he, too, was eavesdropping.

"No, we don't mind, Mother. You may marry him whenever you like," His face reddened. "Don't start having more children. I don't think we would like that very much."

"Thank you both," Gail said grimly, pressing her lips so close together they disappeared. "Both of you go upstairs and stay there, please."

They pushed past. She saw Vincent wink at Geoffrey, and Patricia give him a beaming smile.

"Apparently the children know what is right. Please marry me, Gail."

She felt angry, annoyed at the pair of them, annoyed that Geoffrey thought his money meant so much to her, and annoyed at herself that it actually did.

"I'll let you know Sunday when you come over to collect us. I feel quite angry right now, and because my children are mercenary does not mean you can railroad me into this *alliance*, Geoffrey. I think you're catering to their whims to get your own way."

Her children, she fumed, what callous small people they had become. Turning away, she watched as Robert swing on the now sagging front gate, arguing with the extremely filthy Alf.

Geoffrey blew out a breath and patted his pockets to make sure he had not forgotten anything. Gail knew he always did that; another of his habits, like shaking his food.

"Very well, Gail," he said without much warmth.

She went outside with him and waited until he got into the car, talking to Robert about the new aerial mounted on the back that brought in short wave stations.

"Are you going to marry Mr. Haslett, Mummy?" Robert asked, hanging onto her hand as they went into the house.

She looked down at him. "Where on earth did you get that idea?"

"Oh, Vincent and Trish were talking about it in the garden. He's got piles of money, Trish said," Robert turned on the scullery tap to wash his dirty hands as Gail stood by with the towel. "I wouldn't have to call him Daddy, would I?" he asked worriedly. "No, I 'spect not." Quickly answering his own question when he saw his mother's face. "Anyway, he would buy me a dog, I know he would. Will you marry him, Mummy, then I can have a dog? Trish could get a horse, too." He looked up at her, serious and wide eyed.

"Marrying someone is not so you can have things, Robert. Marrying someone is for a life with someone you love. I don't love Geoffrey. I like him a lot, but I *don't* love him."

"You don't have to love him," Robert said with the wisdom of youth. "You can only love our Daddy and he's gone, and we don't have anyone else. Still, you can pretend he's our Daddy, can't you? Daddy would let me have a dog, I know he would." He put his head back, looked at the ceiling, closed his eyes and steepled his hands. "Please, Daddy, tell Mummy to marry Geoffrey so I can have a dog. Tell her please, Daddy. Okay? Amen."

"Oh, Robert," Gail said her eyes prickling with tears, as she stooped and hugged her young son. "Come here and give me a cuddle."

He was a treasure this one, a real treasure. If only the other two were as uncomplicated, she would have less to worry about. Vincent and Patricia wanted her to marry Geoffrey so they could have a life of ease. She was livid to think they had eavesdropped, but it was too late now to alter anything because they heard the conversation. She could not erase the conversation from their minds. If she married Geoffrey everything between them would be fine as they would think she had done it for them. If she turned him down, she shuddered to think what they would have to say, Patricia especially.

Why was she so worried about two children and what they thought? It was her life, not theirs. She knew why, though. John was gone, she was all they had, and it was her job to ensure they were happy and well looked after. Giving them back the life they enjoyed when John was alive was, in her present circumstances, impossible. However, if she found John's money, she would not be in this position. Living with two sullen uncommunicative children was not her idea of heaven, but that was what they would be if she rejected Geoffrey's proposal.

To heck with it; she would marry him to make it easier on herself mentally and physically. She could always divorce him, for heaven's sake. Why was she fretting? Suddenly she had no problems, felt no guilt. It was as though her acceptance of Jill and Geoffrey's offer lifted her burdens, and her mind suddenly relaxed.

It would be a marriage in name only, she knew. She need not fear any advances, although she might welcome them eventually. Then hadn't his mother said she could have a lover if she were discreet? This misalliance could bring her the best of both worlds, then too maybe he would become more romantic. Who knew how things might turn out? Geoffrey was so attractive and marriage to him was infinitely preferable to her accepting welfare, or returning alone to an uncertain future in Canada.

She would make the commitment.

CHAPTER SIXTEEN

When she heard the news, Jill, excessively pleased, kissed Gail on both cheeks, a real kiss, not her usual air kiss.

Then she took over. "My dear, come along and tell me your thoughts concerning the ceremony. In anticipation, I talked to the best wedding consultant in London, and this is what Mr. Charles suggested." she said as she handed Gail a huge leather folder bearing the royal insignia. "I pride myself on my superb organizational abilities."

Astonished, Gail sat on the couch with Jill at her side and read the papers. Jill, the busy bee, through Mr. Charles, had taken care of everything: from the church to the gown, to the catering to the guests.

"As you see, we decided to keep it select. Only close relatives and friends." She put a hand on Gail's arm and leaned toward her, saying in a honeyed voice, "Unfortunately we don't have many relatives, and those we have are sadly in their dotage, so the smaller salon at the Savoy should suffice. We invited Geoffrey's business associates and their wives because business always takes precedence in the legal profession, you know. Then, of course, because you've been married before, white is out of the question and we, Mr. Charles and I, thought you should wear rose pink. It would do wonders for your complexion and we could arrange the decor to suit."

The complicated forty page organization, where everything had been considered, stunned Gail. Was there nothing the woman would not do? Already she was running everything. Flabbergasted, she stared at an excited Jill, who continued chattering. For some reason Gail had thought they would be married in the local church, a church the Hasletts apparently bankrolled.

"I thought we were being married at St. Matthew's?" she said timidly.

"Oh my dear, this is to be a town wedding, right in the salon. Our vicar will officiate, of course, but since most of guests own town homes, we thought we would celebrate in style. Mr. Charles said pale pink roses would be flown in from Holland to fill the place with perfection. He knows someone with greenhouses who could supply pink and mauve orchids for your bouquet. No carnations, though." She raised her eyebrows. "A very common flower, don't you think? Dark red lace toppers on plain white linen cloths for the tables with pink roses centerpieces, silver candle sticks and candelabra, and the wedding cake could also have pink roses. Oh my dear, planning this has been wonderful, wonderful."

"Yet you didn't know what my answer would be until today," Gail said blankly, staring at her with consternation.

Jill laughed in her tinkling way, completely imperturbable. "Oh my dear, you would be a foolish woman to turn down our offer. I knew once you thought it over, you would realize the children came first. As for yourself, we can work together on your diction and social skills. We're going to have such fun." She smiled a supercilious smile, her chin rising proudly and her back straightening perceptibly.

The Queen has spoken, Gail thought, beginning to wonder if she had made a huge mistake. She looked at Jill, her thoughts going a hundred miles an hour, already Jill was taking over, and all because Geoffrey needed an heir. Jill seemed disinterested in anything but carrying on the line her impotent son could never achieve unless married to a woman who already had children.

"Tell me something, Jill," she asked quietly, "Why didn't Geoffrey marry someone from your own social circle? Surely in this country has many eligible widows with children. Why me, a socially unskilled foreigner?"

Jill laughed prettily and merrily before she spoke. Her attitude showed her pride, now all her plans had come to fruition. "That is easy to answer, Gail. Geoffrey likes you, and he does not often like females, as I told you. Personally, and this is most important, *I* like you and find your children delightful. They are receiving a superlative English education, are strong, healthy and have good looks." She patted her hair, preening at her success. "I find Americans feed their young children properly so they all possess such clear complexions and strong white teeth. We need you, Gail, we need you and your children to help this house continue the line." Jill dabbed at her eyes with the minuscule lace hanky that always hung from her sleeve.

"I see." Gail wondered whether to speak her mind and decided inevitably she must somehow get through to this controlling harridan that she was her own woman. It irked her that Jill thought her an American, and felt a surge of patriotic love for Canada. Taking a deep breath, she said, "I'm not an American, Jill, I am a Canadian. Could you please try to remember that? As for Geoffrey's choice for a wife, what you really mean is that everyone else was too wise to accept him. That being the case, suppose we discover we are not compatible, and I decide to divorce him?"

Jill gasped and put a hand to her mouth. She stared at Gail as though she were looking at a mad woman.

"Oh, my dear, please never say that. I think you and Geoffrey perfectly suited. I can see it, and you must realize it yourself. As for divorce, well, we have never had a divorce in our family. Never!"

As if that makes any difference to me, Gail thought. *You aren't dealing with a born and bred English upper class twit here, Jill, you're dealing with a common woman who has the courage of her convictions.* Then she asked herself why *was* she marrying him? She knew: the answer was that Geoffrey was attractive and masculine, no matter what his physical problems. She was marrying him because she liked the way other women looked at him, and the way he looked at her. Maybe one day he would find he was not as impaired as he imagined.

It could be her personal challenge to bring back his manhood. Yet surely she was living in dream land, the land of romantic stories, stories so far fetched they could never be real.

She should tell Jill the truth and steeled herself. "I'd like you to know, right now, before things go any further, Jill, that if we don't get along I will demand a divorce," she said firmly.

"Of course you would prefer to think so," Jill seemed understanding. "However, I can assure you, once you marry my son you will *never* want to divorce."

She sounded as sure of that as she was this house was hers, and Gail grudgingly felt admiration for the strength of Jill's convictions. Anyway, at the back of her mind she knew she would do what her heart ordained, but meanwhile she may as well let Jill think she was right if it kept her happy. Arguing would not achieve anything, and as Geoffrey's wife she would have more clout, with Geoffrey on her side.

The wedding went off without a hitch, and so it should since the Hasletts had spent a fortune. The Savoy and Mr. Charles, the wedding consultant, outdid themselves. Patricia and Vincent were in their glory, Trish wore a designer gown while Vincent had his own tailor-made morning coat, complete with top hat. Robert wore his new best suit with long pants and strutted around importantly.

Gail's full length gown was of soft pink embossed satin and suited her admirably. Jill chose both fabric and design, not that Gail much liked that, but, after all, Jill insisted on paying for everything. Reluctantly Gail had to admit Jill knew what she was doing. With the gown she wore the Haslett family diamonds and felt like a queen in her finery. Geoffrey looked perfect and she found herself looking at him with lust in her heart, and something akin to deep affection.

In the weeks before the wedding, it had not taken her long to perceive that, if she went along with Jill's edicts, everything was effortless and pleasant, so she simply stood back and let her get on with it. Why not? Though it was her wedding, she might as well enjoy letting someone else do all the work. Jill's many minions dashed around frenziedly as Jill composedly sat in the comfortable living room, taking messages and giving orders.

At Gail's suggestion, they honeymooned at Niagara Falls, visited New York City, went to Toronto, Montreal and Quebec City before they flew back to River's End and took up residence in the newly decorated west wing. They were away only five weeks since Geoffrey was in the middle of a protracted court battle, at least that was the explanation both he and his mother gave. Gail felt annoyed as she had wanted to go to Paris and Rome, but Geoffrey promised that when his case was finished, they could take the trip at their leisure.

Unsatisfactory though it was, she accepted it, though she sensed that once the case finished Geoffrey would immediately start another. The honeymoon proved disappointing, being more like a holiday with a close friend. Geoffrey lavished gifts on her, bought her new clothes, took her to the finest restaurants, and kissed her gently on the cheek before she went to her room. He spent hours on the telephone talking to his colleagues about the case. Was there ever such a peculiar honeymoon? He did not like Canada, she could tell by his remarks. Nor did he like the States where he pronounced everything too flamboyant, too vulgar. Their recent experiments with the Hydrogen bomb annoyed him. Geoffrey preferred things understated, elegant, and had no time for ostentation, nor warmongering.

It was with a sinking heart she steeled herself for their homecoming, and with relief found it pleasant. The west wing was exclusive and private, so much so that she found herself wondering why she had wanted her own establishment. She need not see Jill because they even had their own dining room and kitchen. A maid served food from their kitchen, though the chef cooked the meals in the main kitchen. How wonderful not to have to worry about cooking and food shopping. Now each morning she spoke to the housekeeper who came to their wing to receive instructions for their meals.

The furnishings were expensive and plush. Antiques interspersed with modern seemed to blend together perfectly. Jill, of course, had employed an interior decorator, and the man obviously knew his business, Gail could find no fault in anything and felt at home immediately. Her bedroom was a cosy haven, painted and papered in a soft shade of lilac, with two easy chairs and a small round table in the bay window. What a wonderful placed to sip morning tea, she thought, looking outside at the manicured grounds and distant trees. The bed was queen size and covered in a matching bedspread and wore a mound of pillows edged in lace. Her bathroom was fantastic, with a both whirlpool tub and a shower. Heated towel rails held the finest Egyptian cotton towels, and a matching bath robe hung on the back of the door. Jill had forgotten nothing.

Geoffrey's suite of rooms was across the hall from hers. The children were on the lower floor, each with their own bathroom, each bedroom giving access to the gardens. To her disappointment, Geoffrey did not come to her rooms, nor, feeling peculiar about this arrangement, did she go to his. Irked at what she considered a snub, she realized she was truly a wife in name only.

Still, what had she expected? The British upper class lived differently than the masses, even she knew that. No, she would give Geoffrey more time to become accustomed to having her around. Someday she would visit his suite, if he did not come to hers.

Geoffrey asked that they ate at least once a day with his mother, so at first they saw Jill at breakfast and again at tea time. She could not grow close to her mother-in-law since she felt disheartened by Jill's social skills, intimidated by her knowledge of everything British.

One day Jill took her to London for a shopping trip and Gail enjoyed herself immensely, letting Jill shower her with gifts and clothes. The stores delivered all their purchases, so they never had to tote parcels. This was the way to shop, she thought, no more lugging carrier bags, hands free and carefree. Their conversation, however, amounted to nothing more than polite chitchat because Gail could not open up to this constrained, correct woman.

At school holidays, the kitchen staff catered to the children during the day. They had the run of the house and grounds, ate lunch and what Jill called 'nursery breakfast' upstairs in the former house school rooms. Gail saw them after breakfast in the garden room and at tea time in the dining room where everyone assembled.

The children soon became fit and brown, their perfectly styled hair bleached by the sun. They had tennis tournaments and swimming meets with the children of the Earl of Switham who lived at Switham Manor about three miles away. It became a habit for the Earl's chauffeur to drive the children over early in the mornings twice a week to spend the day at River's End. Twice a week Jill sent Vincent, Patricia and Robert over to Switham Manor by car, from where they returned in time for tea, weary and happy.

Two days before their return to school, she and Geoffrey took them to London and outfitted them from top to bottom with new gear. This outfitting cost hundreds of pounds but Geoffrey charged everything, insisting the children have things they were not sure they even needed. They were excessively happy and Patricia, running true to form, climbed all over Geoffrey to con him into more outrageously expensive things for which she had no use, to see how far she could go.

In the late afternoon Gail sat in their cosy living room that looked out over the rose garden. The radio played softly and the strains of "Some Enchanted Evening,' had her humming along. Pinkish white doves fluttered around the dovecote and purled soothingly. How peaceful. How comforting to be free from money worries, how relaxed she felt. For the first time in years she felt at peace with herself. How silly she was to worry, how many hours she had wasted in futile wishing. Geoffrey was attentive and amusing, and they went out three or four times a week to dinner at the homes of Geoffrey's friends who fussed over her.

He spent four or five hours a day in London, working on his case and had stayed over once or twice, but since they were still honeymooning, as Jill said proudly, he tried to get home each evening. They also went to London for the theatre and supper, usually staying overnight at the Savoy. This is the life, she said to herself, looking around the plushy Savoy double suite with satisfaction. I surely made the right decision.

Gail still found it enervating to attend social events with Jill and

Geoffrey. When they went out as a couple, she could cope by taking her lead from her husband, but when Jill was present things were more formal. She must be aware of her movements, watch her tone of voice, say the right things. Jill made each social occasion torture for Gail, although this she felt was her own fault for purporting to be something she was not.

A life of conformity to the morés of the upper classes soon exhausted her. To behave according to the rules of polite English society meant she had constantly to guard her tongue - not something that came easily to someone accustomed to speaking their mind. These rules of etiquette had been inbred in most of the people with whom she came into contact. Manners were everything to them, though she could bet in the confines of their own homes they were as crass as the people they snubbed. Apparently how they comported themselves in front of other people was all that mattered.

Nevertheless, she told herself as she lay drowsing in a bubble bath, it was not too much to put up with when she thought of what she had gained. A life of ease, a life of luxury. Unruffled peace pervaded her days and Geoffrey was still attentive at their journeys to the theatre or dinner parties. He was, she admitted, not at all sexual. Maybe time would change that and she lived in hope, because he was so attractive.

CHAPTER SEVENTEEN

"...So tomorrow I shall have to stay in town," Geoffrey concluded. "I'll probably be back on the weekend. I've got a full calendar, what with court cases and disclosure meetings."

Gail wished he were not going and sighed.

"Could I come with you, perhaps?"

"Good gracious, Gail, it would bore you to tears. I shall be out most of the day and well into the evenings. You would be all alone in that tiny flat. No, my dear, you stay here with Mother." He took her hand. "You know, I am delighted that you get along so well. I'm sure you can arrange some outings to keep you busy."

Sure, Gail thought. *Leave me with your mother who is still trying to convert me into a charity worker.* Jill was out and about most days, visiting the sick with baskets of goodies, in her chauffeur driven car, of course. Attending committee meetings in the surrounding cities or going up to London to see her hairdresser, her dentist, her chiropodist, her accountant. For a lady of leisure she was not often home.

"Very well, Geoffrey, but you will telephone me now and then, won't you?" she said wistfully. She missed him, even if they were not a couple.

"Of course I will, my dear. I will also be seeing you on Friday afternoon. The Christie auction, remember? We'll stay at Claridges overnight as we're having supper with the Wilson's at their Grosvenor Square home."

"Oh, of course," she said thinking how odd it was that they were attending an auction to buy art, when they had already covered each wall in the house in museum quality paintings. Jill had explained that it was an investment and said they also had large selections of their artwork on loan to museums and art galleries.

Geoffrey tootled off with a wave and she sat on the large front terrace watching the gardener and his young assistant removing the summer annuals from the front borders to replace them with chrysanthemums and fall asters.

"Ah, here you are, my dear," Jill said from behind her. Come along, you and I are going to have elevenses. It really is too bad that Geoffrey has to keep going to London, but that's where the practice is, and that is where he must go." She continued talking as they headed for the morning room where Jill attended to correspondence and took her morning tea break. "He will not even entertain taking an office in Guildford or some location closer to home. Weybridge has grown substantially these days and so many commuters now live there. I'm sure that if he put his mind to it, he could make the move."

No, Gail thought, Geoffrey would not want to have an office close to home in case he had report home every day. As she grew to know more about him, it surprised her that he had managed to find enough backbone to take the London flat. It had not taken her long to realize he was afraid of his mother. Love her he might, but he feared her more.

Jill, armed with that knowledge, used it and turned Geoffrey from a forthright man into something a little more pliable and subservient to herself. Sadly, Gail realized that he liked domination.

"Today I'm going to Guildford to attend a meeting of the Ladies League against Child Abuse. I do hope you'll come along. I've told them to expect a guest. You will fit in so well with that very worthy cause. Now that I have my children around me, I feel much more strongly about this activity."

Gail looked at her curiously. Were the children around her

different from Gail's children, or did she think that *they* were *her* children?

She half listened as Jill continued. "To think that some men beat not only their children, but their wives. It does not bear thinking about." She shuddered genteelly. "We should all strive to make this a better world for children, don't you think?"

Later in the crowded salon, Gail sat at her side as a masculine looking woman expounded on halfway houses for battered wives and children, the need for more support from the government, the proposed changes in legislation submitted to the local Member of Parliament, and various methods of fund raising.

Before she knew it, she was on a committee with Jill and had a new learning experience ahead of her. At least it will keep me occupied while Geoffrey is away in London, she thought, looking around at the obese or portly ladies who sported hats full of feather. flowers and tulle, wore mink coats and designer clothes, and who obviously knew nothing about living with a wife beater.

They, as was the practice in their social strata, saw their children once when they were born. Nannies took the inconvenience of babies and infants off their shoulders, and after the birth they rarely saw the children unless the nanny had dressed him or her in their best, and the child was on its best behaviour. This only to show them off to visitors or relatives. The offspring were kept at the top of the house in the care of servants, sent off to boarding school at the first opportunity and became real to them only when they were young adults and could deport themselves properly in company.

Oh well, she would have a quiet giggle at the presumptuousness of the matrons of the committee and not let it bother her. To her it was all a waste of time as they could easily toss a thousand pounds each into the kitty and let someone with the youth and energy of the so called 'lower classes' get on with making the world a safer place for wives and children.

Charitable work was all right she supposed, thinking that her time could be spent elsewhere on more worthy causes than those proposed by the rich bitches who sat on the committees. Still, with the children away at school and no transportation other than the chauffeur driven Rolls, which she thought ostentatious, Gail felt smothered at River's End.

She began writing long letters to everyone, even to the children, whom she knew would resent having to read pages of what they considered drivel. Again she wrote to the Canadian Embassy to find out what headway they had made in finding John's money. The thought of finding the money had ceased to be urgent and she had almost forgotten it, but was still important to her. She simply had to know.

Suppose she did divorce Geoffrey (some days she could have cheerfully left him without a backward glance), and suppose she had to support herself again? Of course she would need money to support them all. Then too, John had worked very hard for that money, wherever it may be. Yes, she would pursue it more actively now she had the funds to make it easier.

She hired a private detective and gave him the information. Jill immediately spotted the sparrowlike man arriving at the front in his Austin mini and, of course, wanted in on the meeting. Anything and everything that happened at River's End was her business.

After the man left, she sent for tea and while they waited, said, "Why are you throwing money away on something as silly as finding a few paltry pounds, my dear? You have money enough without needing the niggardly sum your deceased husband might have left."

Gail bit back a sharp retort, thinking Jill had a nerve. Fancy speaking about John in that manner when she had never known the man. "It isn't that, Jill. It's the principle of the thing. John worked hard for that money and I need to know where it is. After all, it should go to his children."

"Suppose you find that your husband was supporting a mistress? I'm sure you would not want to discover that. Leave well enough alone, my dear."

Gail glared at her. So she thought John was a womanizer? How dare she? "No, Jill, I will find it, and I'll do it my way. That's before you start telling me what I should do. John didn't have a mistress and, if he did, he was very discrete about it. He couldn't afford one really," Gail said laughing. If she were pleasant about things, Jill would sometimes drop the subject.

Jill shook her head sadly. "I still think you should leave it alone. I should hate for you to discover something vulgar."

"Well, I won't. John wasn't that kind of man," Gail said firmly. "Thank you for worrying about me and what I do, but I am an adult, Jill. Thank you all the same, but let me do things my way."

"Very well. I must warn you, Gail, that things can sometimes be very upsetting when it comes to men and their secrets. Prying can sometimes cause irreparable harm."

"I suppose so," Gail said, and considered the matter closed, switching the conversation to something Robert had written her.

CHAPTER EIGHTEEN

It seemed no time at all before the children were expected home for Christmas. Jill decided to allow them each to invite one school chum to stay. This time Gail found herself eagerly anticipating their arrival. She and Jill had gone overboard on presents for them this year, and spent two days in London shopping at the best stores. Geoffrey also was like a small child as he did his own shopping, telling Gail about his purchases when he arrived home.

Now a young chestnut mare waited in the stable at The Beeches for Patricia. A racy red sports car sat in a locked garage for Vincent, and for Robert they had lodged a cuddly, purebred old English sheepdog pup with the gardener until Christmas day.

Soon the sounds of children resounded. Calling to each other, playing blind man's buff, and hide and seek around the house. Nowhere was sacred from their invasion and a very red faced young friend of Vincent's, looking for somewhere to hide, had surprised Jill in her bath.

Hearing her relate the story at tea time, (the children had tea in the kitchen, because so many children did not make for a peaceful meal), she made it sound quite hilarious, but Gail knew she was furious at the invasion of her privacy. Jill then confined games to the downstairs portion of the house. The kitchen was out of bounds, and they were forbidden to enter the dining room with its glistening parquet, mahogany furniture and cabinets of silver and china, unless an adult was present. Soon the children were all playing outside in the stables and gardens, chasing each other wildly through the shrubbery and driving the gardener crazy with their crashing around in the greenhouses.

Christmas was wonderful. An experience unlike anything in her life. The food was delicious and, wonder of wonders, she never went near the kitchen. Geoffrey presented her with the keys to her own black Jaguar saloon and she was mobile at long last. She had bought him, on the advice of his mother, who knew everything he needed even now, a new set of lounging wear consisting of maroon silk pyjamas with a matching silk robe. Idly she wondered if she would ever see him wear them.

The children were thrilled with their gifts and kissed Geoffrey often and hard. Jill got her share of sloppy kisses and seemed on the verge of tears. Gail sat and watched them, her older children. Much to her chagrin they did not seem to care about her anymore, now they acted as if they were Jill and Geoffrey's children. They talked mainly to them, deferred to them, and as for herself they tossed the odd remark in her direction. That was the only dark spot on her holidays.

Of course Robert loved her to bits, but he spent most of his time playing with his puppy, who he named Alf much to Jill's annoyance who had wanted him to have his English Kennel Club registered name of Hampton's Rapscallion. Robert became most annoyed when Jill stated that Alf must stay in the stables instead of in Robert's room. Gail knew that he smuggled the puppy in anyway, thrilled that he had the intelligence to get around the orders. That was what any red-blooded young lad should do. He was learning fast, was Robert.

When they went back to school, the house seemed empty and quiet. Even Alf was living with the gardener until Robert's return. Jill said, "While I was so pleased to see them initially, I am relieved to see them go. We can now get back to our life of charitable works and organized routine."

Geoffrey stayed away more often once the holiday season was

over. Now, with her new car, when the weather was good and she could get away from Jill, which took some doing, Gail drove around the countryside exploring, seeing places she had never seen. It was on one of these jaunts that she met Richard Talbot.

She was sipping tea and reading Time magazine's report on Hemingway's Nobel Prize for literature in a tea shop in a tiny market town near the Sussex border.

"Excuse me."

Gail looked up to see a handsome man wearing a jaunty Tyrolean style hat with a sable hair brush in the band, looking down at her curiously. She felt a prickle of sexual excitement.

"Haven't we met before?" he asked. "I'm Richard Talbot, of Talbot, Talbot, Rank and Greaves, Barristers & Solicitors of Green Lane, London. I think we've met before."

She smiled. Yes, they had and she had felt attracted to the handsome solicitor. "Yes, we have, Mr. Talbot. My name is Gail Haslett, Geoffrey's wife." Gesturing to the empty chair. "Would you like to join me for tea?"

She felt shocked at herself. Picking up men was not her forte, but she was picking up this one. astounded that she knew exactly what she was doing and did not care. He was so very good looking, tall too, and had very white teeth.

Their attraction to each other was obvious. It was easy to chat about the evening they met at a dinner dance for Geoffrey's law firm. The conversation swung around to Richard, which she found fascinating. Obviously he was his own favourite subject.

He was the son of Richard Talbot Senior, now a Queen's Counsellor. Richard Junior was a senior partner in the family law firm in the old city and lived in Horsham, which was a few miles from *River's End*. Stopping in the tea room for a packet of cigarettes, the only place open, it being a half day, he had spotted Gail.

"You must excuse my rudeness. It isn't done, you know, to walk over to a woman and start a conversation," he'd said after accepting the invitation to join her.

"Why ever not?" Gail found the English customs amusing and

archaic. What you could do and not do were so confusing and sometimes so stupid that she always deferred to Geoffrey when they were out socially.

"I've discovered that the fair sex dislike men to treat them as if they were available ladies, if you know what I mean. One should always approach a lady through a third party, then she'll know your intentions are honourable." He raised his eyebrows.

"Are your intentions honourable?" Gail asked, flirting outrageously. It felt so good to let go for once.

"But of course," he said, but the lascivious grin on his face meant he had no intention of being honourable. She laughed with him at how silly it all sounded.

They sat chatting in the tea room until throat clearing noises from the counter made them aware that the place was about to close. He took her to a small pub about a mile away and they sat in the snug. For some reason Gail didn't want to leave and he made no move to go, appearing content to sit and talk with her. They hardly knew each other and yet both found something in each other's company that they liked. By the time they parted, she felt more than a little attracted to him.

"My wife will worry about me if I don't head off home," he said glancing at his watch. "I was down visiting my maiden aunt who is in a convalescent home nearby. I usually pop down to see her once a week. Usually Wednesday," he said raising a quizzical eyebrow. She knew that he wanted to see her again, as much as she wanted to see him.

CHAPTER NINETEEN

s she drove home, she thought about his hands. Nice hands with square, shiny, clean nails and black hair on the backs. His hands looked soft and warm and she would like to feel them on her body. Although she was alone, she blushed to find herself thinking such things.

Geoffrey, her honest to God husband, had never even kissed her properly. He gave her sociable little pecks and that was that. He would put his arm around her waist when they were out in company or across her shoulders, as if to prove his ownership, she thought, but nothing more intimate. Gail wanted someone to cuddle her, wanted a man to hold her in his arms. The sex she could live without, yet the warmth of a human body next to hers was something else.

The following Wednesday she sat in the tea shop, surprised to find herself trembling with excitement. It was like being a young girl again, waiting in the coffee shop to see if that special boy would notice her, or even talk to her. When she saw Richard's Daimler pull into a parking spot, her heart gave one almighty thump like someone had banged it like a gong. As she watched as he walked across the road, her pulse raced fast with anticipation. Richard, tall and well built, carried no spare weight and she could see he kept himself in shape.

"Hello, Gail," he said as he took off his overcoat and sat across from her. "You look lovely today," he said, admiring her otter brown velvet suit and the peach satin blouse that made her complexion shine. She had taken very special care in her choice of clothes today and felt glad Jill had not stopped her before she made her getaway.

"Thank you, Richard," she said, pleased he had noticed. "Did you have a good visit with your aunt?"

"Yes." He picked up the small menu. "Now what will you have? We could have a light lunch and then drive to Hampton Court. I remember you saying you'd never been there. It's very interesting and I'd love to show it to you." He looked at her over the handwritten menu.

"What a lovely idea. At least the weather is good. Yes, I'd like that. Shall we have an omelette?"

Five hours later she felt exhausted. The walk about had drained her energy. They sat in a waterfront pub, recovering over a large drink.

"I'm glad we came in separate cars," Gail remarked as she looked at her watch. They had decided it would be best if they took both cars if they were going to see everything, to avoid having to drive all the way back to pick up the other car. "It's getting very late and Jill will wonder where I am. What about your wife? Won't she worry about you?"

"Oh, Phyllis?" He shrugged her off. "No, she won't worry. I told her I wouldn't be home today. She thinks I am going back to London when I've seen the old lady." He smiled at her over his large brandy. "Have I told you how very attractive you are?"

"Many times, Richard, many times, but don't stop, please." Gail loved his flattery. It made her feel female again.

Soon they regularly met each Wednesday at the tea room, and the lady who ran the place saved the window seat for them. Each week they would visit a place of interest. Richard loved showing Gail 'his' England.

Gail fell in love with him without realizing. It was not the heart stopping kind of love, the 'til death do us part' kind of love, but it was love, a yearning kind of love. Falling in love with such a good looking and attentive man had been so easy because she received no love at all at home. Or was it lust? Oh heck, what was the difference?

Wasn't it strange that even as your body got older your feelings remained the same? She felt like a teenager with her first crush, experienced the same heart stopping nervousness whenever she thought about him, felt the same tingles running along her limbs if she saw someone who vaguely resembled him.

Richard took her hand as they strolled around Wisley Gardens which unfortunately did not look their best and, stopping under a trellis that would be beautiful in summer, covered as it was with wisteria, said, "You know that I love you, don't you?"

Gail held her breath. As she looked up at him, her eyes filled with tears. This lovely man loved her and yet she had opted for a loveless marriage and, too, he had a wife and family. What were they going to do? She put her arms around his neck and they kissed. Gail felt weak in the knees.

"I love you too, Richard," she said when she got her breath back. "Are we going to have an affair. I hope?"

"Yes, my lovely, we're going to have an affair. Now come along, I can't wait any longer." Laughing, they rushed out into the car park and drove off to a country inn near Ripley.

They adored each other. Richard was a good lover and she found herself doing things she had never done with John. Suddenly her life had new meaning and she forgot Geoffrey and his domineering mother, her children and the world. They made love for hours and eventually sated and tired, ate a meal in the dining room.

"You are very beautiful, my love," Richard murmured taking her hand.

Gail felt beautiful. She felt that she was glowing and radiated happiness, felt beautiful because she was in love. Everyone should always be love, it made the world a better place.

CHAPTER TWENTY

Jill never asked where Gail spent her Wednesdays, but her old eyes told her that Gail seemed more relaxed, was easier to get along with, even when she ordered her around out of force of habit. Gail apparently had a lover. Jill did not mind that at all and one afternoon she spoke to Gail about it.

"This lover of yours is doing wonders for your complexion, Gail," Jill said suddenly.

Gail stared, startled. She knew? Did everyone know? Was it that obvious?

"You've also shed a few pounds and look so much trimmer. Lovers are wonderful, aren't they? So good for one's ego, too." Jill smiled at her blushing daughter-in-law over the teapot.

"There's nothing to be embarrassed about, my dear. I'm very pleased for you. We've had this discussion before. You're at perfect liberty to entertain a man friend, if you are discreet. Discretion is always the key word."

"Oh, we are discreet," Gail murmured.

Jill leaned forward as she said softly, "I myself had many affairs in my married life. My husband was not very sexual, you see. He was far older than I." Jill smiled and put her head back, closing her eyes as if thinking about her lovers.

The large silver framed photograph of the wedding party sitting on the mantelpiece in the lounge showed Jill as a slim pretty young maiden while her stout and elderly husband stood stone faced and grim.

"He never knew because I was terribly discreet. I never knew about his affairs, but I think he had them. It was a marriage of convenience and brought together two families who were landowners and investors. It was too bad that I never conceived again after Geoffrey was born. We needed more sons to carry on the line. My husband was the last son of his generation. His brothers lost their lives in the war."

"What a shame," Gail said, wondering to which war she referred.

"Yes, it was rather, but then they passed everything down to my husband. After he died, it came to me, and it will pass to Geoffrey when I go. So you see, my dear, you will be very affluent and, bearing this in mind, must be discreet. I realize that you are not born to this kind of life, but I had thought you would soon adapt. You and I do not spend much time together these days, not while you are carrying on this clandestine affair, but please be very circumspect."

Gail thought about the conversation later. Did Jill honestly think she was going to go around flaunting a lover? Then of course she was ignorant of anyone who knew about Richard, because she knew so few of the people in Jill's social circle. People could have seen them often without her knowledge. She decided the public walkabouts would have to cease. They would concentrate on their affair in private at the out-of-the-way inns Richard seemed to know so well. She had to wonder if he had done this before, but then decided that she did not care: he was such a good lover.

One week she missed seeing him when they took Robert into hospital with appendicitis. Gail drove to the school to be with him when he came out of the anaesthetic and stayed over for two days until he was feeling better. The worry had driven everything else out of her mind, and as she drove home she suddenly thought about Richard.

Had he missed her? They had no way of getting in touch with each other if anything untoward happened. Each had said that if they were not at the tea shop at two-thirty then they were not going to arrive. With a pang of regret she later realized that she had not missed him at all, and sadly the bloom had worn off her affair with him. What had started as what she believed was love had deteriorated into common lust. She might never see him again unless it was at a law society dinner.

She thought about him for some weeks afterwards, but knew she was better off without him. Gail analysed the affair as though it were a school project, and was not sure she liked herself very much. He had read only too clearly the need she carried around with her. Richard had recognized her sexual wants, but was not interested in her as a real person. Her problems were not his and he had no intention of becoming more involved with her than their hours in bed.

At first she found it strange that he was always mentioning how sorry he was for his wife. Did he really think she could care? Then she figured it out: his wife was his protection, his security from predatory unattached women or someone like herself who might think that they could force him into a meaningful relationship. He *had* to keep mentioning her.

Yes, she also felt sorry for his wife. Maybe she was a nice woman unfortunately married to a womanizer. Who knew? She felt sure he had no more feelings for his wife than he did for her. And it was not as if she would ever have asked him for legal assistance of any kind since he was a friend of Geoffrey's.

Richard, in his supreme egotism, she reasoned, thought he was doing her a favor. She didn't doubt that for a second, for he was so very superior when he made her climax twice or more, as though he were a god bestowing his blessings. It had made her feel good, she had thanked him for that, though not aloud. Now she thought about it, she had not given a fig about how he felt.

In a way she was glad it was over because, now she had figured it out, all she represented to him was some way of getting his jollies without responsibility. She was safe and helped him gratify himself, nothing more. Mind you, she had been more than willing. In retrospect, it made her think less of herself.

She had not thought that way while it lasted because she was using him too. He was never grateful for what she allowed him to do, that was what rankled. No, she would keep herself to herself and get on with her life as Mrs. Geoffrey Haslett as best she could.

CHAPTER TWENTY-ONE

Things were not going well at River's End. Gail, despondent since the end of her affair, attempted to browbeat Geoffrey into finding them a house of their own. She had come to resent Jill's now constant forays into their part of the house. Nevertheless, he was adamant and stated that he could never allow his mother to live alone. Gail visited several estate agents and brought home many brochures. Geoffrey lost his temper when he heard this from his mother, who had seen them on the coffee table during one of her snoops.

She and Jill were not getting along these days. Gail felt nervous and jumpy, so much so that Jill's constant orders drove her to distraction until she felt she could not tolerate the continual aggravation. When the arguments started, she commenced house hunting, which was difficult because she had no idea how much Geoffrey could afford. When she realized yet again she had no idea of her husband's finances, she sat in the car and cried at her own credulity.

Then, what started as an innocent remark, was blown out of all proportion, and Gail soon paid for it.

Over the school holidays Robert wanted to ride Patricia's mare, but everyone warned him to avoid the stable as the horse did not get enough exercise and was skittish. Patricia's expensive whim stood around eating its weight in oats and hay, rarely getting any exercise other than when a gardener's assistant, who job was to look after her, took her out for a trot.

Nobody was in the stable yard when Robert took a rope and formed it into a noose around the horse's neck. He then opened the bottom half of the stable door, hoping to lead the horse down to the pasture beyond the gardens. The horse, a canny creature, sensed he could not hold her and, feeling fresh air on her body, took off for the fields. Gamely Robert hung onto the rope as the horse dragged him across the yard. He yelled and screamed for it to stop, ably helped by Alf who barked frantically. After a short chase, the gardener and his assistant managed to halt the horse. Poor Robert, who had refused to let go of the rope, was left with skinned knees, badly bruised feet and wounded pride.

Gail treated his wounds and told him off, not seeing Jill standing in the doorway to the bathroom.

"Don't you ever, ever do anything like that again, Robert. Do you hear me?" she said grimly. "That horse could have killed you. It's not some seaside donkey, you know, it's a highly strung thoroughbred. Now promise me you won't go near the stables again, young man."

Robert looked up at her, his large eyes filled with tears. "All right, Mummy. I promise, honest."

Gail looked to see if he had crossed his fingers, for a promise made that way did not count with Robert.

"I shall buy you your own pony, Robert," Jill said, startling them both. "The mare is many hands too high for you. You need something easy to control, and it is time you learned to ride on some decent horseflesh instead of the mules and plough horses they stable at that school of yours."

"Honestly?" Robert looked around Gail to Jill. "Gee, thanks."

"'Gee' is not a word for polite conversation, Robert," Jill said coldly, "People use Gee to control horses, not to talk to human beings. Try to remember that."

"Yes, madam," Robert said, downcast.

Jill pulled herself up, moved forward and towered over him. "Yes, madam' is an American expression which I understand they use in gangster films about the manageress of a brothel. We do not talk in that manner in England. Desist from using slang, Robert, it does not suit you, or your station."

"Yes, er, er," He didn't know what to call her and Gail hid a smile. "Yes, Mrs. Haslett."

Jill regarded him down her patrician nose. "Did you take your dog for a walk today, Robert? Did you brush him and make sure his kennel is clean? Does he have clean water?"

"Jill," Gail said in warning. How dare she chastise Robert right now? The incident had injured his pride, and also his knees.

"Yes, ma…er… Mrs. Haslett," Robert said looking at the bandages on his knees.

Jill did not stop. "That is your dog, Robert. You are the one to feed him, clean his kennel and brush him. Grooming is important to an animal. I get Green, the gardener, to brush my dogs every day. I personally brush the cats so they will not get fur balls."

"Good for you, Jill," Gail said, livid at Jill for chastising her son. "That must take you all of five minutes seeing they are all short haired and run a mile when they see you coming." It came out so nastily. She could have bitten off her tongue.

"Gail! Please remember your manners. Robert is young and cannot always act properly, but you should know better. One has to set a good example to children. " She tossed her head in the way she affected. "I can see where they get their bad habits. Now, young man, please assure me you will see to your dog immediately."

"Yes, Mrs. Haslett," Robert said, twisting around on the toilet seat. He wriggled out of Gail's grasp and ran past Jill, pushing her aside in his haste.

Jill looked furious and followed him. "Robert Haslett, you come back here at once," she called over the bannister rail, "At once! Do you hear?"

Robert heard and Robert ran.

"Robert Haslett, come back immediately," Jill called in her genteel voice. As if that will do any good, Gail thought. He slammed out of the house and Gail, though she was angry, smiled when she thought of what he was saying to himself Robert, once aroused, could swear like a trooper, but only did it when he thought no one could hear.

"I think we need to have a serious talk, Gail. Follow me," Jill ordered and regally swept down the stairs, leaving Gail to follow.

Gail pulled a childish face at Jill's retreating back and went upstairs to her bedroom where she sat on the bed. How dare the woman call her son Haslett? His name was Montgomery, and she had refused point blank to let Geoffrey adopt them legally. Hadn't Geoffrey told his mother that?

As for the children, Gail knew Vincent didn't like Geoffrey, though he liked his money well enough, and had told Gail he would never allow anyone to change his name, unless it was to claim an inheritance. Meanwhile, he wanted to remain a Montgomery. To Patricia it made no difference, since she would change her name on marriage.

Robert was a different story. Robert was the spitting image of John and had inherited his sunny personality. Gail's memories of John now turned him into a knight in shining armour, though she had to admit he was never that perfect. Still, people always did that with dead people, turned them into the wonderful fault-free people they had never been. She decided not to lose the one thing that reminded her of her husband. Robert was *her* son, her pride and joy.

The resulting argument over tea was not pretty and now they were hardly speaking. Jill said in minced tones that she considered Gail inconsistent in her control over the children. "Children needed proper rules by which to live," she pointed out, "One does not change the rules day by day, nor does one let children run ragged with no parental control. While Geoffrey is in town on business, it is up to you, as their mother, to exercise this control."

This infuriated Gail who had tried hard to teach the children normal everyday values. She countered the argument. "Why then, do you and Geoffrey treat them as if each day is their birthday, accede to their demands and hand out pound notes like pennies?"

Eventually, after arguing in circles, Gail refused to let Jill have access to Robert. She could, she said, give orders to Vincent and

Patricia but not to her Robby. Robert, warned by Gail, tried to stay out of Jill's sight, which made Jill doubly annoyed when she could not find him.

She accused Gail of turning him against her. The result of this new altercation was Jill's issuance of many orders that Gail, in turn, stalwartly ignored. This inevitably led to further animosities until Gail felt like she could not remain in the same house for another minute.

Jill had taken to stalking unannounced into the west wing, something she had never previously done. When Gail was out, she pried and poked into everything, yet when accused of it, turned to Geoffrey for support. According to Geoffrey, Jill felt Gail callous for treating her so cavalierly in her own house, especially since she was giving food and shelter to the entire family.

Gail heard a conversation as she came in through the French windows. "I should have expected this to happen, Geoffrey. Blood will out, as they say," Jill was reporting to Geoffrey via the telephone.

The location of the telephone was another thing Gail disliked. The sole telephone was kept in the living room. Anyone making calls did so as Jill sat and listened attentively. Since when the receiver was picked up it made a pinging sound, Jill homed in immediately from wherever she was in the house. Gail learned to use the telephone only when Jill was out on her missions of mercy, but resented getting the third degree when the bill arrived. The statement itemized each call and Jill demanded to know to whom she had made each call.

"It's too bad that I did not look further into her background." Gail listened quietly as Jill paused and sighed wearily, the world's worries on her shoulders. "Since I found no insanity or any criminality, I thought she would suffice, but now I sense dodgy breeding in her line. It appears she isn't what she at first seemed, and we may have to make the best of a bad bargain. I feel glad we got hold of the youngsters before much harm could be done. However, if Robert cannot learn to comport himself properly, we must send him to a military school. You and I need to talk about this, Geoffrey, and soon." She put the telephone down without saying goodbye; her usual practice. Once she had said her piece, further conversation was a waste of time.

Gail saw red and burst into the room. "How dare you," she said, to Jill in a low savage voice. Jill shrank back, startled. "How dare you talk about me and my children like that? Who made you God? Why do you think you can run my life and that of my children? I'm telling you, you can't. Why don't *you* behave properly yourself instead of trying to interfere in other people's lives? You're not so special yourself. I shouldn't wonder you don't have a pirate or highwayman in your bloodline about whom you don't talk. It's very strange that, since I was the paragon of virtue who was the right person for your beloved son, you now brand me as a scarlet woman and a disgrace. You could hardly wait for me to marry Geoffrey, and now you are talking to him about me as though I were the plague."

She was pacing in agitation by this time, her hands clenched into fists as Jill smirked and posed in her high-backed chair. Gail knew each word of castigation would only exacerbate the situation but could not stop herself.

"How dare you think you can get away with this! I will not have you interfering in my son's life, any more than I'll let you interfere in mine. My son Robert will not go to military school, nor will he change his name to Haslett. His name is Montgomery! Don't ever try this again," she warned, "I'm as stubborn and intractable as you, Jill. You'll never get the better of me."

Gail, shaking with emotion, felt like striking out at Jill who sat cool and calm with not a hair out of place, a supercilious smile on her lips.

She spoke softly which made Gail feel twice as boorish. "Yet my dear, I *acquired* you for my son. Geoffrey wanted you, so I got you for him. He doesn't regret the bargain he made with me, but I am beginning to regret my acquisition of you."

"You did not *acquire me*, and you did not buy me!" Gail shouted.

Jill stood and took a step back, a hand to her mouth. How uncouth and uneducated, her action said, though she still smiled condescendingly. "Think before you speak, my dear. I really did buy you, didn't I, Gail? If it were not for me, you would still be living in a damp cottage in Rycroft. Your beloved sons would be at a lesser public school, and you would still be working as a servant in a public house. Oh yes, my dear, think about it, I *did* buy you."

Gail looked at her in horror. Jill was right. She *had* bought her. The children would still be at school thanks to the trust fund, maybe not the prestigious schools they now attended, but a public school at least. As for everything else Jill was correct. How stupid she was, how short-sighted. Why had she thought she could handle a situation like this? Why had she married the man?

Sitting upstairs in her living room, she deliberated on the situation, knowing that doing something, anything, was imperative. She could leave, but that might prove difficult as she had no money left from her allowance since she had spent too lavishly at Christmas. She did, however, have her Canadian funds. Too bad that the Canadian Embassy, unable to trace a bank account in the surrounding county, had been unsuccessful with the London banks.

Her latest obsession was to discover what John had done with the money. It remained a mystery. If she wanted to get away, how could she go with no funds with which to support herself? Right now she had little money in her local account, as Geoffrey, probably on the instructions of his mother had not given her any clothing allowance. He made muttering noises about having to wait until his company year end, which she knew to be a lie.

She could sell something. Yet what? She owned nothing and even her car was in Geoffrey's name. The situation was becoming intolerable, and she had placed herself in the same perilous financial situation. Would she never learn?

Right! She would go to London and have it out with Geoffrey when the children returned to school.

CHAPTER TWENTY-TWO

Gail put her foot to the floor hoping to make it to the station before the train left Woking. It halted there for ten minutes or so awaiting the tail-end of a connecting train from the north that they hooked on before it continued to London. With seconds to spare, she got into the first class compartment and, settling in a corner seat with a library book, made herself comfortable.

Train travel was the norm in Britain and the number of people at each station always surprised her. In Canada trains were something she rarely used and only for special trips. Here it was simply public transport and everyone used the train to commute or go to town for shopping. After driving the typically narrow British road with its horrendous traffic, taking the train that went in a bee line to your destination, was faster and more comfortable. She mused that without the trains, Britain could well be at a standstill.

In less than an hour, she took a taxi her to Geoffrey's flat. When they were first married, Geoffrey had given her a key to the flat, although she had never used it. Right now, Geoffrey would be at work so she could relax with a cup of tea until he arrived home.

The door man looked at her strangely when she gave him her name, but eyeing her mink coat and handmade shoes, said nothing.

A very discerning man, she thought, noticing how carefully he noted her appearance. She went to the lift and made her way to the flat.

Unlocking the door, she pushed it open. It opened onto the living room where Geoffrey and a man were grappling on the floor, completely naked. It only took her one second to realize what was happening. She turned around and dashed to the stairs, running round and round, down and down until she reached the ground floor where she rushed past the doorkeeper, the horror still on her face.

Gail sat in the pub and drank a double brandy, shaken to the core. Perspiration ran from under her hat and she dabbed her forehead with a shaking hand. She knew Geoffrey was not like other men, but how horrifying to catch him in the act and how deplorable to think about it. Gail had no idea he was a practicing homosexual, though she had suspicions. It was as if, in ignoring her qualms, the reality would not exist.

Still incredulous, she remained at the table, keeping her head down, staring at the initials carved in the table top. This was something she had not bargained for, and it made her wonder why someone had not let a hint or two drop in her ear. Usually the people with whom they associated were only too keen to gossip.

Did they all know she was living a lie? Did they snigger behind her back at the horrendous mistake she had made? They must think she was really ingenuous and more than dense. How could she face him after seeing him like that? Did his mother know? She could bet Jill did not.

She stopped herself from grinding her teeth. Her neck muscles felt tied in knots and she had a headache. *When, oh when, am I going to smarten up? I've placed myself in jeopardy again. I lack money, I married a homosexual, I have a barracuda for a mother-in-law, and am estranged from my older children. John's sudden death caused this mess. His death left me so confused and angry that I've done things I shouldn't. Yet how am I going to extricate myself from the situation? A situation of my own making. How can I ever face anyone again? Drat, I never think, never weigh the consequences of my decisions.*

Gail quickly decided and made her way to the Canadian Embassy.

Mr. Johnson was pleasant. He listened to her story, his expression growing ever more unbelieving. *Well,* she thought listening to herself, *it sure sounds like a cheap soap opera. Here I am, an adult woman, ignorant of her husband's financial affairs, widowed and penniless, who married a homosexual to keep a roof over her head.*

Eventually Mr. Johnson called the office that investigated her husband's bank account and requested the file.

Gail sat and drank tea. They also gave her two arrowroot biscuits and she ate quickly since she had eaten nothing since breakfast. The two double brandies were playing havoc with her stomach.

Mr. Johnson went through the file. "I find this interesting. I wonder why no one pursued this."

"What is it?" Gail asked, her interest quickening.

"A bank in Weybridge reports that a Mr. Montgomery used to buy bank drafts once a month. He paid in cash. Interesting, wouldn't you say? This sounds like your husband was buying drafts with his money and sending it on elsewhere."

Gail felt a surge of hope. "Does it say to whom he made them payable?"

Mr. Johnson shook his head. "Bank drafts are simply drafts. The payee is the remittor's business, although drafts are legal-tender as a bank note. The money could have gone anywhere, I'm afraid."

Gail felt the germ of hope dying.

"Well, at least we know he was doing something with the money," she said sadly. ""If only I could find out where he sent it.""

"I wish we could help you, Mrs. Montg…, sorry, Mrs. Haslett, but we cannot trace anything further. You could hire a private investigator."

"I'm afraid I already did that, Mr. Johnson, twice. Neither investigator came up with anything of value. This information might be of help, though. Could you give me a copy of the sheet?"

He stood and looked at it. "Well, it's unusual, but let me see what I can do." As he went to get a copy, Gail wondered about this latest revelation. Was she any closer to solving the puzzle? What should she do now?

She sat on the train staring at the copy as if it could tell her what she longed to know. So John was buying bank drafts, yet for what purpose? To whom had he sent them?

She got in touch with Mr. Ranson, the small, painfully thin man who previously tried to find information. Jill stalked onto the terrace as Gail stood talking to him on the steps.

"Do invite your friend inside, Gail," she said effusively, "Would you like a cup of tea, Mr... ?"

Gail snapped at her. "No, he does not want a cup of tea, Jill. Please go away so we may continue our conversation."

Mr. Ranson gaped at the two of them, his scrawny neck swivelling.

Jill did not move and Gail refused to talk in front of her. "Come along, Mr. Ranson," she said, "We'll sit in your car. We can always drive away if she won't go inside."

"Urgh," Jill growled like an angry puppy and strode into the house, head held regally high.

"This might prove a considerable help," Mr. Ranson said as he read the report. "Yes, I'll continue my investigation from that point. Do you have a recent photograph of your husband? A clear one from which I can make copies?"

Gail nodded. "I think I could find you one. Come around to the west wing, you can wait in my living room. It might take me a while to find the albums. The photographs I keep around are not of John. I don't think my present husband would appreciate it."

Gail found the box in which she had hidden the photograph albums and found a clear shot of John at a company dance. Mr. Ranson went away whistling, which she took as a good omen.

After her ill-fated trip to London, Gail took the obligatory daily tea with Jill with much trepidation. Obviously, Geoffrey had not telephoned his mother about her surprise visit because Jill would have immediately told her so and visited the west wing to relate his every word. Had Geoffrey seen her when she opened the door on them, she wondered, or had his passion for the lover made him blind to everything around him? She could not remember now if she even closed the door. Pictures of them on the floor came into her mind at odd intervals. Geoffrey's closed eyes and his look of utter rapture gave her nightmares. Strange that she never really thought about what homosexuals did. Never could she ignore what happened, forget what she had seen, and did not relish the confrontation to come.

Right now she wanted nothing more than to leave *River's End*, and take her children back to Canada. Finding a writing pad, she started a letter to her parents who surely could advance her funds until she arrived back in Canada, which now seemed far more civilized than Surrey. Old England had somehow lost all its charm.

Jill's walking into their private rooms had become customary. To fetch the mail was one excuse, after she thoroughly examined it, of course. Gail often wondered if she steamed it open before she delivered it and carefully examined the envelopes for proof of tampering. Another excuse was to bring flowers fresh from the garden, normally the housekeeper's job, or she would pop in to ask a question. They were excessively polite to each other. Jill spoke with controlled authority and Gail was positively subservient. It was all so very, very civilized that it made her flesh crawl.

Each morning Gail faced the day with apprehension for surely Geoffrey would soon arrive home. Would it be today? What he would say might be bad enough, but what she herself would surely blurt out caused her more concern. She knew only too well that once she wanted to say something, nothing on earth would stop her.

Too, the children would soon finish their term and head home for Easter. Should she take them away then? Making them suffer for her mistakes did not somehow seem right, but suffer they would, and so would she, if she took them away from their exclusive schools.

Vincent and Patricia enjoyed the scholastic life, while Robert wrote that he wished she lived near the school so he could be a day boy and come home each evening as others in his class did. The elder two, however, were content to hang out with their snobby mates, imagining they, too, were ancestrally upper crust and affluent.

What to do? The private investigator was slow in sending any information and she wondered whether Jill had appropriated her mail. She wouldn't put it past her. If she wanted to use the telephone these days, she drove to the village. Getting through to Mr. Ranson was difficult as he did not have a secretary or answering service. Five times she telephoned, and his telephone rang and rang but no one answered. Driving all the way home only to come back later was silly, she thought the last time, deciding to visit the library to read the latest magazines.

Mr. Ranson never did answer and she went home annoyed at her wasted day and the lack of information. Once back home she wrote a letter to her Canadian lawyer hoping he could learn what John had done with his salary. She had earlier sent letters to those people she knew John had business dealings with in Toronto, using the address book and records she found in his briefcase. Not one came back with anything she could use, all said they were sure John would have made allowances for his family. Somewhere some investment or bank account existed that would solve all her problems. Somewhere a clue existed. The one bright spot was that the children's education trust fund was doing so well.

As Gail was sealing the envelope, Jill came into the room with a magazine.

"Ah, here you are," she said brightly, walking over to look at the address on the envelope as Gail applied the stamp. "I was wondering what had happened to you. Where did you go today?"

"That is none of your business," Gail said bitterly. These days Jill's burbling annoyed her. "Do you ever think of knocking?"

"My dear, this is *my* home. I can walk into any room I like, without knocking or asking permission," Jill said, her smile pasted on, her eyes cold and dead.

"Don't I know it," Gail said, shutting the desk drawer. "Excuse me. I have to go to the postbox."

Jill put out her hand. "You can give that to me. It can go with my correspondence when Green takes it later today. We have already missed the last pick up at the pillar box so your letter will not be going anywhere until tomorrow morning."

Gail put the letter under the blotter. "No, thank you, Jill, I want to go myself. Anyway, I have to get a breath of fresh air. It suddenly got stuffy in here."

Jill gave an impatient hand flutter. "Do we have to snipe at each like this, my dear? I'm sure my Geoffrey would not wish to hear us behaving like fishwives. We should try for Geoffrey's sake."

Her Geoffrey, would she never let him go? Gail simmered with animosity, careful not to display it in her tone. "I refuse to make any further effort for Geoffrey. I doubt he has any feelings for me at all. All he ever wanted were my children. No, pardon me, that's not right, all *you* ever wanted were my children."

Jill shrugged and sat in the wing chair. As she spoke, she checked each tiny detail of the room looking for anything out of line. "Please Gail, do try to use some understanding. You did the right thing in marrying Geoffrey, and I know he feels a great deal of admiration for you and your little brood. Why you won't let him adopt them legally is beyond my comprehension. I only pray they have the good sense to change their names when they are old enough to do so. They cannot inherit unless their name is Haslett."

Gail lost her temper. ""I wouldn't let them change their name to Haslett even if they could become kings and queens of this crackpot little island." Vehemence filled her tone. Should she blow the whistle on Geoffrey? No, his mother probably condoned his sexual predilection.

Jill became all exaggerated patience and understanding. "Must we argue about it, my dear? Let us attempt to live amicably and graciously. Your children will do what is best for them when they reach the age of majority and, no matter what you or I have to say on the subject, it is in their hands, is it not? I did so want to have a home full of life, but I had not expected verbal sparring as the dominant sound." Suddenly she smiled and her voice changed to one of warmth. "When are the children expected home? We must plan a marvelous birthday party for Patricia."

"Yes, I suppose," Gail said, beaten. Trying to get through to Jill who, would live her own life her own way, was futile. Everyone around her would have to accept it and conform. Jill never fought, not really, she found lucid arguments that sounded so much like common sense that it was all over before you realized she had gotten the better of you.

Jill rose and smoothed her pleated silk skirt. "Come along, my dear, we will sit in the conservatory and have tea while we make our plans."

Gail went, not happily but she went, mentally kicking herself for being so weak. Nevertheless, her life was not bad if she overlooked Jill's bossy ways and Geoffrey's perversity. Surely she possessed the tenacity to stick with it until she found John's money? She had known what she was getting into, although she stopped insisting that Geoffrey find them a new house. He refused to discuss money or a mortgage with her, so house hunting alone was senseless. Because of this, she thought herself weak and pitiable, annoyed at herself for being so meek. Her self image had diminished considerably since she finished with Richard, and she didn't know how to change her feelings, or what to do, apart from running away. That seemed too much like a cowardly solution.

CHAPTER TWENTY-THREE

The children came into the house like a whirlwind. Patricia brought home two girls without asking permission and was presently wheedling Jill into letting them share a room in the main part of the house.

Vincent was taller and broader and, with surprise Gail realized his face was now that of an adult. He immediately strode off to the garage to tinker with his beloved sports car.

Robert, taller and slimmer, was still the same sunny boy she loved. He stayed with her as she unpacked his case and told her about a dorm end-of-term party that they held after lights out.

"It was really super, Mummy. Everyone pooled their remaining pocket money to buy goodies. We had those little wrapped up Cadbury cakes, and some crisps and pop from the tuck shop. We had sausage rolls that a chap smuggled in from the village shop. They were nice, but not as good as if we ate them hot. We put oodles of hot mustard on them, and that made them taste super. Then Norris Minor barfed right onto Blake's bed. It caused an awful stink, both ways, if you know what I mean, and Blake had to sleep on the floor. It soaked through the mattress and everything." He held his nose."Whew, the dorm smelled really atrocious. It was super, Mummy, really super. We didn't half laugh!" Throwing himself on his bed, he rolled around laughing and laughing at the thought of Norris Minor throwing up over someone else's bed and poor old Blake sleeping on a hard floor. Gail laughed with him, thinking he might not have thought it so hilarious if it had been his bed.

Patricia got her own way, of course, and the two girls now shared a large double bedroom in the main part of the house, far grander than the guest room in the west wing. Trust Trish to figure that out, Gail thought, Trish was definitely out to impress the two plain, gangly girls.

Why don't their parents get their teeth fixed, Gail wondered, when she met them. Surely they would look better without the Bugs Bunny teeth? They must come from an important family, Gail thought, annoyed at herself for looking for ulterior motives on Trish's part. Jill, the walking Debrett, immediately recognized the names, Frederica and Wilhelmina Shillingford, and her manner changed to one of gracious hospitality as she catered to their every need.

Gail did not care what Jill did now, and in this instance it was converting Trish into the daughter of the house, letting Trish give the impression they were a substantial family - which they were not. It stuck in her throat when Trish called Jill "Grandmamma" and Jill gave her a hug and a kiss. *Little toady*, Gail thought, *wait until I get Trish alone.*

Later when they were all sitting in the conservatory eating fancy cakes and scones at tea time, Geoffrey breezed in. He kissed the top of her head saying, "Hello, darling."

No, he did not know of her visit. She smiled and greeted him, relieved.

He kissed his mother and took a seat on the couch next to Patricia who twinkled up at him. Gail waited with murder in her heart thinking *if she calls him father, I'll kill her.* Trish saw her glare and said nothing but a small "Welcome home."

Wilhelmina and Frederica, or Freddy and Willy as they asked that all call them, shared a wicker bench and ate like horses. Usually the food served at tea time was enough to feed a small army, though most went back to the kitchen. Today all the platters were cleared. When the maid came in with more milk, Vincent said he could manage some more crumpets if the kitchen had any, glaring ferociously at the sisters who had eaten so ravenously.

"Do you know if your father is going to give his paper next week?" Geoffrey asked the girls.

So Shillingford is an MP, Gail thought, listening to their toffee nosed accent and plummy utterances. She knew then where Trish had picked up her manner of speaking. To her ears it sounded garbled, although no one else found it unusual. Gail realized she was too long in the tooth to change and the British accent, which branded you to a particular social stratum when you opened your mouth, was beyond her.

Geoffrey had explained it to her. "Your speech tells listeners not only where you originate, but which school you attended." She could not detect the difference, but Geoffrey always knew if someone had attended Eton or Harrow without the benefit of an old school tie. The Queen spoke an upper class cockney and Gail could understand every word she said, even if she did speak in a nasal soprano with no low tones.

Patricia appeared much impressed by her guests and frequently asked them to tell Grandmamma about such and such. Geoffrey looked amazed the first time Trish called his mother Grandmamma and seemed to swell with pride, as if he always knew the children would come around eventually. Over my dead body, Gail thought, glaring at them.

They decided to hold Patricia's birthday party on a Saturday and Jill issued invitations to each child of consequence who lived in the surrounding district. They needed many to swell the ranks, Jill explained to Gail, waspishly remarking that Patricia would know few of their neighbors, and said the party was a perfect opportunity for her to meet the better local families. "After all," she said to Gail, "the young woman is nearing marriageable age and should meet suitable young men."

Rather than cause any animosity, Gail let Jill organize everything, knowing Jill would tell her everything was under control, or that Gail did not know how they handled such social occasions in England. Still, she enjoyed watching the party taking shape, Jill making the arrangements, without lifting a finger herself. Yes, Jill could all accomplish it without Gail's inferior opinion.

The day of the birthday was fine and, looking from the bedroom window, she saw Geoffrey in the garden supervising the men who were erecting a red and white striped marquee. Weather permitting, they would hold the party outside under cursory supervision of the adults, who would stand by in case needed.

As the guests arrived both by car and by horse, it was an oddly dressed gathering. "Gels" in bouffant skirts and high heels stood talking with young chaps in jodhpurs and boots. Youths wearing polo shirts talked to young women with beehive hairdos and a great deal of real jewelry. The juniors took their places at the long tables in the marquee, while the adults sat at a small table set at one end. They ate smoked salmon sandwiches and made small talk among themselves while Patricia, dressed in a chiffon tea gown purchased in Paris, and a thin diamond necklace belonging to Jill, presided at the head table, holding court.

After the adults had eaten, they left the children to themselves and the caterers. Jill had hired a social director to supervise party games inside the marquee and outside on the lawn. The highlight would be a scavenger hunt that would take them all over the district by car or horse. Later the festivities would culminate in a dance on a portable parquet floor laid down in the marquee.

Gail went back to the house to sit in the conservatory with Geoffrey and Jill, sipping sherry, and talked desultorily about things in general. She wanted to get Geoffrey on his own to face him down, or did she?

CHAPTER TWENTY-FOUR

Gail finally got through to Mr. Ranson to ask if he had anything to report and ask why she had heard nothing. Today Jill was making one of her regular charity visits to the hospital so Gail waited to make sure the chauffeur had driven down the driveway before she ran to use the telephone.

"Yes," he said, "I mailed you the information two weeks ago, Mrs. Haslett. I discovered that your late husband… wait a minute now until I get my notes, I want to be sure I get this right."

Furious at Jill who obviously had taken her letter, she heard his footsteps recede on an uncarpeted floor and waited impatiently, looking out at the driveway.

He came back on the line. "Ah yes, here it is. The lady who often made up the bank drafts was most helpful. A Mrs. Greenwin. She remembers your husband well. A pleasant man, she said, always ready with a merry quip and a smile."

Yes, yes, yes, get on with it, Gail thought testily, but Mr. Ranson would get to it in his own sweet time. He obviously enjoyed showing off his superior investigative skills. She listened impatiently until his description of what he had done and how he found out, wound down.

"Then she told me she would have to think hard about what he told her. She recalled that he mentioned a company once or twice, but the name would not come to mind. On your behalf I paid her fifty pounds, with the promise of more if she could remember the name. I trust that was all right? It is my usual practice, you know. People will remember many important, though insignificant, details when the prospect of a reward appears. As you know, the bank does not enter the payee on a bank draft, but the buyer fills it in at his, or her, convenience."

Gail felt annoyed when he asked if she were as pleased with the results as he, because she was still seeing red, knowing Jill undoubtedly had stolen her mail. Now she wondered how much more Jill had removed from the post. Anyway, no point in worrying about it. Jill would not change for her or anyone else: she would simply claim it must be lost in the mail. The information contained in the letter was not particularly helpful and could do Jill no good. Until this Mrs. Greenwin remembered the company name, she would remain in a loveless marriage, still penniless, while surrounded by luxury.

"Please telephone me when you have more information, Mr. Ranson, Do not send anything by mail. This is too important to me to have your work go astray as your last letter did."

He agreed and said he would check with Mrs. Greenwin on an almost daily basis.

Geoffrey returned to London before she said anything. Obviously he had not seen her in the flat doorway, so she must have shut the door, after all. She was still mortified at what their acquaintances knew, thinking how silly she must appear in their eyes. Right, she would stay at home and to heck with them. When she found her money, she and the children would be out of here. She never did mail the letter to her mother, embarrassed at being thought stupid, already hearing her father's derisive comments.

Mrs. Greenwin, now richer by another fifty pounds on regaining memory of a conversation with John Montgomery, recalled John telling her about "his company, that's right, Mr. Ranson, he said *his*

company, in Canada. He told me he was a partner in an import-export company dealing in high tech merchandise for business and industry. The name of the company, as near as I can recall, was Monterey Enterprises. Yes, I saw him write the name on a registered mail envelope because he addressed it as we chatted, but I can't recall the address."

Gail was thrilled to bits to discover John had a partnership in a company. Surely now her troubles were over? Immediately she wrote to the Toronto lawyer, Mr. Ludlow, asking him to make enquiries from the partner running the concern and report back. Soon, she promised herself, soon she would be back in Canada, with what she hoped was a profitable company, and enough money to support them all. She hoped to take the children back to Canada when they arrived at River's End for the summer holidays.

She wondered why John was sending money each month if he were a partner. Surely the company should be paying him? Maybe it was, and she had yet another bank account to discover. On the other hand, maybe he was buying back his partner's share in the company. Who knew? Another mystery to solve.

Gail felt Jill's eyes on her as, with pleasant thoughts filled of a secure future filled her mind, she hummed over the flowers she was arranging in an antique Chinese vase.

"You sound pleased today, Gail. Have you had good news?"

Gail decided not to say anything. "Not particularly. Sorry if I seem happy. I know you seem to prefer me silent and cowed," she said with more than a touch of asperity.

"Now, my dear, let us not resort to sarcasm. You know I want you to be content. I know," she lit up with an idea, "Let's go to tea in Guildford today. I do so like that new little tea shop the Clock Inn has made out of their stables. We can meet there with Nancy Carruthers and Edith Warburton They'll be so pleased to see you. I told you they were upset because you rejected the offer to help with their "Clothing for Orphans" committee."

"No, thank you very much," Gail said firmly. She had long ago given up on the so-called charitable works in which Jill participated.

Of course, Jill's involvement stretched only to attending meetings: actual work of any kind was never considered.

"I would rather die than go to tea with those two doddery old biddies. It annoys me immensely when I think they could dip into their own full pockets and buy new clothing for half the county instead of having a bunch of do-gooders collect old clothes from people they coerce? Most of them still need those clothes for their younger children."

Gail placed the vase on the window sill and stood back to admire her skillful arrangement.

"Never put flowers in direct sunlight, Gail," Jill said caustically. "They wither almost immediately. You did remember to put a penny in the vase, I hope."

"Of course," Gail looked hard at her and stuck out her tongue like a child, but Jill was busy rearranging the roses and ferns Gail had arranged in an ancient Spode soup tureen on the coffee table.

All day long she had thought about her conversation with Mr. Ranson. Please God, she prayed, let me find out that I'm wealthy in my own right, then we can get out of here. Tempted to call Canada, but reluctant to do so from the house as it would show on the telephone bill, she collected odd shillings and florins to make a call from the call box in the village. She must talk to the lawyer. Funny how lawyers were always so damned slow to set the wheels in motion. They're bad enough in Canada but here they worked at a standstill. Thank God she didn't rely on a local solicitor.

At three, Mrs. Carruthers and Mrs. Warburton strode into the hall, ignoring the maid who tried to take their coats. They walked straight into the living room where Jill was showing Gail some photographs of Patricia's party the housekeeper had brought back from the chemist's shop.

"Here you both are," Mrs. Carruthers, the more raddled of the two, said. "I must say it's nice to see you again, Gail. We wondered what on earth had happened to you. Jill said you were unwell and must have a complete rest, so we thought we'd pop in and see how you are coming along."

Gail glanced at her mother-in-law knowing she had made that excuse rather than tell her friends of her refusal.

"You look quite well now, dear," Mrs. Warburton said as she plopped into an arm chair. She wore a moth-eaten mink coat and a flowered hat resembling an upturned plant pot. Face powder in a too dark shade clumped and clogged her myriad lines and wrinkles. To this stucco finish, she had applied violent blue eye shadow and false eyelashes. Gail, smothered a giggle, thinking she resembled a pantomime witch.

Mrs. Carruthers sported a new brick red wig that clashed with her florid features and decidedly port wine nose. In contrast, Jill looked positively young and radiant, which was probably why she enjoyed their company. That and the fact they came from titled families and were old money.

Gail listened to them as they skillfully destroyed people's characters with a few well-chosen words. All they seemed to do was gossip, gossip, gossip and anyone absent was fair game. Even the Royal Family came in for discussion and Gail had to hide her smiles as they pulled the Queen to bits, along with Princess Anne, Princess Margaret and Prince Philip. She could bet they had never been within a mile of these personages but subscribed to Queen Magazine, or the countless other papers that reported everything concerning the royals. Gail had to smile when they spoke as if they had personally informed Elizabeth or Margaret of their opinions.

"She has a terrible time with her husband, Lord Parker, you know. They say he's one of those," Mrs. Carruthers said of a local acquaintance as she flapped a limp wrist. "Of course, you can see that by looking at him."

"Oh, you can tell if someone is one of those by looking at them, can you?" Gail asked, not bothering hiding her grin.

"Oh, of course, my dear. They stand out even in a crowd," Mrs. Carruthers assured her, taking a large bite of an eclair that dripped cream onto her ample bosom.

"How about the Major next door? Is *he* one of those?" Gail asked.

"Oh, come now, my dear." Edith looked shocked at the thought.

"Tush tush, Major Benny Leighton is an officer of the old school, and his morals are definitely above reproach. Why would you even suggest such a thing of a man who often graces my table?"

"Really, my dear," Jill also looked aghast, "That is taking things too far. Your insinuation is appalling."

Gail grinned and chuckled. "Have you seen this morning's edition of the Surrey Examiner?" she asked, going to fetch it from the hall table. "Look at page five, down at the bottom," she said on her return as she handed the paper to Mrs. Carruthers.

Mrs. Carruthers took old-fashioned tortoiseshell spectacles from her handbag. She opened the paper, where on page five a police report stated that Major B. Leighton, an already convicted pedophile, was caught interfering with a young boy in the public washrooms at Paddington Station. The police charged him with sodomy and corrupting the morals of a minor and bound him over. They would hear his case next month in a London court.

"Well!" she gasped. "Look at this Edith. He's a pedophile. Whatever is that? It can't be good if they charged him with being one. Well, at least he isn't a homosexual."

Gail laughed aloud, saw Jill's glare, tried to keep her face straight, and said. "You apparently don't know what a pedophile does. It means he likes little boys, the younger the better, so he *is* a homosexual and a deranged man. So you say you can spot them, eh? How on earth did you miss the Major? Surely you would have spotted his leanings when he came to dinner at your house."

"Well really! I always spot those who are *real* homosexuals. We met enough of them the year I was presented. Didn't we, Edith?"

"Oh, my yes," Edith nodded her head and made all her overblown hat roses bobble. "They were all over the place. Daddy, the Earl," she added for Gail's benefit, "...had to vet them when they came over for tea. He didn't want our blood lines mixed with them, you see."

How a homosexual could continue anyone's blood line was a mystery. The two old bats' attitude revealed they had no idea what homosexuality involved. Gail listened to their chatter, amazed.

Jill said, "I must say this news about the major surprises me and must surely have been the result of a mental aberration. No way would an officer and gentleman deport himself in such a manner if he were not suffering a nervous deficiency. The doctor will probably place him in a sanatorium until he comes to his senses."

"What about Geoffrey?" Gail asked slyly.

"What?" Jill cried, her eyes wide with shock. "Have you completely taken leave of your senses?"

"No, of course not." Gail turned her attention to the ladies. "What about Geoffrey, Mrs. Carruthers? Is he one of those?"

Mrs. Carruthers gasped. "Not at all, not at all, my dear. What on earth would make you ask such a question? I know Geoffrey as a normal well-educated man who has nothing to fear from that type of sexual proclivity. I really must agree with Jill. What a terrible thing to say! And about one's husband! Really!" She subsided into a simmering mass and drained her tea cup. "Come along, Edith, we must be going. This conversation is not at all to my liking." She gathered her belongings and started walking out of the room while Jill ran after her uttering soothing murmurs. Edith continued talking to herself, as she walked behind them.

"Talking about the Major like that," she mumbled, "Then casting aspersions on Geoffrey's character. Tsk-tsk-tsk. Her own husband, oh my my."

Gail could hear them plainly.

Nancy chimed in, raising her voice. "You can't expect proper manners from foreigners. I know Canada is a satellite of ours, but that woman is not from good stock, or she would never have expressed such a thought in public. Poor Geoffrey and poor, poor Jill. What you must have to put up with, darling. What appalling manners and to think you have taken her under your wing."

They went out onto the terrace and Gail quickly headed to the west wing and locked herself in the bathroom, unwilling to argue with Jill over her pansy son.

Things went rapidly downhill. Jill absolutely refused to speak to Gail and spent hours on the telephone. She also told Geoffrey what Gail said and what she had done. Gail heard her quite clearly as she happened to pass through the lounge and, on seeing her, Jill did not lower her voice.

In retaliation, Gail spent time calling Toronto to speak to the lawyer who promised he was working for her, although yet he had nothing to report. Then she called the Toronto-Dominion Bank to find out if they could tell her how much they had transferred to the Barclay Bank for John. They told her to make her request in writing. She called Mr. Ranson, who was hardly ever home, to ask if Mrs. Greenwin might have remembered anything else.

Jill sat visibly fuming while these conversations took place, but said not a word.

CHAPTER TWENTY-FIVE

Geoffrey was gloriously angry. While he did not mention homosexuality, she instantly knew Jill had told him everything. He sought her out in her suite and stood towering over her like an avenging angel. Gail remained seated while he told her, in what she was sure were the longest words he knew, that she must learn to live amicably with his mother, or she would have to find herself other accommodation. The children, of course, would stay at River's End over the summer holidays.

"I feed, clothe and house them now," he said, obviously trying to make a point. "I even paid their next term's extras. Robert will be transferring to Eton. Vincent plans to attend Oxford when he gets his results and is sure he will pass. Patricia has expressed an interest in a school for young ladies in Switzerland, which she tells me the Shillingford girls are to attend."

She felt angry that they had not consulted her. "You have no right to do that, Geoffrey. They are my children, not yours."

"Nevertheless, my dear, the law is on my side. You are my legal wife, ergo they are my children, and definitely my responsibility. If I choose to send them to good schools, to house and feed them, then I have a say in their well being. You cannot afford to do what I have done as you have no income other than that which I grant you. You would be a bad parent to prevent them receiving a good education. I don't know of a judge in the country who would be on your side, mother or no."

She felt like someone struck with a two-by-four as she realized he was right. Geoffrey and his mother had bought her children, lock, stock and barrel. She could never compete.

Arriving home in the style to which they had quickly grown accustomed, the children climbed gravely out of the Rolls, contemptuously ignoring the chauffeur who held open the door. Shades of Jill, Gail thought watching them, supercilious and disdainful like her. Geoffrey had journeyed to the station to meet them and here they were, but neither Vincent nor Patricia seemed particularly pleased to see her.

Robert ran to her and hugged her around the waist, saying, shouting, "Mummy, Mummy." She kissed his cheek and ruffled his hair before he raced off to the stables to see his dog, Alf. How much he looked like John, she thought, especially his disarming smile.

Tension charged the atmosphere because Patricia and Vincent were being respectful, too respectful. They talked to her with a peculiar politeness, not as their mother but as though she were a casual acquaintance. What *had* Geoffrey said on the trip home?

"Sit down, both of you," Gail said when they came out of their bedrooms and were passing through the living room on their way to the main house. "We need to talk."

"Really, Mater, I don't think we have anything to discuss," Vincent said snippily, throwing himself into a chair and regarding her with wary eyes.

Vincent had grown considerably, Gail noticed, and was now a young man. He was taller than she and had broadened out, suggesting that in a few years he would run to flab unless he pursued some healthy outdoor activity. Already she could see signs of his father's weaknesses in him.

Patricia was a young woman now, though girls matured earlier than boys. Now as tall as her mother, she had inherited Gail's trim figure. Out of the outrageously large allowance Geoffrey bestowed on her, she had purchased a most unsuitable dress with plunging neckline and fitted skirt. This she chose to wear to travel home.

Gail was dying to mention it, but her mother-in-law had earlier forestalled any comment she had, by saying, "Oh Patricia, that dress is most becoming," while casting an eye at Gail, who knew Jill could not possibly like the dress. It was cheap looking on such a young person; which meant Jill made her remark hoping it would start another argument. Gail thought the dress made Trish look like a tart.

Sitting head held high in a straight chair, Patricia regarded Gail as if she were something that had crawled out of a sewer.

"Why are you looking at me like that, Trish?" Gail asked sharply.

"Like what?" Patricia said nonchalantly, trying to pull down her skimpy skirt to cover her knees. When she lifted her head, she looked across at Vincent and winked.

"What is going on with you two?" Gail demanded. "Why are you acting like this?"

"Acting like what?" Vincent asked all wide eyed innocence. "What on earth is your problem, Mater? We are home for our hols and you act as if you had lost your mind." He turned to grin at his sister, nodding. Facing Gail again, he said, "Maybe Geoffrey was right about you. I thought it odd when he told us, but I can see what he means. Come along, Patricia, let's talk to Grandmamma."

They walked out and left her standing open mouthed with the blood pounding in her ears. What had that stupid pansy said to her children? She searched the house but was unable to find him, and when she checked the greenhouse, the gardener said Mr. Haslett left ten minutes earlier, in a taxi.

When she found the children, they were in the conservatory playing a game of happy families. How ironic, happy bloody families, that was a laugh!

Jill looked up from pouring tea. "Isn't this nice, Gail? Our children home for the entire summer."

Gail regarded her with relief. At least Jill pretended things were peaceful. As for herself, her head ached and she knew such pretense would surely end in acrimony.

"Oh, we are going to have such a lovely time, my dears," Jill said to her young audience. "We'll take some day trips this year, perhaps to France and then to the Channel Islands. I must have Geoffrey bring the boat out of dry dock. We haven't used it for years. You'll all enjoy that."

Being their first day home, Jill was happy surrounded by the children, and they were happy at being pampered and cosseted. Patricia touched her now and then, smiling a secret smile as if Jill really were her grandmother. Vincent deferred to her, listening to her chatter as if to a professor. Robert simply basked in being home, smiling and eating.

Trish, she noticed still glared at her while Vincent completely ignored her. Only Robert was the same little love and showed her a dead butterfly that had found its way out of the enclosed portion of the conservatory. It was royal blue and iridescent green with black and white eye markings.

"I shall start my own collection like Geoffrey's," he announced, carefully carrying his find to the study where Geoffrey's collection was kept in glass cases. "I bet this is better than any of his."

"I understand you wish to attend school in Switzerland, Patricia," Jill said, offering a plate of tiny watercress sandwiches.

Trish took four and placed them on her plate meticulously. Gail found her new social skills wearying, everything was done so carefully, each movement contrived. "Oh, I simply *have* to go, Grandmamma. Freddy and Willy are going, also Cynthia and Beth. Willy says it is *the* school for young ladies, that you haven't been properly *finished* unless you attend."

Jill looked over at Gail, triumph in her eyes. Gail could have killed her at that moment, then slain her daughter without a qualm.

"I'll need an entirely *new* wardrobe, of course," Trish said, "Willy says we should all wear couturier clothes unless we want to appear drab compared to the girls from Saudi or Europe. Will you take me to Paris, Grandmamma, or shall we buy from the English designers, do you think?"

Jill sipped her tea, smiled her little smile and looked at Gail as she answered, "A little of each, my dear. I'm sure your mother will come along to advise us," Jill suddenly appeared to offer an olive branch.

"Mother advise us?" Trish said scornfully. "You've got to be *joking*, Grandmamma. What does *she* know about clothes? I want something with *style*, something with *class*."

That did it, Gail exploded. "Patricia Montgomery. Get to your feet and follow me," she ordered with a face as black as thunder. Inside she fumed. *This little snippet is not going to talk about me in such a manner, nor is she going to continue calling Jill Grandmamma. I've already told her a million times to stop doing it, but she blithely continues to say that.*

"Oh tosh, Mother," Patricia said, carelessly waving a lily white hand and sounding bored. "Do stop being so bloody *melodramatic*. Geoffrey said you were having *problems,* but none of us realized you were going off your *rocker*. Do sit down and stop waving your arms around. You look quite potty."

Gail, speechless, rushed from the conservatory in tears and ran into Robert who was coming out of the study.

"Mummy, it's better than all of Geoffrey's," he said grinning widely, "Some of his look moth eaten. Will you buy me some cases of shiny wood with white insides? Mummy? Are you crying?"

She enfolded him in her arms as he held out his arm stiffly so she would not crush his butterfly and cried into his neck.

"Don't cry, Mummy," he said, patting her neck with his free hand. "Let's go upstairs and you can tell me all about it. Come along now, Mummy."

He took charge like an adult and she followed as if she were the child. Robert held her hand all the way and sat her in a chair. Carefully putting his butterfly on the bureau, he poured her a glass of whisky as though it were lemonade. She smiled as he carefully carried it across the carpet making sure he did not spill a drop.

"Here you are, Mummy. This will make you feel better. It always made Daddy feel better. He told me that once, and it made him smile a lot, remember?"

She took the too full glass from him and put it on the side table, pulling him to sit by her side in the chair arm.

"What on earth would I do without you, my little man?" she asked through her tears. "You bring the sunshine into my life."

"Oh, Mummy," Robert wriggled uncomfortably He was reaching the stage where anything mushy embarrassed him.

"I'm so sorry, Robby. I was crying because of something Patricia said."

"Oh, her," Robert's tone was scornful. "She's a bitch."

Gail gasped. Robert talking like that?

"I know she is," he continued, "because my friend Alf used to say that about her. That's 'cause she said niggers should go back to the jungle and not to let her see him again, or she'd report him to the authorities for being an illegal."

"Oh, Robert," Gail said giving him a hug. He had carried that around for a long time.

"She said Alf was a wog, Mummy, and he had no real father, that he was a bastard. It made Alf cry a lot, Mummy. She *is* a bitch and I hate her, and now she made you cry, I hate her very much."

Gail hugged him. "You don't hate her, Robby. She's your sister. You're annoyed at her, that's all. Don't ever say you hate her."

He shook his head. "She made you cry and she's hateful, so I do hate her," Robert was firm in his convictions. Gail wondered how she could change his opinion of his sister.

He's right, though, she thought, Trish is a bitch. She has learned all the bad manners that go with upper crust snottiness and none of the good manners the school aimed to instill. She cared nothing for anyone else, considering her own little world as the only thing important. Gail had often wondered how she could make Patricia into her own child again, but Jill and Geoffrey between them had turned Trish against her. Not that Trish needed much persuading when they dangled money and possessions in front of her greedy eyes.

They sat companionably in the arm chair. Robert chattered about butterflies as Gail hugged him close, and thought about how things had turned out. They needed to be a family again, but the people in this dysfunctional house would never be a family. How foolish she had been to marry Geoffrey, knowing now she had also married his mother. She could not possibly begin to compete with their familial relationship.

Gail finally managed to corner Trish alone at bed time. She went into her room and found her lying in bed reading a Vogue magazine.

"Selecting your trousseau, are you?" Gail asked sarcastically.

"I didn't hear you knock," Trish said coldly staring at her mother over the top of the magazine.

Gail did not like this room, decorated as it was to Trish's specifications. She glanced now at the bedroom suite of bleached, almost white birch, the pale blue walls and carpet, a mirrored wall behind which were the closets, the pure white en suite bathroom. The only real color was Trish herself, vibrant in manner and action, the color of the magazine cover and her dressing gown of royal blue.

"I don't need to knock in my own home," Gail said, hearing Jill say the words. "You are my child and I can walk in on you anytime."

"That's the problem with you, Mother," Trish put the magazine down and glared. "You *have* no manners at all, not proper English manners. You are too Canadian." Her tone became more patronizing, "It is *not* done to walk into someone's private room without an invitation." She paused and sighed. "Geoffrey was right about so much. I mean, all this business about you having a nervous breakdown, and not to upset you. That's a lot of piffle, isn't it?"

Gail stared at her. What was she talking about? What nervous breakdown? Was Geoffrey turning her children completely against her?

Trish settled back on her lace trimmed pillows. "It is really a shame that you have no education and no manners whatever. *And* he said you wanted to take us out of school. How *dare* you? Geoffrey is looking after my education, thank you very much. He and Grandmamma are doing well without your input. You're *jealous* because we're getting the education you wished you had. Anyway," she narrowed her eyes, cat like, "You live on charity, don't you? It's all their money, isn't it? Some day it will come to me and Vincent when they die, but you won't be getting any part of the estate."

Gail ripped the magazine out of Trish's hands and flung it into the corner of the room. She took Trish by the shoulders and shook her, as angry as she had ever been.

Trish gasped and cowered as Gail yelled. "Don't you ever talk to me like that again, do you hear? I have as much education as you will ever have, if not more. I have a university degree to prove it, and I do have manners, along with common courtesy. I suppose if Jill walked in here without knocking, you'd be kissing her on both cheeks, you mercenary little brat. She is not your "Grandmamma," no matter how often you say it. She is no relation to you whatsoever, apart from my marriage to her son. How dare you call her your grandmother! You will call her Mrs. Haslett from now on. Do you hear me?"

Trish lay back against her pillows and smiled condescendingly. "Oh yes, Mother, I hear you. The entire *house* can hear you. Geoffrey won't like this, you know. He's pleased when I call Jill "Grandmamma" and if you really want to know, he *suggested* it. Now, do you mind." She turned on her side and pulled up the sheets. "Shut the door quietly on your way out."

Gail, livid, wanted nothing more than to tan Trish's hide, however knew it would not solve anything. Storming out of the room, she slammed the door as loudly as she possibly could. The little bitch. Yes, Robert was right, Patricia was a bitch.

Robert came out of his room rubbing his eyes. "What's the matter? What's that banging, Mummy?"

"Nothing darling, you must have had a dream. Go back to bed. Come on, I'll tuck you in."

As Gail watched fondly, he fell asleep the minute his head hit the pillow with the goodnight smile still on his lips. Robert was the only thing that really belonged to her, yet Geoffrey wanted to send him to Eton to become another public school boy.

She had read and heard about Eton, the relationships that resulted between boarders, how many homosexuals graduated - Geoffrey being a prime example. She could not allow it to happen to Robert, although she felt Robert was strong enough to avert any unwanted advances, at least she hoped so. To get back her family and regain some semblance of sanity was to take them away from this place, and soon. How long had she been saying that? Forever, it seemed.

CHAPTER TWENTY-SIX

Gail made it a habit to telephone her Toronto lawyer each Monday morning to ensure he realized the urgency of the matter. Jill would stare and listen to every word, making no attempt to appear disinterested. Gail stared back at her as she drew out the conversation, knowing Jill was mentally assessing the cost of the transatlantic call.

"We are moving ahead, Mrs. Haslett," Mr. Ludlow told her. "I have a private detective working on it. I'm sorry about the extra cost, but unfortunately Mr. Elie Rejistan denies all knowledge of your husband and claims Monterey is his own private company. We are investigating further. I will say, though, the company registration has been checked thoroughly. It appears, however, that Rejistan has worked a flanker and we cannot find Mr. Montgomery's name anywhere on anything. We are acting as diligently as possible. I, for one, get the impression Mr. Rejistan has something to hide."

"Please continue to look into the matter, Mr. Ludlow. I'm sure you're correct in assuming the man is a crook." Gail felt a cold hand on her heart. Was this pressure never going to end?

As she hung up, Jill cleared her throat. "Having problems, are you, dear?"

"Not really," Gail said, heading for the door to the garden.

"It appears that you are going out of your way to be troublesome,

Gail. Do stop this petty sniping and let us get on with life as best we can. I realize little love is lost between we two, but for the sake of the children, you really should attempt to be more pleasant."

Gail smiled coldly. "I'm pleasant when the children are around. I work at it, knowing how you have been poisoning their minds against me. Why don't you get off my back, Jill? I would appreciate your not trying to turn my children against me, and I resent the devious underhanded way both you and your precious son are driving a wedge between me and my children. I resent it very much." Gail moved back into the room as she was saying this and stood in front of Jill, as she sat in the brocade wing chair looking every inch the reigning monarch, fastidious to the nth degree.

"Oh my dear," Jill stood and took Gail's hands in hers. "I am not trying to do anything to cause any friction between you and the children. How could I possibly do that? You are their natural mother, the only mother they will ever have. While I realize certain conversations of mine, and my interference in your relationship with my son have been, at the best, dubious, I agree that I might have caused problems between you. After all, Geoffrey and I are mother and son and understand each other. Nevertheless, I assure you that I'm not trying to be vindictive. You must forgive the ravings of an old lady and try to make allowances." She smiled warmly and squeezed Gail's hands.

"Yes, well," Gail said, moving uncomfortably from foot to foot. She did not really want Jill making peace with her, she wanted to go on hating her for the interfering old schemer that she was.

"I can also assure you that Patricia's newly found habit of calling me Grandmamma," Jill continued, "is not earning her any bonus points, as enjoyable as I find it. I understand from Geoffrey that you take exception to her calling me such, and understand your feelings. I am not her grandmother, that is an undisputable fact, and I will never be her grandmother." Jill smiled and squeezed Gail's hands so hard that her rings cut into Gail's fingers. "Oh, my dear, observing her as she goes through these phases must be difficult for you, but I assure you that this is simply a phase, one she will soon grow out of and recognize as foolish. Let us, as adults, use some common sense and face facts. She is simply being as silly and juvenile as any other young person of her age. Patricia is nice to call me her grandmother, but you and I both know Patricia is looking at me with her greedy little hand outstretched."

Gail looked at her with surprise. So Jill was not as willing to allow Trish to cuckold her as she appeared.

Jill resumed her throne and motioned to Gail to the other chair. "To her I represent wealth and property, and she is at that age when such things are the meaning of happiness. However, Patricia will soon learn that being pleasant to me is not going to be much help to her when she goes out into the real world."

"I suppose I should be glad of that," Gail said, her voice trembling, wondering whether Jill was speaking the truth or again trying to whitewash things. Jill always had an ulterior motive, but for the life of her she could not fathom the reason for this latest olive branch.

"Now shall we have tea?" Jill said smiling brightly, positive they had resolved the latest skirmish. "We'll invite the children to join us in the lounge, shall we, to discover how they deport themselves in an adult environment." She pushed the bell to summon the maid

An invitation to eat in the grand living room with its brocaded upholstery and Kirman Oriental carpets was an honour, since the children ate most meals in the kitchen or the conservatory because Jill did not like crumbs or sloppy manners.

Patricia, who had changed into a smart slubbed silk frock, was in her element and sat poised and regal in a wing chair aping her "Grandmamma." Gail found it farcical, but sad.

The splendor of the room overcame Robert. Because he was afraid of Jill, he refused his favorite chocolate biscuits in case he dropped crumbs on the furniture. Now Gail watched as he carefully set his thin bone china cup and saucer atop his napkin on the small inlaid table at the side of his chair as he ate a small fairy cake in one mouthful, his other hand under his chin. She watched as he chewed and chewed, then swallowed and swallowed, staring at his tea cup, appearing nervous about picking it up again.

Vincent, wearing a suit and vest complete with old school tie, accepted the occasion with a languid air, sitting with legs casually crossed, as if he were accustomed to drinking tea and making polite conversation in such a palatial setting.

Jill talked at length on the state of the government which bored Robert and Patricia, although Vincent was knowledgeable and spoke his mind on the state of the current economy with such flair that his command of the English language and his interest in politics took Gail aback. She could tell Jill was pleased with his discourse, finding it acceptable. Gail assumed that Vincent, as eldest, would inherit from Geoffrey. With Jill's permission, of course.

Then the summer wound to a close and the children were again thinking of school. They had accepted Vincent at Oxford and he walked around with his nose in the air and a definite attitude of superiority. Patricia, busy organizing her journey to the Swiss finishing school, spent hours closeted with the Shillingford girls, who had come for another week's visit. They spent their days talking about clothes, boys and Switzerland. Robert was no longer looking forward to his sojourn at Eton after Geoffrey told him tall tales about the ancient system of making the younger boys into personal slaves.

While this was going on, Gail contemplated a visit to Toronto thinking she would like to see this Mr. Elie Rejistan for herself. Consequently, she decided she needed to prove exactly how much money John had sent the man and to do so must visit John's bank in Woking. To check, she would need copies of all his bank statements.

In protracted correspondence, the bank manager informed her that he required a letter from her solicitor requesting the release of the information. On receipt the bank would supply her with back copies of the account. Typical red tape, Gail thought, frustrated with the slowness of things in Britain.

"This is the nineteen-hundreds," she said when she called him, "not the Victorian era, surely you could handle it more expeditiously?"

He could not.

"Yet you know John is dead," she argued. "We have been through all this before. Shall I bring another copy of the death certificate?"

"I'm sorry, Mrs. Haslett, but anyone can get a copy of any death certificate once it is a matter of public record. No, I'm afraid the bank requires a solicitor's letter. Rules, you know."

"Yes," Gail sighed with annoyance. "I know about the rules in this country. This country should be sinking slowly into the sea under a mountain of red tape. It must be top heavy."

She went to see the solicitor, who was charming when he saw money walk in the door wearing a mink coat, and, for the exorbitant sum of twenty-five pounds, she received a letter that took his secretary three minutes to type.

Leaving the letter and a copy of all pertinent papers with the bank manager, she was assured he would telephone her when the copies of the required statements were available.

A week later he called and, as Jill sat staring at her, not wanting to miss a single word, Gail kept her words short and said she would collect them.

"Collect what up, my dear?" Jill asked. "Do I understand that gentleman was a bank manager? What bank? Do you have an account there?"

"Don't be so nosy, Jill," Gail said smiling because she felt so much better. Soon, her heart sang, soon she would know exactly with what John had been involved. "It has nothing to do with you," and snidely added, "my dear." Going into the garden through the French windows, she called for Robert.

After cleaning him up after his wild romp with Alf, they drove to Woking to collect the statements. Having Robert along made it seem like a picnic. He was always so full of life and chattered on about his butterfly collection that now consisted of four he caught with a net in the meadow and the one he found in the conservatory. Constant handling had tattered all his catches and the dust was almost off their wings, but he was so pleased with himself, determined to outdo Geoffrey's collection before he went back to school. Poor Robert, Gail thought, he did not realize that doting mother Jill had probably bought Geoffrey's collection for him because the butterflies were all exotic species. She decided not to tell him, realizing he would soon figure it out for himself when all he could find in the countryside were cabbage whites, admirals and monarchs.

The bank manager was all unctuous charm and offered them tea. Gail found it pathetic that once he knew who the Hasletts were, he bent over backwards to ingratiate himself. What a change from their first meeting when she was plain Mrs. John Montgomery, penniless widow.

It turned out that the safety deposit box key found in John's jacket belonged to this branch and she had earlier opened it to find nothing more than a canceled insurance policy and a copy of an old will of his father's that showed that the money he had left for his one-time housekeeper, now his wife, was to be paid from a trust set up for her and that John was to manage. So that explained the other Mrs., Montgomery. It had been a real blow to her to discover there was nothing of value in the box.

Later they went to a shopping centre where Robert picked out a new collar for Alf who was now almost fully grown. He was an affectionate dog and Robert had his face washed repeatedly by the large shaggy beast who resembled a perambulating haystack. Only the large pink tongue revealed which end was which. The back of the store held cages behind a glass wall where tiny puppies and kittens, along with rabbits and hamsters were on display. It was difficult to pry Robert away from their charms. Given his druthers he would have bought them all.

After an enjoyable afternoon they went home to join the others for the afternoon tea ritual Jill held in the conservatory each day at four-thirty. Gail felt at ease and more comfortable now she held the secrets to John's financial dealings in her purse and could hardly wait to go into them in detail.

At the first opportunity she escaped to her living room and laid out the statements in date order. Taking a pad, she listed the dates of each deposit and the dates of each withdrawal. John had withdrawn approximately nine hundred pounds each time the company made a deposit. Some portion of this withdrawal had to be his share of the house rent and the housekeeping money. When she added up the withdrawals made, presuming half of which went to buy bank drafts, it astounded her to see the amount was for more than fifty thousand pounds. It was also possible John paid these amounts out of his pay when they lived in other places. At the rate of ten thousand pounds a year it represented a considerable fortune. She wondered how she could find out exactly how much was involved. *Had* he been buying the company from his partner?

It was now imperative to travel to Toronto and investigate for herself. First, she planned to visit the warehouse where they stored their effects so she could search through the bureau and his desk. Then she would see the bank manager, go through John's safety deposit box, and visit the lawyer. Tomorrow, whatever else she did, she must go into Woking and make travel plans.

"You want to go where?" Geoffrey snapped, furious when she told him of her intention. "I see absolutely no need for you to go on a wild goose chase, darling. I support you and your family well enough. Your dead husband's estate is only piddling amount, not worth pursuing. You will stay here and look after Mother."

"Is that an order?" Gail asked, her face flushed with anger.

Geoffrey saw her expression and said, "No, no, I never give orders, my dear." His voice became warmer. "In any event, I think it advisable for you to stay here to look after Mother. The children will be at school, I will be in London and she will be alone. You know no one is here to look after her if you go."

Gail laughed. "Come off it, Geoffrey! Your mother has the strength of character and stamina of a steam roller, and can look after herself. Of course, you never count the servants, do you? Are they not people?"

He made a moue of distaste. "Really Gail, sometimes your lack of background leads me to wonder if I made a mistake."

She stared at him. "I thought your mother had already established that."

Geoffrey flushed and she realized they had discussed her shortcomings at length. "Servants are servants, my dear; one does not fraternize with servants. They know their place, as we know ours." He sighed deeply, resigned, "I do not want you to go abroad, but I suppose you will do exactly as you please. I don't think Mother will receive this news at all well. No indeed, I can assure you of that."

Gail looked at him, sitting in his chair, so well dressed, so fastidious in his person, so queer. Her stomach lurched at the thought of his physical relationships with men.

"You and your mother are always assuring me. Maybe you think you rule the world, Geoffrey, but you don't rule my world, wife or no. This is the age of liberation. You seem to live a completely liberated life, so why can't I?"

Geoffrey stiffened in his chair. "I beg your pardon Gail. Do I detect a veiled reference?"

"You said it, brother." Suddenly Gail was tired of the pretense. "I came to your flat and caught you rolling around on the floor with your lover." He gasped and stood as if to run. "Didn't you know that, did you, Geoffrey? Well, it doesn't surprise me because I could see how overcome with passion you were. It was the surprise of my life, you and a man! I think I always suspected it, so it wasn't too much of a shock, but somehow I don't think your mother realizes you're a practicing homosexual. She thinks, how did she put it when she proposed to me? 'He does not take to women,' and that *she* spoiled you for other women. I can tell her a few home truths, if you like."

Geoffrey became still as she spoke, but now he strode around the room waving his manicured hands in agitation. "My God, Gail, do you mean you came to the flat, or is this some huge joke?" he spluttered, white faced. "Are you trying to upset me?"

Gail suddenly felt sorry for him, knowing she was destroying his tiny world, the world he had enjoyed for so many years.

"No, Geoffrey," she said softly, "It isn't some joke, and I understand why you are upset, but I *was* at the flat, ask the doorkeeper. I didn't say anything before this for reasons I can't fathom. I was upset, but I learned to live with it because, after all, it is not as though we share a bed, now is it?"

He stared at her with flat, lifeless eyes. Somehow, in a flash of understanding, she perceived what her discovery meant to him. Poor man, he had lived a lie for all of his adult life and here she was stomping on his social facade as though she were crushing his butterfly collection. He looked suddenly old and smaller, as if someone had deflated him, and she experienced a pang of guilt at being the villain of the piece.

Quickly she reassured him. "Don't worry, Geoffrey, I won't say anything to Jill. You have my word that I won't say anything to anybody. After all, it makes me look like such a idiot, doesn't it?"

His eyes moved over her face as if seeking the truth of her words. "I suppose this is blackmail," he said in a shaky voice. "You won't say anything to Mummy and I let you go to Toronto, is that it?"

"Got it in one!" Gail said, smiling. "Don't make waves, Geoffrey, and we'll get along famously. You scratch my back and I'll scratch yours."

He grimaced, already feeling better. "Really, Gail, *must* you use those horrible expressions?"

The smile left her face. Once he thought her Americanisms funny and endearing, now they annoyed him immensely.

He looked away as he said in an even voice, "Well, whatever. You are correct in assuming that we must pull together for the sake of the family and outward appearances. Be discreet, that is all I ask. By the way, I heard about your lover. You were wonderfully discreet with that affair, and Mummy was so pleased. Congratulations."

Gail looked at him in amazement. It was curious that Jill had found out about Richard Talbot, and all the time she thought they were being so circumspect. She supposed the association of upper class twits were everywhere, the upper classes who spent their time bed hopping and married mostly for convenience. Why should she have thought she could get away with it? Then too, maybe Jill had someone follow her.

When Gail made her announcement that night during dinner, Jill was decidedly frosty. "Really, Gail, what *am* I going to do without you? I will rattle around in this empty house on my own, depressed and miserable." She put her hanky to the side of her eye, almost as though she were acting in a Victorian melodrama. Gail almost laughed aloud.

"You lived for years on your own, Jill," she said calmly without looking at her, gazing instead at the garden where a revolving sprinkler created a rainbow in the last of the evening sun. "You can surely manage for three weeks."

"Three weeks? Why on earth would you want to go for three weeks? What is so important that you have to desert us this way? I know you are curious about Mr. Montgomery's affairs, but this is ridiculous." Her eyes narrowed. "I sincerely hope you are paying for this trip yourself." Jill turned to her son. "It would upset me greatly, Geoffrey, if you were wasting money."

"Yes, Jill, I *am* paying for it myself," Gail lied knowing that without the money Geoffrey had given her, she could not afford to go anywhere.

"Hmm," Jill said looking hard at Geoffrey who was eating, eyes firmly fixed on his food.

CHAPTER TWENTY-SEVEN

Toronto seemed so alive after laid back, cultured Walton on Thames. The airport was packed with people greeting arrivals, saying goodbye to departing passengers, watching planes, begging quarters, selling roses. It was so noisily tumultuous in the terminal that the atmosphere felt quite different from her last visit.

Taking the airport bus to the Royal York, she registered in a suite. The rooms were lovely, newly decorated as part of an upgrade that had been ongoing for years. Sighing with pleasure, she sank into an easy chair and flipped on the large screen television.

What a difference in programming from the BBC, she thought. *River's End* had only one television that Jill had housed in the study disguised as a cabinet. She did not believe in television. Any time the children went into the study to watch a program, Jill always found something else for them to do. Television was not educational, she said, and anyway the children always wanted to watch inane cartoons. She did, however, switch on the set for the BBC news, Shakespearean plays, high class boring documentaries, or National Geographic specials. Sole handler of the TV Times, each week she read it cover to cover, then wrote a list of those programs she considered suitable for digestion.

Gail sat back after ordering tea from room service and watched with pleasure as the MC awarded a prize for picking the correct door to a fat lady dressed as a chicken. She laughed aloud at the antics of the audience and realized that England had starved her of mindless entertainment for years. That was what she missed, entertainment, a good laugh now and then.

The following morning, she rose early and took breakfast in the coffee shop then stepped outside onto a Front Street as busy as ever. She paused at the door to look across to Union Station, watched the hundreds of people coming and going. Then quickly she strode along the street to a street car stop and boarded a tram to the Queen's Quay facility where she had an appointment to search the items in storage.

It was an old brown stucco structure, rising seven storeys. It looked like a building made from a cardboard box with its narrow windows. Seedy, she thought, wondering about its original purpose. A grain silo?

A security guard escorted her into the huge warehouse and, after consulting a listing in a small corner office, took her to the sixth floor and along a corridor. Off this corridor were many storage bays, and his purpose was to help her in moving large pieces so she could find the boxes holding their papers. The bay was enormous and several other people had furniture and effects stored inside. Huge shelves held chesterfields and sideboards, chairs and bookcases. To one side smaller shelves held boxes and crates all clearly tagged, numbered and labeled. It all smelled of ancient dust and mice.

Having found her goods, the guard consulted the master inventory list, found two huge storage boxes and then began looking for box number seventeen. Gail sat on a kitchen chair to open one of her smaller boxes that now rested on a felt-covered bureau belonging to someone else. It took more than four hours to check all the boxes, but armed with a large stack of papers she decided might be useful, covered in dust, her head aching from the bad lighting, she took a taxi back to the hotel.

After a quick shower, she sat on the bed and sorted through the paperwork. John, a pack rat, kept all kinds of rubbish along with necessary documents that could prove useful. She found another copy of a former will, but not the latest one. Other papers included bank statements and these she eagerly spread across the bed so she could see the pattern of withdrawals.

Yes, according to the oldest statement, that went back ten years from the time before they moved to England, he had withdrawn money. Surely this money must be an investment? John must be deeply into this company as he had invested so much, she thought. She packed up everything to take to the lawyer the following day.

Then scanning through an old diary she discovered a safety deposit box key taped to a page and prayed the box contained John's will. The will would answer so many questions, would bring to light all those matters of which she was unaware.

In one heap, she stacked the canceled cheques and started flipping through them. Disappointed to find no cheques payable to Monterey Enterprises, and realizing John had only issued bank drafts, she carefully examined each cheque. He had made many payable to Wood Gundy, a stock brokerage and she could pursue that avenue tomorrow. Several cheques payable to Harrison, Lawson and Reeves also were curious.

As she lay in a relaxing warm bath, tired from the day's activities Gail knew she had been right to take a three-week trip. It might take her that long even to begin to find out about the estate.

Two weeks later she realized she was still at an impasse. She checked with Wood Gundy, whose manager was searching their old files as recent records showed John Montgomery was no longer a client. It was possible, they said, that he had purchased stocks under another name. They were contacting the broker who dealt with their small investors who had recently retired to Prince Edward Island.

Harrison, Lawson and Reeves, a stock brokerage, were out of business, so that was a dead end.

The next afternoon she decided to call on Monterey Enterprises. The building was on Bay Street. While looking quite modern from the outside, she knew it could simply be a facade. Entering a marble clad lobby, she watched as a security guard checked each visitor in and out. She announced her name, asked to see Mr. Rejistan and the guard made a phone call. Soon a dark haired, dark eyed young man came to escort her to an office on the tenth floor.

Elie Rejistan, a dark swarthy man, was not effusive in his greeting. He looked shifty and his eyes never rested on her face. Gail immediately sensed she had been wrong in making a personal visit. Rejistan might seem devious, but his plush offices and the fact the company owned the ten storey office building, all pointed to a thriving business.

Politely he shook her hand after the young man ushered her into his sumptuous corner office overlooking the distant lake.

"Would you like a cup of coffee, Mrs. Haslett?" he asked.

"No, thank you, Mr. Rejistan," It surprised her to find the pronunciation was REYjistan, and it dawned on her that the name Monterey used part of John's name and part of his. That she considered proof enough.

"How can I help you?" Mr. Rejistan was excessively polite. She decided her mink coat had probably set his mind at ease. Maybe he thought she was bringing him business, but she knew from their year in Beirut that Middle Eastern men never talked business to women. In the eastern world, women stayed indoors, looked after the families and never worked outside the home. Mr. Rejistan was probably of that school, a male chauvinist of the highest order.

"It is how you can be of assistance to me," Gail said smiling. She noted his expensive suit, hand made shoes and silk tie. Three of his teeth were gold capped making his smile blinding but phoney. What would his reaction be when she told him of her mission?

"I would like to talk to you about my husband." He was still semi-attentive and at ease, his eyes gazing at a picture behind her. "My dead husband."

"Your dead husband?" He glanced at her, puzzled, obviously wondering what she wanted. She knew he would not know anyone named Haslett and could almost see him searching his mind.

"Yes, my dead husband, John. John Montgomery."

His mouth dropped and he looked stunned. Quickly he pulled

himself together and she saw his eyes dart around the room, as if looking for somewhere to run.

"I have come to take out the money my husband put into this company as your partner," she said triumphantly. A confrontation was obviously the best way to treat this man. The lawyer had not had any results from his letters or investigation.

"I do not know this John Monty," he said, licking his lips.

You liar, Gail thought, watching him squirm.

"Oh, but you do, Mr. Rejistan. Between you, you made the company name partly of my husband's name - the "Mont" of Montgomery and the "Rey" of Rejistan, did you not? I have copies of the bank drafts he sent to you for all these years and I now demand my share of this company."

He was all oily smarm. "My dear madam, you are mistaken. I do not know this man and am sole owner of this company." A sudden thought came to him. "Aha! You are the person who sent that lawyer to harass me," He pointed a finger at her accusingly. "You have no grounds for this harassment, as my legal advisor has stated. You will leave my office and you will not bother me again." He pushed a button on his desk and the male secretary came into the office.

"Yes, sir?"

"Show this woman out and do not let her into my building again."

"Yes, sir," the secretary said, coming to grasp Gail's arm as if she were a prisoner.

Gail held her ground and looked at Elie. She was mad as hell and vented her anger.

"You have not heard the last of this, Mr. Rejistan. You are a crook and a liar. I will not allow you to take away my children's inheritance, nor will I let the matter rest until I have found justice."

Gail sat in a coffee shop across the road and watched people leaving and entering the building. Oil rich Arabs arrived in limousines; successful business men with well-padded stomachs came and went, lesser salespersons ran up the steps with sample cases, businessmen and aides, couriers and messengers. Whatever business area Elie was involved with was in did exceptionally well. She asked the chatty waitress at the counter if she knew anything about Monterey.

"Oh, they come in here a lot for sandwiches for their meetings and such. We get a lot of them coming in for lunch, the girls mostly. Ever so successful they are, from what I hear. They import and export high tech stuff. They got a six milliondollar contract with some eastern country to supply the government with equipment. I read it in the Telegram."

Gail found this most interesting and pumped the waitress for more information. Unfortunately she did not know much more than she had already related.

Later that afternoon she went over her findings with Mr. Ludlow. His icy and acidic tone revealed how upset he was at her intrusion into things that she had paid him to do.

His face a mask of disapproval, he said, "Mrs. Haslett, I think your visit to Mr. Rejistan most ill advised. Dealing with these people in the proper legal fashion is necessary, and that takes time. I can only hope your visit has not entirely ruined our chance of a disclosure of the company assets."

"Why should it?" she asked, miffed. "I have the proof my husband put money in that company. I *know* he was a partner."

"No, you do not have proof," he said coldly. "We have no proof of his partnership. In legal terms it is strictly hearsay, nor can you prove where Mr. Montgomery sent the money he withdrew. You have no concrete evidence."

"Well, we'd better have something, Mr. Ludlow. I'm tired of this waiting game. I need to be able to support myself, to look after my children properly."

He smiled mirthlessly. "You have since made a good marriage from all accounts. Look here, Mrs. Haslett, handling things properly is legally imperative if we are to win our case. Haste is not important. We can lose everything if we do anything impetuous."

Gail stood and looked down on him. "Well I *want* speed, and I *need* haste. If you can't hurry this up, I'll find another firm to handle the case. I don't think you realize how desperate I am, Mr. Ludlow."

Gail had not realized how desperate she was either until the words came out of her mouth. She needed to get out of her sham marriage, needed to be able to support herself and the children.

"Mrs. Haslett," Mr. Ludlow was then all concern and charm. "Please don't upset yourself. I assure you that I will personally attempt to hasten things." He sighed. "Alas with the law, these things take time."

That did not impress Gail. "Yes, and time is money, is it not? The longer the case goes on, the more money you make. You charge every second and that's how you make such a good living. My husband John had no time for lawyers, which is really why I'm in this mess right now. Very well, Mr. Ludlow, I'll leave you to move it along. My time is also valuable."

"Please keep in touch, Mrs. Haslett."

"You may have no fear of that, Mr. Ludlow, I will be calling you daily until I know how we stand." She left his oak paneled office without even shaking his hand, annoyed that he was such a wimp and so unproductive. Still, better the devil she knew.

Later Gail returned to the hotel and rested for the remainder of the afternoon, watching mindless game shows, enjoying them immensely.

Her present good humor was attributable to a visit to the bank where she found the safety deposit box contained the latest copy of John's will, and wonder of wonders, a bank book showing more than fifty thousand dollars deposited in a Swiss bank. The bank manager was helpful and wired the Swiss bank to ensure the account was, in fact, still open. It was.

Now as she lay on the couch, she felt much richer and pleased with her day's work. Feeling gratified at the day's results, she decided to take a few days off to enjoy herself and visit old friends.

CHAPTER TWENTY-EIGHT

The time she spent with acquaintances in her old hometown recharged her spirit. With renewed vitality and the knowledge of financial security, she continued her efforts to discover more about John's dealings.

Wood Gundy's retired broker recalled John had invested heavily under the name Monty Philip. Philip was John's first name. They held a numbered account in trust pending his further notification. Again she went through the paper chase, providing identity papers and a copy of the death certificate. So far John's death was the mostly widely verified of anyone she had ever known. When they made her a copy of the ledger, it gratified her to discover she had accumulated another twelve thousand dollars worth of stocks. Wheels were set in motion to transfer the account into her name. Wood Gundy's man, too agreeable, held her hand one second too long. It did not take her long to realize that money made her more attractive. Now she felt new born and alluring.

Although it was time for her to return to England, the matter of Monterey Enterprises had moved not one iota. She became furious with Mr. Ludlow, telling him plainly that he must get a move on as she wanted the matter completed. Surely, she said, this was becoming a major court case?

Jill displayed delight when she arrived home, even if she were a trifle distant after Gail's three week desertion. When Gail entered the house, Edith Warburton and Nancy Carruthers were sitting in the living room drinking tea and eating cakes.

"Gail, my dear, how lovely to have you home." Jill kissed the air on each side of Gail's face and patted her arm.

"Right in time for tea, my dear. Come, sit here and tell us all about your trip," Nancy said, butter on her chin from the crumpet she was devouring. Gail noticed she had changed her hair color to more of a honey blond, but the salon had styled this wig in tight curls that made her look like a tart, or Harpo Marx in drag.

"Oh my, yes," Edith twittered. "It must be so nice to jet set around the world. Of course, *you* are a young woman. Flying is not for me. My blood pressure would never stand it," she said, as she stuffed her face with butter cream choux pastry. Because her false eyelashes had come unstuck in the outside corners, they made her look like a quizzical, plump rabbit.

Gail said a lot which amounted to nothing and left them gorging on cream cakes. No way was she going to talk about her private affairs to those two old harridans. It was bad enough having Jill as inquisitor.

When Geoffrey arrived home early Friday evening, he seemed pleased enough to see her, and while he asked about her trip, she could tell he was not much interested.

"Oh, by the by," he said, "Vincent telephoned me at the office today. He needs extra money for accommodation. Apparently the chap he rooms with on campus has developed a nasty habit of drinking night and day, and inviting his chums in to help him get drunk. Poor Vincent can't get a decent night's sleep so he found himself rooms in a small boarding house in Oxford. I wired him money, though, so he should be all right now."

"Thank you, Geoffrey," Gail said, realizing Vincent also found Geoffrey an easy touch.

When, a day later, Jill received a letter from Patricia written in purple ink on pink paper in which she pleaded for extra money to buy a special outfit for skiing. Gail knew without a doubt that if she refused, then Patricia would write to Jill who would send her the money. Oh yes, "Grandmamma" was overjoyed when any of the children wrote to her and made much of their letters. "See how intelligent Vincent is," or "Look at this word, twelve letters and Robert spelled it correctly." and "Patricia is *such* a caring girl, look how she worries about her best chum." *Sure, Jill, as if! Trish never worries about anyone but herself.*

Robert sent his mother pathetically tear stained letters. At least Gail liked to think they were tear stains, but they could have been anything. While he said he did not like the school much, reading between the lines Gail could tell he was happy in the company of other boys his age and had adjusted admirably, as always.

It was still her intention to take them all out of school and back to Canada soon as she possibly could, although the opportunity had not yet arisen. Her funds would remain frozen while the various institutions went through the rigmarole of passing around paperwork, signing forms and issuing directives.

Although Geoffrey had not been the slightest bit interested in her trip, he perked up when she let it slip John had left money and investments. Apparently this seemed of great interest as he talked about it for a long time, then bluntly asked her how much was involved. Feeling he had some ulterior motive, she cut the sum considerably although she left him with no doubt that she could look after herself. Geoffrey did not greet this snippet of information, she noticed, with any great enthusiasm.

The next afternoon she found him in deep discussion with Jill, which ceased when she entered the room. What were they plotting now, she wondered?

On receipt of the news that Wood Gundy had released the account, she sent a letter requesting them to liquidate half the investments and forward the proceeds to the Barclay Bank in Woking where she opened an account. The manager oozed all over her, delighted to gain business from the wealthy Hasletts. She sent Robert a money order for twenty pounds, just because she could.

The money, when it arrived, made such a difference to her outlook on life. She could come and go as she pleased without any thought of cost. To celebrate, she purchased a Thunderbird from a dealership in London. While a 1959 version, it was comfortable and had automatic drive that was a godsend on the winding, hilly roads of southern England. To heck with Geoffrey and his car. This was more her style. She planned to visit Robert at Eton soon; still car mad, he would drool over the flashy two seater T-Bird.

"What on earth is that enormous vehicle doing on the drive? Do you have a visitor from America?" Jill asked as she looked out the picture window when Gail came in for tea.

Gail smiled at her disapproving back. "No. No visitor, Jill. That is *my* car. I picked it up this morning," she said and moved over to Jill's side where she eyed the sweeping lines of the pale blue car with immense satisfaction.

"It's vulgar, don't you think, with all that chrome?" Jill said looking at it with aversion. "It is *not* a car for a lady. It looks much too racy."

"That's true," Gail said with a great deal of gratification. "Geoffrey would never drive one, would he?" She smiled, "Or would he?" She added cattily. "I happen to like it and since I'm going to be the only driver, I wouldn't let it worry you, Jill."

"Oh my dear, I'm not at all worried," Jill hastened to assure her. "It's simply that it is so ostentatious and not a conveyance with which I like to be associated. People will eye it with such abhorrence."

Gail laughed, how petty minded Jill seemed. "Nevertheless, I bet if the Queen drove one, you'd have one yourself, eh?" Gail said, smirking at Jill who was such a terrible snob.

Jill wrinkled her porcelain-like brow. "I seriously doubt the Queen would ever switch to such a conveyance, and even the Prince of Wales drives a Bentley. That monstrosity, I am sorry to inform you, is extremely common looking. You should drive an English car, one people recognize."

"It didn't have a common price, though, Jill," Gail said with satisfaction. "It cost me…,"

Jill cut in before she could finish. "Please Gail, try to behave like a lady. One does not discuss the price of one's possessions. It is impolite. One's satisfaction comes from personally knowing the price paid, not in flaunting money in front of other people to impress. They say the only people who know how rich they are, are the poor. They are the ones who put price tags on everything. Still, then again you were poor, were you not? Now I know from where Patricia gets her inclinations."

Gail's fingers curled into fists. "Patricia didn't learn that from me because I never had any money worth mentioning, as you so kindly pointed out. She learned her condescending attitude from her school chums."

"I doubt that," Jill said caustically. "This country's public school system is the finest in the world. People send their children here from abroad to give them the benefit of a good education. I can assure you, Gail, money never enters the equation."

"No, but the fact that these people are willing to spend money to send them to the school in the first place, is snobbery at its finest. To say that your child is going to Eton or…,"

"Please, my dear, do not attempt to convert me to your point of view. Canada may be a large country, but it cannot, in any way, match the English school system. It is too new, too brash and uncultivated. Anyone who is anyone in Canada sends their sons here to attend Oxford or Cambridge. As for the other Dominion universities and colleges, you, I'm afraid to say, are probably the best example of what I mean."

Gail glared. She could say nothing to rebut the words, knowing her ignorance would glare and embarrass her. Oh, why did Jill always get the better of her in any conversation? It was giving her an inferiority complex. She was aware that all Jill had going for her were old money plus a haughty arrogant attitude that was an acquired trait and not one taught by the schools. Educated by a governess, she had attended a finishing school before her debut. Yet it appeared that Patricia was picking up the same supercilious attitude without the slightest trouble.

Gail spent the afternoon driving around the villages, stopping to browse through small shops, then took tea in Camberley. That was where she met Steve.

Steve Cochrane was not a courteous person, she instinctively knew, after speaking to him for only one minute. Within five minutes, she found him brash and loud, but what he did have was the looks and build that attracted her. She missed what she had found with Richard and, since the end of their affair, she'd had no other lover. Right then, Steve was a gift from heaven.

By six o'clock she was in bed with him at the Ship Inn in Weybridge, thoroughly enjoying herself. He was not a proficient lover, but she could teach him. At least he was willing to learn.

Her mink coat and American car impressed Steve, who talked about the car nonstop and stroked her mink covetously. She even let him drive back to Camberley. Having soon seen through his veneer, Gail had no intentions of letting him know where she lived.

"You look like the cat who got the cream, my dear. A new lover, perhaps?" Jill said quietly as Gail entered the dining room.

Gail said nothing as the maid served her meal.

"How does the machine run?" Jill asked.

"The Thunderbird?" Gail said, Jill made a moue of distaste as she did not even like the name, so vulgar, she said. "I presume that's what you mean." Gail continued. "It runs like a dream. I mean it's so great to feel all that horse power at your command. I love it."

Jill put down her wine glass. "Oh my! It sounds extremely dangerous. I don't think Geoffrey is going to like it."

Gail stared at her. "I really don't care what Geoffrey likes," she said hotly.

Jill raised her chin, assumed her imperious pose and spoke in a soft, meaningful tone. "A wife must do as her husband wishes, my dear. If Geoffrey does not like the car, he will send it back from whence it came."

Gail hated her air of smugness. "He can't touch it, Jill. *I* paid for it out of *my* money. It is in my name and I have no intentions of selling it, not for you and not for Geoffrey. Try to get it through your head, Jill, that I don't answer to Geoffrey, nor to you for that matter."

"Au contraire, my dear. While you are enjoying my hospitality, you do indeed answer to me, and I do not like that infernal machine.

It cheapens my home and I sincerely pray you conceal it in the garages whenever possible. We will see Friday evening, when I'm sure Geoffrey will let me know what we will do."

Yeah, sure, as if you ever let Geoffrey decide anything, you old hag, Gail thought as she ate lobster Newburgh. They finished dinner in silence after which Gail went into the west wing, leaving Jill to her own devices.

The next day she met Steve in Weybridge and he drove the T-Bird into London where they spent the afternoon. After tea at the Hilton hotel, where she openly stared around hoping someone would recognize her, they checked into a small inn on the outskirts.

It was a pleasure to have found someone as virile as Steve as he was the never satisfied type. Gail missed sex and while she never cheated on John, accepting his absence as part of marriage, she felt the need for the comfort sex brought her after his death. Now she lay on the rumpled bed in all her naked glory and let Steve have his way with her body.

CHAPTER TWENTY-NINE

Almost before she knew it, the Christmas holidays were almost upon them again, and Geoffrey and Gail had become even more estranged. Geoffrey must have found himself a new lover, Gail thought. When he came home at weekends, he wandered around fidgeting, impatient to return to the city.

Her affair with Steve ran its course, and when he started asking for money, she dropped him. Thankfully, she'd had enough foresight not to tell him her real name or where she lived.

Again she journeyed to London with Jill and they Christmas shopped for the children. This year they purchased sensible things.

Robert was to have a remote-controlled plane that Gail knew he would love. The other two were to receive money to purchase their own gifts. Gail did not much like that, so bought little toys to amuse them. What was Christmas without surprise presents? She realized Patricia and Vincent were young adults now and would probably scoff at her waste of money, but she thought her offspring should have some nonsensical gift, simply because it was Christmas.

While it was cold outside, it was still summer in the conservatory. Tropical plants bloomed and perfumed the moist warm air, the birds chattered and sang in the aviary. Gail relaxed in the wicker chair, her feet on a footstool, watching two butterflies as they flittered in a courtship. She and Jill had spent the morning wrapping gifts for the staff and the children, and were taking a well-deserved break. Jill had mostly supervised, chosen paper and ribbon and written the gift tags in meticulous lettering.

It was strange really, Gail mused as they chatted, that they behaved in such a civilized mannerly fashion when neither liked the other. Jill, of the old school, paid careful attention to all conversation, was careful not to disturb the status quo, even when she barbed her remarks and smiled like a barracuda. Gail, tired of arguments and knowing she could never win, attempted to appear cordial. She found it less stressful.

After tea, they sat making small talk about the weather. As Gail was wondering how to make her escape, the maid announced a visitor to see young Mrs. Haslett.

"Are you expecting a visitor?" Jill asked with surprise. Gail made it a point never to bring anyone to the house after Mr. Ranson had been embarrassed.

"No, I am not. Who is it?" she asked the maid, whose name she never knew for they changed as often as she changed her shoes.

"It's a gentleman, madam," the young woman said, mortified because she had not asked the name.

"Go away, girl, and get his name," Jill ordered. "Honestly," she said to Gail, "staff these days have no training at all. I cannot seem to find one young person who knows the correct way to answer a door, and surely that is simple enough."

The River's End servants, Gail quickly learned, did not receive acknowledgment, never did Jill say "please," or "thank you," never said "well done," never saw them as human beings. Gail found that deplorable, although she noticed the same attitude at the homes of Jill's other acquaintances She thought it barbaric. Still, most of the servants stayed and must accept the fact employers treated them as lower class, so who was she to say it was wrong? As for herself, she always said "please," and "thank you," to the servants, much to Jill's displeasure.

Gail watched for the girl's return. Who could it be? Her mind sifted through the men she knew in England. The list was short.

The red faced maid came back and stood to attention as she recited from a business card. "It is a Mr. Steve Cochrane from the firm of Cochrane, Cochrane and Blair, madam. He is here on business of a personal nature."

Jill, eyebrows raised, sat up straight, exceedingly interested at this announcement and stared at Gail, who sat white and stone-like at the news. What the hell was that crook doing here? How *had* he found her?

She rose and started out of the room only to discover Jill right at her heels. Suddenly she stopped, and Jill bumped into her.

"Please don't disturb yourself, Jill. This is personal. I'll take him to the west wing and deal with him in private."

Jill tutted. "I sincerely hope this is not one of your paramours, Gail. That would be very vulgar and…,"

"Go away, please," Gail said loudly, which she knew was not the way to talk to her mother-in-law, but could not stop herself. "I said I'll deal with this myself, thank you very much."

"Really, my dear, raising your voice in that very annoying way you Americans have is quite unnecessary. I will accompany you to the living room as chaperone. In polite society it is not the thing to entertain a man alone, even if it should be a lawyer or doctor. One must follow the conventions of society."

"Go away, Jill," Gail said, not moving. "That might have been etiquette back in Queen Victoria's day, but I can assure you I'm quite accustomed to talking alone with a man, whether it be an acquaintance or a businessman. Emancipation is history, you know. I think you must have lived under a rock for the past forty years."

She stood stiffly with her arms at her sides, full of tension. Knowing Steve was not here to ask about her health, she became anxious for Jill to back off from her etiquette protocol. What on earth could Steve want, she wondered?

"Well!" Jill said, eyes glittering with anger. "You cannot talk to me like this in my own home. While you are under my roof, you will live by my rules."

Gail suddenly decided she would not allow Jill to run her life a second longer. Not now she had her own money. "Good! I agree with you, that's exactly what I wanted to hear. I will move out from under your roof so I can live by my own rules and take my children with me!" Gail stated as angry as she had ever been. "Who do you think you are, Jill?" *Or is that whom?* flashed through her mind. "I'm not a prisoner here, surely? I'm entitled to live my own life, set my own standards. So you can get your precious son on the telephone and tell him I have left this establishment, that is, if you can prise him away from his latest lover." She let her tongue run away with her and rued what she said even as she said it. "I must say the men he chooses would never measure up to your excessively high standards."

Jill regarded her, paling, then her expression turned to horror. She put out one hand, held onto the door, then slumped to the floor, white and still.

"Oh, my God," Gail said, running to ring the bell for the maid. She took Jill's head onto her lap and was smoothing the hair back from her forehead as the maid came running.

"Ooh, madam!" She stood dithering, twisting her hands. "Should I call the doctor?"

"Call an ambulance right away, forget the doctor. We have to get her to a hospital," Gail shouted.

"Ooh, madam, only the doctor can order an ambulance. We *have* to call him." The girl scurried to the living room to use the phone.

Jill remained unconscious and Gail put her head down on the floor. Placing a cushion under her head, she opened the boned, high-necked blouse. Then she stood, wondering what other stupid rules the National Health System had that she was not aware of, when the maid ran back.

"He's coming, madam," the girl said, twisting her hands nervously. "Can I fetch anything for you, madam?"

"Yes, bring a double brandy quickly and get rid of that man. Tell him I can't see him today."

The maid brought the brandy and Gail quickly tossed it back as the girl stared at her in horror. She obviously thought it was for Mrs. Haslett.

"Well? Don't stand there catching flies. Get rid of that man, immediately," Gail ordered, dismayed to hear herself talking like Jill.

She sat on the floor holding Jill's hand until she heard footsteps along the flagstone passageway. Eagerly she looked up, expecting to see the doctor.

"Well, well, well, what's the matter, Jane, or should I call you Gail?" Steve asked as he leaned against the sofa back.

"What the hell are you doing here? Go away." She scrambled to her feet. "My mother-in-law has collapsed and I'm sure your arrival brought on this spell. Get out of this house and stay out," she shouted.

"Now, now, shouldn't we get her onto the couch?" He bent over Jill.

"Leave her alone! The doctor said not to move her," Gail said angrily.

Steve took off his overcoat and put it over Jill. "You should keep her warm to prevent shock."

Gail was going remove it, when the doctor, who lived four houses away, bustled in, followed by the maid.

"Good, good, you kept her warm I see." He knelt at the side of his patient and took out his stethoscope.

Steve grinned at Gail as if to say "I told you so."

"Call an ambulance," he said to the maid, "Give them my name and tell them to get here as quickly as possible." He turned to Gail, "I'll call the hospital when you have arranged that to book a private room."

He brushed off his knees. "I think we can move her onto the couch, if you wouldn't mind helping me."

He looked inquiringly at Steve, who said, "Of course, of course, doctor."

Gail walked through the house and went to the west wing, leaving Steve and the doctor to move Jill.

Her mind was in chaos. It was her fault that Jill had collapsed. Oh God, suppose she had suffered a heart attack? She should never have shouted that about Geoffrey. However, the old woman had to know sooner or later, and she was tired of being treated like a second class citizen.

Why was Steve here and what did he want? The only thing that came to mind was blackmail. Well, he could try if he wished because she had decided to leave the house, no matter what. She wandered around the living room picking things up and putting them down as she tried to decide what she must do first.

As an ambulance transported Jill to the nearest fully equipped hospital, Gail drove over in the Jaguar followed by Steve, who drove a flashy red two-seater. Numbly she sat in the large waiting room while Steve went to get her some tea. In a way she was glad he had come, though she dreaded his reasons for turning up in the first place.

They did not yet know whether Jill had suffered a heart attack or a stroke, the doctor told her. It was possible the attack could probably impair her physically, and possibly mentally. Gail, feeling numb, shaky and very guilty, followed a nurse to the intensive care unit and was shocked to see how frail Jill looked. She always thought of Jill as a being well built, but maybe it was her air of confidence and arrogance that made her appear bigger.

Later when she left the unit, Gail told Steve she could not talk to him and although he seemed reluctant to leave, eventually he left with bad grace. He warned, however, that he would return when her mother-in-law was back at home. She sat in the waiting room and watched him go with a feeling of impending doom.

Geoffrey arrived a short time later. Gail had called him from the house. He was jittery and befuddled when he returned to the waiting room after seeing his mother. Gail felt sorry for him and wondered what would he do without Mummy to direct his life. Sitting with his head in his hands he was silent, but she could see his lips moving as if in prayer.

The white painted, plastic furnished waiting room smelled of disinfectant, stewed tea, dirty ash trays, and grief. Somehow it brought back memories of John's death, and this made her feel even more sympathy for Geoffrey. She moved to his side.

"Don't worry, Geoffrey, she'll pull through this. She's a very strong lady." What could she say that would help?

He looked at her through red rimmed eyes. "I know she will, but she won't be the same. Mummy would not like to be dependent on anyone. This is going to be awful for her." Tears threatened to overwhelm him and she put a hand on his arm. She knew from experience that a simple touch could make the difference to someone in grief.

"Shall we go back to the house?" she asked. "We can do nothing here and she's in good hands."

"I'll stay and wait for the doctor's report," he said staunchly. She looked at him as he stared blankly at the wall.

Gail rose and put a hand on his shoulder. "I'll go back then, Geoffrey. I'll call the children and let them know. We should inform them quickly so they can send her cards and letters to let her know she's in their thoughts. Jill will like that. I'll ask them to stay with school friends over the holidays as the way things are. I don't think we should celebrate at the house this year, at least not until we know how minor or serious Jill's condition is now."

"Yes, yes," he said impatiently, wanting her to go so he could be alone to lick his wounds.

As Gail drove back to the house, she tried to sort out her feelings. She wanted nothing more than to be done with the Hasletts, wanted to go back to Canada, but the children presented a problem. Vincent would object to leaving Oxford where he was now involved in student politics; Patricia would never leave the snobby finishing school in Switzerland.

All she had left was Robert. Her dear Robert who would not object to leaving Eton, no matter how settled he had become. On the other hand, she asked herself if she were doing him any favors by taking him out of such a prestigious school, a school for which many aimed. Eton accepted few, and those awarded a place, got in through connections. With an Eton background, Robert would be welcome in any society, for the very name carried a cachet of solid contacts and old money.

Her own situation became secondary at a time like this. She may not love Geoffrey, but she did owe him something. After all, she had gone into the marriage with her eyes wide open, knowing what it would be like and accepted it without equivocation.

As she sipped tea in the living room, she placed calls to the children. They all expressed concern, Trish and Vincent assuring her they could stay with chums, but she could tell they were not much interested. It did not seem to bother them as it made little difference to their school lives. Serious illness did not come into their realm of experience.

Robert was the only one to express any concern, though he really did not like Jill, and told her to send a spray of white roses, Jill's favorite flower, with a get-well note from him. What a lovely lad Robby was.

Steve popped up again a week later when they moved Jill out of intensive care. They moved her to a private room where well wishers now surrounded her. Nancy Carruthers and Edith Warburton were there, arriving almost each day in full war paint. They drove the nurses and matron to distraction by continually requesting tea and biscuits. When these were not forthcoming, they brought their own spirit lamp and tea things, and ate snacks served by Nancy's maid, fetched along for the purpose.

Jill, thankfully, was not too badly impaired. She dragged her leg slightly and had restricted use of her left hand and arm. To ease this, they sent her for therapy to the large room on the ground floor, along with other patients who had suffered strokes or accidents. Jill wasted no time in objecting to the mass session, demanding a private therapist so no one would see her inability to make her limbs work to command. Eventually the doctor arranged that an ambulance would take her once a day to a clinic for private sessions. On hearing this, Gail smiled. "Wonderful what money can do, isn't it?" she said.

Jill spoke with a slight stammer although her speech had been the first thing to return. Her face looked uneven, the left side definitely droopy. Although she was ailing, she lost no time in letting Gail know Gail was to blame for her "incident" as she called it. Gail felt her heart sink as Jill spoke, knowing Jill could make her life a living hell if she did not get away.

Geoffrey would not speak to her after Jill told him what caused her collapse. He blamed Gail and treated her like a servant, ordering her to do this and that as though she were an imbecile. Steve's unwelcome visit had ruined Gail's life, much as it had ruined Jill's.

Steve now told her categorically that he expected money or he would tell Geoffrey and Jill about their affair. Gail eyed him with aversion.

"Do as you please," she said calmly. "I don't have any money and my marriage to Geoffrey is only a sham. You can do nothing to me that could make any difference." She prayed he would go away.

He did not believe her and gestured at the luxurious house. "Come off it, darling! This place is worth millions. Look at it. You can't expect me to believe you don't have pots of money lying around."

"Personally I don't have one red cent," she said, raising her voice, but then quickly pulled back her anger. Shouting would get her nowhere. "I don't even have a bank account." She lied skillfully and without blinking. "My husband has his own flat in London, but I stay here to look after his mother. I don't run this house. She does. It is her house, not ours."

"I checked all this, you know."

"Then you know she owns this house."

"Sure, but then the son inherits everything after she kicks the bucket, which might not be long from what I saw. I can bide my time, so don't you worry your pretty little head. I *will* get what I want because I have the photographic proof."

Triumphantly he removed an envelope from his pocket and thrust a bunch of snapshots at her. They were crude black and white shots, blurred but she clearly saw her face, and his.

She felt disgusted to think he had set her up, and shoved them back at him. "Do what you want with them, Stevie boy," she said calmly as she walked away. "I could care less and my husband could care less. He knows I have affairs, as does his mother, and they condone them if I don't flaunt them." She felt confident that he could not harm her.

Steve rushed after her and blocked her path. "Hang on a minute, my fine lady, don't you dare leave until I've finished what I have to say. That might all be very well, but does he want this to get back to his partners in the law firm? Will his mother want copies sent to her friends?"

She gasped.

"Ah-ha! I see by your expression that you never considered that possibility, did you? We have more than one way to skin a cat, as they say."

"You wouldn't be so cruel as to let her see them! She's a sick woman." Gail was shocked to think Steve would upset an ailing woman. He had seen Jill, knew how bad she was, even gone to the hospital with them. How she had ever become involved with this man, she could not fathom, knowing she spotted him for what he was almost when she met him. How foolish she had been, to take up with him for physical release.

Gail saw herself now as a scarlet woman, a woman who cared nothing for other people's feelings. She'd had an affair with Richard and enjoyed it, but then again, Richard was a gentleman, whereas Steve was a con man. So why had she gone with him? Frustration, lust, because she wanted to flout society, wanted to get her own back on a homosexual husband? Whatever made her do it, she now rued it, shuddering to contemplate a public branding as an adulteress. She regarded him with hostility, seeing his too wide tie, his after-five bristles, his greasy hair.

"No," he said "but it'll make either you or your husband cough up the moolah, won't it?" He rubbed his fingers and thumb together and winked. "Well now, I'd better go leave you to think about it. I expect your husband pops down a lot to see your ma-in-law in the hospital. I'll be in touch, darlin', see you soon. Ta-ra."

Gail sank onto a chair feeling her skin prickle with nerves, knowing he was nasty enough to do as he threatened. While neither Geoffrey nor Jill would be particularly upset about her having an affair, the fact that somehow Steve managed to take indecent photographs and was using them as blackmail, would be abhorrent to them. It was peculiar that she, a loyal and faithful wife to John had come to this. A fallen woman being blackmailed by an unscrupulous swindler. It was unbelievable that she had allowed feelings of lust to overcome her better judgement, but she had, and the fault was all hers. She had nowhere to turn because as with all blackmailers, if she attempted to pay him off, he would come after her again. In American TV shows they always made the point that nothing could buy off a blackmailer, who would soon surface again to demand ever more money. Gail considered that, wondering if an accusation could ever bring Steve to court.

Should she, under the circumstances, go to the police? No, that would drag the Haslett name through the mud as surely as publication of the photos. To appear in court would be harrowing to the Hasletts, and all those people sniggering at their indiscretions might probably kill Jill.

With a heavy heart, she went to bed trusting she could think of some way out of the dilemma by morning. Her whole life seemed like a soap opera. And soap operas never ended.

CHAPTER THIRTY

As she sipped her breakfast tea, she listed prospects. She crossed out the lawyer, knowing she could not consult the family solicitor in case word got back to Geoffrey. A priest might help, they never told what they heard. Yet she didn't know of a Catholic church in the neighborhood, bastion as it was of the Church of England. The doctor might be the best bet. After much thought, Gail decided to ask Dr. Reese, who she had seen a week previously about a sore throat. Doctors were accustomed to keeping confidences, she reasoned: they were men of the world and he could surely advise her.

It did not take her long to blurt out the real reason for the office visit, and he listened attentively to her tale of woe. Again she thought that if anyone made her story into soap opera, no one would ever believe it. She told him everything.

He said nothing until she finished. Even saying it aloud made her feel better, she realized. It was cathartic. Now if only he could help.

"This is in complete confidence, of course, Doctor Reese," she finished.

"Dear lady, that goes without saying. Now let me tell you this, not a blackmailer in the world would let go once he sank his teeth into you. You must go to the police immediately."

Gail twisted her gloves nervously. This was not what she wanted to hear. "Still, won't they charge him or something, and won't it go to court?"

"Not necessarily. Ensuring it goes no further is possible, if you are well connected, which you are. Then again, the threat of legal action may be enough to scare him away. I'm sure your solicitor will find ample grounds to have him confined, then he'll cause you no more trouble. From what you tell me, he probably has a criminal record." He was placid, as if he heard such fantastic stories every day.

Gail glanced around his consulting room. It was comfortable here and she felt at ease. It was cramped and full of filing cabinets, shelves filled with medicine bottles, a scale. The furniture was old, well used. The doctor's leather chair squeaked as he moved and somehow brought back memories of an old doctor in her hometown of Sarnia who told her she need not have her tonsils removed.

She looked at him, unsure. "Are you sure my husband and his mother will never hear about it?" Gail asked, reluctant to consult a solicitor or tell the police. Still, that had been her first solution so it was probably the best recourse.

"Unfortunately I cannot guarantee that, Mrs. Haslett. However, I do feel the fact they condoned your adultery in the first place should give them pause to forgive this indiscretion. Surely they cannot ostracize you if this does not attract any publicity? Do yourself a good turn and see the police immediately. Have no fear of embarrassment, they have heard far worse stories than yours, you know."

She thanked the doctor and left with a feeling of dread that it was not yet over. Wondering what the police would ask, she realized she didn't know where Steve lived, or in what type of business he worked. His elaborate stories about entrepreneurial activities in the city left her with no doubt he was lying.

Stopping at a café, she checked the city telephone book. They listed Cochrane, Cochrane and Blair in Hammersmith and she asked directory inquiries to connect her.

"Cochrane, Cochrane and Blair. Good morning. May I help you?" A pleasant, well-educated female voice asked.

"Mr. Cochrane, please."

"Which Mr. Cochrane, madam? Mr. James Cochrane or Mr. Alfred Cochrane?"

"I wish to speak to Mr. Steve Cochrane," Gail said.

"We have no one of that name here, madam."

"What business is this?" Gail asked. The young woman was so pleasant and correct.

"It is a family law practice, madam. Mr. Alfred joined his father, Mr. Albert, about forty years ago. Then Mr. Alfred took over. Mr. James is his son. Mr. Blair came on as partner two years ago."

"I think I possibly have the wrong number. Thank you for your time." Gail hung up, stunned.

The blasted crook! Steve was not a lawyer, but now she came to think of it he had never suggested he was. He was simply using a lawyer's name to cover his real business, probably flashed cards around to that effect. Now she prayed the maid had not thrown away the card.

This time luck was with her. She found the card in the small drawer of the hall table. She examined it closely. It was a good quality embossed linen calling card, the name Stephen Cochrane raised in a black script. It could not possibly have been a one off, even she could see that. As was the habit with English calling cards, it bore only the company name and his name, nothing more, no address or telephone number. However, one thing was sure, it was a forgery because Cochrane, Cochrane & Blair had no Mr. Steve.

Gail sat thinking about this latest predicament, irritated at being gulled. He had told her a lot about himself during their conversations in the car when driving around. Now she searched her mind for anything that might give her a clue to his whereabouts. She was lucky in that Steve was inordinately proud of his rise from the gutter and liked to talk about himself. If only she had paid more attention, maybe he had said something on which they could nail him.

Originally of the lower class of Cockney, through aping his betters, he managed to attain a thin veneer of respectability. Early in life he realized the advantages of wearing good clothes. In a way, she admired him for pulling his way out of the lower strata to which he was born, but the lessons in thievery and extortion had left their mark on him. Obviously he knew no other way of life.

She struggled to recall the rest of their conversations. She knew he balked at working at a regular job, so maybe he preferred graft, embezzlement and his glib artistry as a con man as his means of support. That Steve thought he had it made was evident in his attitude, but, for all his easy charm, it was clearly apparent he would never amount to anything much. Right now his criminal tendencies probably had him headed for prison.

It was the Thunderbird that brought him back into her life, and as much as Gail hated to admit it, Jill was right about the car. It was so prominent among the dark English cars that it stood out like a goldfinch in a flock of blackbirds. Steve had followed her after spotting her shopping in Guildford. If only she had driven the black Jaguar saloon, then he would never have noticed her. Yet it was too late to worry about that now. He knew where she was, and had those damned incriminating photographs.

As she mused, she looked at the business card she was tapping on her thumb. Surely they could get him on grounds of being an imposter. One could not go around impersonating solicitors and get away with it. Maybe that alone would be sufficient grounds to get him jailed.

CHAPTER THIRTY-ONE

Jill arrived home from the hospital replete with private nurse and a hospital bed. The staff made the large sunny garden room, with its wall of French windows, into a bedroom. The nurse, most annoyed at the inconvenience, found herself installed in a small maid's room at the top of the house.

It was not an easy household with Jill back in charge. Though easily able to get around with the aid of a cane, she much preferred to recline on her bed, propped against huge pillows of goose down, holding court with her many visitors. If she had been Queen-like in her arrogance before her stroke, now she was even more so. Gail found herself feeling sorry for the nurse who on fine days wheeled the chair around the grounds as Jill or her entourage directed.

Geoffrey spent two or three days a week at home, and each weekend. Feeling terribly guilty about the "incident," as both called it, at his mother's bidding he spent time on the telephone inviting people over to visit. This constant stream of visitors resulted in Jill and Geoffrey entertaining gift bearing, chattering women from between eleven in the morning until at least four-thirty.

Gail soon tired of this salon, which both insisted she attend, and invented excuses to leave the room. Yet though this constant parade of visitors was unwelcome, it did keep Jill occupied. Recent days spent alone in the peaceful haven of the west wing were some of the happiest and relaxed she'd had in months. Then when Jill came home, the peace vanished. Geoffrey was more concerned about his mother's welfare than anything else, so tended to leave Gail to her own devices. Although feeling snubbed, and she could not imagine why, this enabled her to complete her plans to return to Canada.

As far as her other worry, the worry of blackmail, she informed a detective about Steve Cochrane and gave him the card. The last word she heard, the police inspector assured her someone would investigate immediately, and they would hold everything in strictest confidence. She was to contact them immediately if Steve came to the house in future. That they were looking after things without publicity, took a huge load off her mind.

Gail planned to travel to Canada at Easter. She decided to take only Robert with her, knowing the other two would decide for themselves. It disheartened her to realize her eldest children were all but lost to her. She had lost them to Geoffrey and Jill, to money and social prominence. Putting herself in their young minds, thinking what she would have thought at their age, she could see the wealth and influence the Hasletts afforded was not something they could easily relinquish. Their mother had nothing comparable to offer. No, they were too accustomed now to having everything handed to them on a silver platter.

Patricia sent weekly begging letters to Jill and got her wish, while Vincent telephoned Geoffrey for money and received cheques. It was so easy for them these days, and how accustomed they had become to the constant hand outs. They did not often write to their mother, but regularly to Jill and Geoffrey, which really hurt when Gail received news second hand. When she telephoned Vincent at weekends, he was always 'on his way out' and could hardly speak to her civilly. Patricia was too far away to call. Yes, they were lost to her and she would never forgive herself for bringing them to River's End, or for marrying Geoffrey.

Of course, Vincent was eighteen, old enough to make up his own mind, but she knew, if given a choice, he would opt for the inheritance. On the other hand, Patricia was so self-centered she thought the world revolved around her. She would never fear for the future, would always expect to be treated well.

Miserably Gail realized nothing she could say or do would fetch back one whit of the love they once had for each other. While she would like to think they might come back to be with her, she didn't hold much hope. She had done it to herself, she thought woefully, and would have to live with the consequences. Maybe one day they would see money was not everything and return to her. She would not, however, hold her breath.

Now that she'd had time to think about the situation, she wondered if Geoffrey and Jill would want Vincent as their heir if she left Geoffrey. Would Geoffrey disown the children under those circumstances? She must ensure that Vincent changed his name by deed poll if he decided to stay in England, it being far too late to have Geoffrey adopt him. As this gave him a ready-made future, she thought he would jump at the chance. Gail planned to visit him at Oxford within the next week.

However, when she approached Vincent with this plan he screamed at her that she was mad. "I don't want to change my name. Why would I want to be the stepson of a poofter?" She gasped and started to say something but he interrupted "Oh yes, I know Geoffrey is a homosexual. I spotted that on meeting him."

Gail felt shocked. Apparently everyone knew... even her own children. After a not very satisfactory meeting, she went home feeling somehow tainted by her alliance with Geoffrey.

She would, she decided, tell Patricia at the last minute of her plans and given the option, Gail knew without asking what she would opt for, a life of luxury and social position. She would, if it were in her best interests, agree to a name change or adoption.

Thinking about it later, she reckoned Geoffrey would not go for adoption anyway, not if he realized Gail was leaving him. Her desertion, broadcast quickly through Jill's coterie, would leave him in a terrible situation. Jill would be furious and make his life intolerable, and his homosexuality, which his marriage had somehow negated, would be the subject of many sniggering conversations. Those who thought themselves better, adulterers all, derided homosexuals.

She agonized over her decision. Was she doing the right thing? Didn't she owe him something? He had, after all, lifted her out of a life of penury and given her status. Should she wait until the children finished school to make her move? That would seem the right thing to do, but no, she could not live any longer in this sham marriage, must make a life of her own before she was too much older.

The past weeks of stress, she was pleased to notice, had slimmed her down. She lost at least two dress sizes and could now wear clothes she had put away over a year ago. So problems did some good, although she wondered why her looks were still so important to her. Selfish, she was selfish, she wanted it all; money, status, looks, a social life… love.

CHAPTER THIRTY-TWO

Later that week Mr. Ludlow wrote to say Mr. Rejistan had left the country. Unfortunately the police investigation of both Monterey and its books failed to turn up any mention of John's name. They even opened old files stored in the basement, but found nothing. However, they found it particularly suspicious when they noticed certain pages missing from record books. Old bank records showed the deposits made to Monterey's account, but, of course, the bank had destroyed the actual bank drafts and the company microfilm entries did not show who sent the money. So far nothing had surfaced to prove John's partnership.

She thought then that Rejistan had destroyed everything. That once advised of John's death, he completely expunged any document that referred to John's involvement. It was also a possibility Rejistan had taken over the company at the outset while John was working elsewhere in the world. However, John Montgomery was not a stupid man and surely would have demanded current data on company finances, would have demanded the audited yearly statements or, at the very least, progress reports. He would never have continued to transfer money into a losing proposition. Why too had he continued to send money if the company, as it had looked to her, was so very prosperous? Wouldn't the company have paid him something for his investment? Nevertheless, she found no record of payments credited to his account. Nor had she found anything in John's desk concerning the company, or found financial statements or records of any kind. This really was a mystery.

Once back in Canada, she decided, she would take everything out of storage and make a thorough search of every item. Knowing John, it was bizarre that he would have gone to such lengths to conceal his investment from anyone, especially his wife. It was unlikely that he was involved in anything illegal, because John was basically honest, apart from his 'swindle sheets.' It must have been for some important reason that he kept it to himself because he never mentioned it, even in passing. Even so, it was vital to find any paper that proved he was involved in the financial affairs or running of the company.

Mr. Rejistan, obviously unscrupulous and, like other old-fashioned Middle Eastern males, thought he could get the better of a mere woman. Well, she had news for him. She had not yet started to fight.

As Easter approached, Gail worried about when she should inform Geoffrey of her impending departure. To sneak off without telling him would be cowardly, and though she did not love him, he had, after all, helped her find her feet. She decided to tell him straight, feeling she owed him that much.

Her tickets were already in her purse, two first class seats for herself and Robert. After she picked them up from the travel agency, she drove down to see Vincent, who, annoyed she was trying to sabotage his life, refused to talk to her. Gail decided not to write or call Patricia, as she knew Trish was too wrapped up in her own life to worry about her senile old mother. Robert seemed thrilled to be going back to a Canada that he remembered as a magical place of hamburgers, french fries and thick milk shakes.

Two weeks before her flight, she sought out Geoffrey and found him walking in the garden. It was not often these days that he was not with Mummy. He had reverted to calling her Mummy since the "incident."

Much to her surprise, Jill never referred to the cause of her stroke. Maybe she had forgotten, wiped it out of her mind, and still treated

Gail the same, frostily. For that Gail was thankful because she felt guilty about Jill's condition.

She found him sitting by the river watching two swans and their cygnets. The sun shone from one of those skies that looked as if painted by Sergeant. A slight breeze nodded the bulrushes, and somewhere a bullfrog boomed.

"Hello, Geoffrey," she said, "Beautiful, aren't they?"

"Yes, indeed. They come back here each year in the spring. All swans are the property of the queen, you know."

She turned away from the swans, eager to have it over.

"Geoffrey, we need to talk."

He turned on the seat to give her his full attention. Gail rarely used her strong voice with him these days. She knew he would withdraw into himself like a turtle into its shell if she tried to be dominating, although he liked that in his mother.

"Well?" He sounded annoyed at her tone of voice.

"Geoffrey, as much as it pains me to tell you this, I have decided we will go to Canada."

"I beg your pardon!" He was immediately red faced and angry. "You are my wife and I have no intentions of going to Canada. My place is here with Mummy, as is yours."

"I have been thinking about this a great deal. It is not a decision I made lightly. My place is back in my own country. I can't live this lie any longer, Geoffrey. I owe you a great deal, and thank you for everything, but I cannot live the rest of my life in this manner."

When he spoke, his tone was soft but snide. "Yes, you do owe me a great deal, and since you realize that, I can't understand why you feel it is your right to leave me. Oh, never mind," he waved his hand as if she were a minor irritation. "Please yourself. The children must stay with me. I'm sure I can explain your desertion."

"I intend to take Robert with me," Gail said angrily.

His face was hard and red as he faced her and took her arms, digging in his fingers. "On the contrary, Gail, Robert will remain here with me. Take Vincent or Patricia, but Robert must, and will, stay."

She shook her head and tried to pull away from him. "Robert

comes with me, Geoffrey. You may keep Vincent and Patricia. That way you get your heir and I get my freedom."

He still held her arms and she found his strength surprising. "If necessary you will stay in the house under a restraining order." Anger clipped his tone, "You cannot lay down the law to me, Gail. I am a barrister. You will remain here as my wife, or you will leave alone. You have no other option."

Gail stared at him stonily. He would force her to leave alone if he insisted on keeping Robert. He had the law on his side, knew all the ploys. Why hadn't she considered this circumstance, knowing how much he loved Robert? From the moment they met Geoffrey really had taken a shine to the boy, had always treated Robert as his son and she had admired him for it. Now he considered Robert legally his. Oh, why hadn't she taken her son and gone?

Geoffrey stood, pushed her onto the seat and looked down at her. "I will inform the school to forbid you access to Robert for any reason whatsoever."

"You can't do that!" Gail said, shocked, not thinking that Geoffrey could be that vindictive. "He's my son, not yours."

"Nevertheless, he *is* my son, just as I am your husband. Please do not attempt anything foolish, Gail. It would be a terrible shame to destroy Robert's future. He will inherit everything, you know, and I have already changed my will. As for Vincent, I know he is the oldest, but I should point out that Vincent is far too set in his ways and remembers his father too well. Patricia is a mere female and not even in the equation. No. Robert will inherit everything, and I will certainly set in motion the wheels to adopt him legally. No more needs saying."

Gail stood, her hands formed into fists. She felt like hitting him, of screaming, but that would not solve anything. "I won't allow you to adopt him, Geoffrey," she said through clenched teeth. "As his mother I have the right to say where he will go, and with whom he will live."

"Don't be so sure, Gail. I have the perfect right to charge you with being an unfit mother. For example, your affairs."

She gasped. Who would have thought he could be so venomous?

"The man who caused Mummy's incident was one of your paramours, wasn't he? People have seen you with other men, people who would act as witnesses to your infidelities. You are really obtuse to think you can hold your maternal parentage over my head."

Oh dear lord, Jill did remember and had told Geoffrey! She shouted now, unable to help it. "You wouldn't do such a thing! *You* condoned my affairs! Both you and your mother essentially gave your blessing if I were discreet. How dare you try to turn things around now? You have never shared my bed...."

He sneered. "Try to prove that in a court, my dear. Casual sex is never that, is it? I hold the winning hand. You seem to forget that I have contacts in high places."

"You bastard!" Gail yelled. Geoffrey motionless, wore a slight smile of pity, watching her work herself up into a rage. "How could you do this to me? I've never done anything to warrant this type of treatment. You can't buy children, you know. I *will* have my son and I *will* go to Canada."

He said nothing as he stood with arms crossed over his chest, smiling condescendingly, blandly watching her make a fool of herself. Gail, well-aware Geoffrey and his mother disliked any public display of emotion, now found his stance extremely infuriating, jumped to her feet and angrily marched away.

CHAPTER THIRTY-THREE

She stood in the largest green house, shaking her head in disbelief. What was she going to do now? She had been foolish to think Geoffrey would let her walk out of his life. Why on earth hadn't she thought of that before she told him of her plans? Hindsight was wonderful, wasn't it? She should have packed, left, and picked up Robert on the way to the airport. Once they were in Canada, Geoffrey could not touch her: at least she didn't think so. Stupidly, she had revealed her hand too soon.

Later, depressed and forlorn, she slumped on the couch in her living room and thought over the situation. Plans and counter plans revolved in her mind until she developed a splitting headache. She would, she decided, contact a solicitor to see what could be done to regain possession of her youngest child. Strangely, she did not feel much concern for Vincent or Patricia, although she realized they would hate her forever. From what he said, Geoffrey obviously did not want them and, if he were as vindictive as he appeared, would probably disown any responsibility for their welfare. She sat crying, knowing tears would not solve anything.

The solicitor, a man she found through the phone book in London, was helpful, though not confident she could regain her son. As he pointed out, she had no proof that she and Geoffrey had not cohabited. His mother, he said, would be on Geoffrey's side.

His face expressed amazement that Jill had done the proposing, although he said little on the subject. If they could find some way of proving Geoffrey was a homosexual, he said, maybe they would have a chance. Would she consider hiring a private investigator to watch the flat? This sounded like a good idea, and was easy to arrange. Gail did not hold much hope of catching Geoffrey in the act, as he was going into London only two days a week these days to work at the practice, and didn't spend much time at the flat.

She traveled back on the train thinking about her uncertain future. To solve the dilemma was going to take a long time, so she could forget trave lling to Canada at Easter. With a heavy heart, she canceled the reservations.

The investigator watched the flat around the clock, but never had anything to report. Gail even went up to London and checked the flat herself. The place smelled musty and abandoned, unlived in, so obviously Geoffrey was not using it much these days. It amused her to find her visit reported in the investigator's weekly report. Well, at least he was doing his job, she thought with a sigh.

Then something happened that raised her hopes.

Geoffrey invited four people to visit River's End for a week. One couple was one of his partners and wife. The other two were male associates.

From the way Geoffrey let his hand rest on Alan's arm, Gail immediately knew Alan was more than a business associate. She watched them carefully. They were almost too circumspect, too careful and too aware of the others. Geoffrey had invited his lover to the house. Yet how could she use the knowledge?

She drove to the village and bought a flash camera and two rolls of film. One of these nights, she decided, she would catch them together and take photos. It seemed so uncomplicated and easy, but would it be in practice? A flash going off would alert them. Could she run away quickly enough?

He stopped at her side one day as she was cutting roses for the dining room.

"Allow me to show you something, my dear." He smiled so evilly that she knew it was something disagreeable. Taking an envelope from his jacket pocket, he handed it to her. Even before she looked inside she knew what it was, that damned Steve had sent him the photographs!

"Now shall we talk? I think discretion is the least of your virtues, Gail. Mummy would not like to think snaps like these were in circulation. Any hint of scandal against you could rub off onto the entire family."

"Where did you get them?" His ownership mystified Gail as she thought Steve would be under lock and key by this time. He had not tried to contact her since she visited the police.

"I came by them as a matter of course. Another solicitor asked that our firm place one of our investigators on a surveillance project, the man's name was Mr. Steve Cochrane, a suspect in a blackmail case. These snaps, along with many others, were found at his place of residence. Fortunately, as it happens, they sent the seized boxes to my office. I recognized you immediately although they are blurry. You were stupid to think you could get away with this, Gail. Naturally I removed these photos from the files and have both negatives and prints. Now shall we talk?"

Her heart felt like a stone. "What can I say? You appear to have the upper hand, as you pointed out earlier."

Gail's mind raced madly like a hamster in a wheel. She must find the negatives and destroy them. She must burn the prints she still held. No way was she going to let him have all the power if she could help it, but she must lull him into thinking he had won.

"I don't think we need say more about your leaving." He smiled nastily and then, she hated him with a passion.

"No, I guess not," she said, composing her face as if accepting his ultimatum.

When he rowed away in a small boat up the river with his "friend" Alan, ostensibly to do some fishing, she went to his suite.

It was the first time she had entered his rooms. They were modern in fashion with long clean lines and finishes of pale laminate. The floors of polished oak planks had small expensive modern rugs scattered here and there. Dominating the room stood his huge bed, on a pedestal covered with a fur throw. Geoffrey's rooms looked much as he did, fastidiously clean and uncluttered. A large walk-in closet held suits and separates hung as though on display in a high class store highlighted by spotlights recessed into the ceiling. His living room/study was Spartan in its furnishings, the desk small with only one drawer that held bank records and tax statements.

Where should she look? She checked the drawers in the credenza to find they held only magazines, writing paper and other miscellaneous papers pertaining to his practice. She searched through the papers but found nothing. The walk-in closet was the only place where anything could be hidden. Then she found the negatives in the inside pocket of one of his jackets. As she had burned the prints, she must now burn the negatives.

All that remained was to get an incriminating photo of him and his friend, then he could not make good any of his threats. Yet it was not as easy to catch him in the act as she thought. Each night she waited inside her living room door to see if Alan went to his room, or Geoffrey went to his. Four days went by, and all she had to show for the time were dark circles under her eyes.

However, with the removal of the threat of the blackmail photographs, she was ostensibly in the clear and he could not charge her with adultery. She sat and thought about it. What other proof could he find, what else could he hold against her? This tormented her, she thought constantly of her lovers, of how Geoffrey could possibly get proof of her infidelity, until she realized he could not, and relaxed.

The days passed slowly, and then Easter was upon them. Robert and Vincent arrived home for the holidays. Robert brought a chum and Vincent, without warning, showed up with a lithesome, languid blond draped on his arm. The sudden and unannounced appearance of this female did not amuse Geoffrey and he said so in waspish tones.

"But, Geoffrey," Vincent said in a buttery voice, "this is my home and this is my girl. I brought her home to meet my mother."

"You might have first telephoned to ensure we had a room available for the young person. This is not a hotel. It is a private home. I might have had people staying as I did last week. What would you have done if we had no room?"

"Oh," Vincent shrugged nonchalantly. "I suppose she would have shared mine. In fact, she might as well share mine, come to think of it."

"I beg your pardon!" Geoffrey was positively apoplectic. "You will not share a room with a female while in this house. You are not married to this… this… this creature. I will not have this, Vincent, and I'm sure your mother will agree with me. I realize today's morals are lax, but they are not lax under my roof. Anyway, Mummy…"

Vincent interrupted. "Please, Geoffrey, don't talk to me about your mother. She never goes anywhere these days other than the ground floor. How could she know what was going on upstairs? If you don't tell her, she'll never know."

Geoffrey spoke through gritted teeth. "You will tell the young lady that she will sleep in the main house. You will sleep in the west wing in your own room. No more arguments, young man. That is the way it will be."

Gail hated the blond on sight. Sybil might be from a good family and talked with the proverbial plum in her mouth, but she was like Patricia, a gold digger. She looked Gail up and down as they talked, her calculating little mind adding up the cost of Gail's clothes and accessories. With Jill she was sweet and went out of her way to do things for her. As might be expected, Jill liked her and talked to her for hours.

Robert and his school chum spent the days exploring the woods and the riverbanks. Each day they arrived home wet, dirty and tired, but happy. Once he asked her when they were going back to Canada, and she told him she had changed her mind and not to mention it to Geoffrey.

"Oh, I see, Mummy. He didn't like for us to go."

It felt odd without Patricia who had gone to stay with a school chum in Paris. She must be in heaven, Gail thought, realizing why Jill had sent two letters addressed to Trish only last week. They probably included funds for shopping.

Soon the boys returned to school and Gail settled into a dull routine. She spent as little time with Jill as possible, although she could not avoid her completely because Geoffrey was now spending more time in London. Each night she prayed the investigator would catch him with Alan or his latest lover.

Her mind was still active with plans for her return to Canada and she suddenly recalled something Robert had written in his letters. He wrote about going into town once a week for shopping. This she asked him about when she next wrote and discovered the boys went into town each Thursday mornings to purchase anything they needed. This window of opportunity would give her access to her child. She could spirit him off to Canada before anyone knew he had gone. She began planning their escape.

Mr. Ludlow was still seeking Mr. Rejistan. His failure to find anything proof that Rejistan had embezzled John's funds appalled Gail since she had set her hopes on Mr. Ludlow.

"Our only hope is that you find any papers Mr. Montgomery kept on file," he wrote, "Mr. Rejistan is a cunning man and has covered his tracks exceedingly well. I advise you to come over for a short visit to learn whether you have any type of document in storage that would help us with this case."

So she *had* to get back to Canada, moreover she had to get Robert back to Canada quickly because Geoffrey had already started adoption proceedings. These, of course, she intended to terminate when they approached her for permission. Meanwhile, she was living on the edge, her nerves taut and close to snapping.

The investigator managed to catch Geoffrey and his lover in the flat and had some explicit photographs, taken from a balcony window across the street, that left no doubt as to their activities. As Gail suspected, the man was Alan. This put a different light on the situation. Now she could blackmail Geoffrey, and she gleefully confronted Geoffrey with the copies when he arrived home Friday evening.

"I think we need have no more of your threats, Geoffrey," she said with a great deal of satisfaction. "I have hard evidence, evidence a professional investigator can support. I also destroyed the negatives of myself and Steve so you can't hold those over my head any more." Gail felt triumphant, giddy with success.

A terrible row followed about her going into his rooms. Gail pointed out that she was, as he said, his wife so why should she not go into his rooms? She used the very words his mother used when Gail discovered her snooping in Gail's bedroom. This violation of his privacy, both by Gail and her investigator, upset Geoffrey terribly. Much to her chagrin, he sat on the bench outside the greenhouse and, putting his head down, broke down and cried. Not crying as a man might cry, but a wailing keen that struck cold into her heart. He cried because she had threatened to show the evidence to his mother, he cried because she was going to shame him by leaving him, he cried for his heir, Robert.

Gail experienced such a pang of guilt, felt so sorry for him, that she cradled his head against her shoulder and held him. What a poor excuse for a man he was, but how keenly he felt this loss, though his histrionics left a bad taste in her mouth.

"Geoffrey, please stop crying. I'm sorry about all this, however, surely you must see that it's for the best. You can have Vincent and Patricia, but I must have Robert. He is my youngest son, the love of my life and I can't leave him with you."

"I don't want those two," he said sulkily, hiccuping sobs. "They are too old and, anyway, Vincent is not the sort I want for an heir. He is too involved with young ladies and politics for my liking." He wiped his eyes and blew his nose on a large white monogrammed handkerchief. "He told me he wants to go into politics when he graduates, and we have *never* had politicians in the family." He was over his sobbing fit and put back his shoulders, angry now with Vincent. "Why can't he read law as I did? I recall he once said he was interested in law."

Gail chuckled softly. "You make it sound as if becoming a politician is akin to becoming an axe murderer, Geoffrey. Come now, let's face it, not everyone is drawn to the law. Maybe he'd prefer medicine or some other profession. Still, no matter what he chooses, you cannot force him into doing something he doesn't want."

"Nobody is trying to force him into anything," Geoffrey said, sitting up straight and wiped his face. He tucked in his tie, straightened his jacket. "That young man has definite ideas about what he wants to do with his life. I have written to him often since I discovered he leans to the left politically. That will not do, Gail, and he has also become involved with a group of radicals. Unfortunately, I cannot make him see the futility of pursuing such a career choice."

Gail could care less what Vincent wanted to do with his life. He could become a politician or a circus clown; it was his decision to make. She would have loved to hear that he aimed his ambitions at a profession, but who was she to decide? A mother could only suggest, and he would never listen to her.

She sighed and said, "I'm sure Vincent will sort it all out eventually. I can't see him becoming a Communist or other radical type. He's probably having you on, Geoffrey."

He pulled a face of distaste. "What does that mean, "having me on?" I do wish you would not use American slang, Gail."

"It means 'pulling your leg,' as you Brits say," Gail said tetchily, "And I know you know what that means."

"Fine, but as I said before, I do not intend to make Vincent my heir. Robert is my heir. That being so, it is imperative that you allow him to complete his schooling in England. When he has reached the age of eighteen, he can then make up his own mind whether he wants to stay here. I still intend to adopt him legally, Gail, and you cannot prevent that."

"I will not give my permission, Geoffrey." Her composure astounded her. This was one battle he would not win. "You cannot adopt him unless I say it is my wish."

"I have ways and means, my dear, ways and means."

Gail felt a pang of fear at the silky tone of his voice, knew he knew something she did not. He could do something to discredit her, or even have her declared an unfit mother to get his way.

Geoffrey paused for a moment gathering his thoughts. "I think you are being very selfish about the boy, Gail. You are cutting off his financial stability because you cannot have your own way. I will say, though, you may leave if you wish. I would not want to force you to stay in England if you are unhappy. Robert will, of course, finish his schooling. You could fly over to see him during the school holidays. It will work out admirably."

"Maybe for you, Geoffrey, maybe for you." Gail knew it would work only if she had enough money to make the constant trips to England. Robert was away at school the rest of the time and would not miss her if she wrote her weekly letter.

Should she go along with this? Maybe it would work. She considered the pros and cons. It could do no harm right now, because since he was at school Geoffrey, could have no undue influence on her son. Her Robert was very much a person in his own right, had enough brains to see what was what and never took things at face value. Making peace, she knew, would mean the other two could finish their expensive education.

She sighed. "You're right in that Robert stands to gain far more than I would lose so taking away a possible inheritance would be selfish of me. After thinking about it, Geoffrey, I have decided that if you draw up and sign a legal document clarifying the situation, I can return to Canada with a clear conscience." Yes, free to pursue Mr. Elie Rejistan.

They talked about it for over an hour, and finally Geoffrey reluctantly agreed.

Gail picked up her airline ticket and went down to see Robert Thursday morning. She spoke to him when he came out of the school with a group of other boys.

All he said was, "Have a lovely holiday then, Mummy," and, happily unperturbed, ran to catch up with the others. Feeling much better for having spoken to him, she phoned to Geoffrey to say she was leaving.

He wished her a good journey, saying she was welcome to visit River's End anytime, with or without notice. Geoffrey sounded so civilized, so incredibly stiff upper lip that she had to suppress a smile.

"I would ask that you not speak to Mummy before you leave. I'll let her know after your departure. She'll be upset, as she is fond of you and this might set back her recovery."

"Somehow I doubt that, Geoffrey. It will probably *speed* her recovery."

The day before she left, she went into the village to pick up a few things and, as she left the chemist, spotted a swarthy looking man eyeing her. She saw him again as she left the Post Office. Thinking it strange, she made a few sorties into other shops to see if she were imagining things, but he stayed with her even when she cut out through the back door of the newsagent and into the florist through their rear entrance.

The man was stalking her! Who would want to follow her and why? Geoffrey would never do such a thing as he knew she had nothing to hide from him. Steve Cochrane, then? As far as she knew, he was away on a short holiday at "Her Majesty's Pleasure." Now she sat in the tea shop and watched the man as he stood looking into the glassed over notices in front of the ironmonger, making notes in a small book, as though he were checking for a room or an item offered for sale. From time to time, he looked up the street and could see her clearly sitting in the window seat. Sitting forward, she stared right at him. Her scrutiny did not bother him, and his glance merely touched, then grazed over her. Taking the newspaper from under his arm, he pretended to be reading the want ads.

Gail felt apprehensive when she realized he was waiting for her. She glanced around the tea room to check if she knew anyone, but saw not a soul who looked vaguely familiar. Nevertheless, she reasoned, she surely would be safer with another person at her side. Tossing a ten pence piece onto the table as two women got up to leave, she left with them, starting a silly conversation, knowing she had to make it look as though they were together.

They were now nearing her parked car and as they drew abreast of it, she quickly opened the door, started the car and frantically pulled away from the curb. Glancing through her rear view mirror, she saw the man still walking. Probably unaware that she had escaped because of the number of pedestrians.

As she sped home, she wondered who could be following her, but not knowing how she could find out without letting them catch her, decided to forget it. She would inform the police before she left for Canada tomorrow. Surely he was not going to follow her there?

When the taxi arrived to pick her up at eight in the morning it was pouring with rain. Even the driver made her feel uneasy as she looked at the back of his head and checked his docket. He was dark, looked like an Arab or Armenian, like the man who had watched and waited. This made her nervous, though he seemed friendly enough and had a cockney accent. A sense of unease niggled at her when she thought about being followed and, as she waited in line to check in, she looked around the airport. A dark haired man watched the line, and his eyes slid away as she looked at him. Was he watching her? Feelings of paranoia overwhelmed her, and she felt sure someone was watching, but *why*? Or was it her imagination? She felt relieved as she entered the first class lounge, glad to be well away from the man. The other passengers seemed normal enough. Was she really painting them all black because of her fears?

Toronto brought bright sunshine and chaos. The international terminal, where four 747's unloaded simultaneously, meant the concourse was packed with people waiting for arriving passengers. It took a long time to get through customs and to the luggage carousels.

The staid Royal York was much the same. Nothing much had changed in the downtown core, she noted, apart from building facelifts and the new gold mirrored glass office towers. It felt like coming home. She enjoyed a long warm bath and sat watching television until hungry enough to order tea from room service.

CHAPTER THIRTY-FOUR

Gail signed a lease on an apartment in Etobicoke, arranged to move in at the end of the month, then notified the storage company to arrange for delivery of her possessions.

The lawyer, Mr. Ludlow, seemed pleased to see her. They talked over the lack of progress in the Rejistan case, but he felt positive she would find some small clue in the stored possessions that could solve everything. Gail returned to the hotel feeling more relaxed and sure of herself. The fact she was moving into her own place made her feel better. Soon she would have her own furniture and possessions around her.

It felt strange, though, to be alone in Toronto. This was their city, hers and John's. Here they met nearly twenty-five years ago, and here he proposed to her. How strange to think she was living a life apart from him, that she could survive on her own. Well, I'm stronger now, she told herself, I could move mountains if I had to, I could accomplish anything to which I set my mind. John's death gave me that strength.

She rented a car, and went to buy a car of her own. Driving along the Danforth, she checked the car lots. Next day she drove back to the hotel in a red Ford Fairlane.

On the Friday afternoon she sat amid the furniture and boxes the storage company dumped in the apartment. The Superintendent and his wife helped her move the larger pieces and, armed with a tire iron, the Super pried open the wooden crates. The three of them pushed furniture around, opened boxes and sorted things into rooms. She was at home at long last, and sent Robert her new address.

Days passed as she sifted through every item. So far she had found nothing remotely connected with Mr. Rejistan. What she did find was another safety deposit box key in an old briefcase with no indication to which bank it belonged.

Robert sent a picture postcard of thatched cottages that said, "Have a nice holiday, Mummy, missing you. Robby," which made her cry. Gail missed him already, which was silly since, even if she were still in England, he would be away at school.

Then, one day as she sifted through a box, she found a business diary in a box of old files. She thumbed through the pages. For what reason had John kept this out-of-date book? During July, on John's birthday, she found an entry on the second page that read "Weltpostrasse 5, Berne," under which something was crossed out. She tried to decipher it, but unfortunately it had many numbers and John had scored over them too often. The address was quite legible. Carefully she checked through the diary, but nothing more of interest appeared.

Was this Weltpostrasse the reason he kept the book? After calling the Swiss Consulate she discovered Weltpostrasse 5, Berne was the Banque Populaire Suisse. Maybe this was the bank to which the key belonged. She put the things aside.

The following day she spoke to Mr. Ludlow about her finds.

"I suppose he had a reason for not mentioning any of this information, Mrs. Haslett, but I would not care to guess why."

"I also found an envelope in a file folder that explains about the other Mrs. Montgomery. Also another copy of a will, his father's, which explained that he had set aside money for his last wife, who had once been his housekeeper." She had told him about her trip to London and her mistaken conclusion that the woman was John's wife.

"John was, I suppose, her stepson as she married his father after being his housekeeper for many years. It was his father's wish that John be executor of the money because she was a known spendthrift. Not that it was very much, only ten thousand pounds, but John Senior knew she would waste it if she got a lump sum. Still, I cannot possibly continue the payments. The bank had only a few hundred dollars left in the account."

"You told me the woman had married again?"

"Yes, to a man named Arthur. If he is a wage earner I suppose she'll be all right. I hate to think she's suffering."

"Mrs. Haslett, please don't take the worries of the world on your shoulders," Mr. Ludlow said. "I cannot see any reason why this matter regarding Mrs. Montgomery should not wait until we have settled your own financial affairs."

"I wish I knew why John had kept all these secrets." She sighed. "I thought he trusted me, but how could he if he didn't want to let me know about things?"

"I'm sure sooner or later we will discover exactly why Mr. Montgomery did not reveal these matters. I'm sure he had very good reason."

Gail snorted. "I think it was the way his family raised him. His father was very much the patriarch, never told his mother anything, either. His mother experienced few problems on his death primarily because his oldest brother had familiarized himself with the estate in his capacity as a bank manager."

Mr. Ludlow sighed. "If you knew that, why then didn't you ask your husband about things?"

He was right to sound so impatient. If she had ever shown any curiosity surely John would have told her. "I never knew about his father until the day of John's funeral when his aunt told me so I really have no idea why John did not confide in me. It's as if I were married to a total stranger. Then again, I have only myself to blame."

They were right about one thing, the naysayers who warned her about marrying an Englishman. The tight-lipped English people were secretive to the point of insanity. For what reason had John kept his father's slovenly wife a secret? Maybe she was not slovenly then, maybe she had deteriorated since his death. Still, what had it achieved and who would have cared?

"Let me know if you find anything else."

"I will. I don't think much is left."

For two more days she searched, taking out all the drawers and searching underneath each, digging under the padding in the couch and chairs, reading each piece of paper front and back, until nothing was left unexamined. She arrived at the conclusion there could be nothing more to find.

Quickly, she decided to go to Switzerland to investigate the safety deposit box while she still had funds. Before she could change her mind, she purchased a ticket for the following day, knowing in her heart it might well prove a fruitless journey. Mr. Ludlow had suggested she write to them first, but Gail was too anxious to wait another moment.

Switzerland was lovely, she decided, though it was not winter and thus the city had no snow. Berne was a busy place, well maintained and clean. Her hotel was modern and comfortable and she admired the Alps from her window. A clear blue sky with the odd white fluffy cloud added to the peace of the scene.

Once at the Swiss bank, she discovered John had registered the box in his name, and, to gain access, used her passport and his death certificate as identification. Had any other woman had to use a death certificate as often, she wondered? Luckily she had not changed the name on her passport when she married Geoffrey and they had honeymooned in Canada. Now filled with apprehension, she waited in the small room until they brought the box.

It was a large box that she had to stand to open. After the assistant used his key, she was left alone to use her key and investigate the contents.

Inside were many documents. She sat back and blew out a breath of relief. Her pulse skyrocketed as she saw papers that linked and tied John to Monterey Enterprises and Mr. Rejistan. An agreement of some kind, written in some language that could be Arabic, showed John's signature and that of Elie Rejistan. One, in English, was an agreement that John would purchase the company. Also, stocks and bonds and two bank books for different Swiss banks showing hefty balances.

It stunned her to discover that, to all intents and purposes, she was a wealthy woman. The mystery was, why John had kept everything hidden from her?

Then she found an insurance policy with herself as beneficiary for a million dollars, issued to Monterey Enterprises. So, this was the reason Mr. Rejistan was wary of her. He thought she wanted the insurance money, money probably appropriated when he heard of the death.

The bank supplied her with a large brown paper bag into which she packed everything. At the hotel office, she had copies made of all the documents then returned the originals to the bank. Scrutiny of the statements showed the money on deposit in the two banks amounted to more than a million dollars and had been forwarded from Canada.

Mr. Rejistan had probably made those deposits, Gail thought. It felt good to know John had not forgotten his family after all, but, still, why all the secrecy?

On the plane home, she mused over John's hidden dealings. She now possessed the means to sue Mr. Rejistan. He would not be happy about that. First, she must find someone to translate the document into English, then take it to Mr. Ludlow with the insurance policy. When she got back, she would open a bank account to where they could transfer Swiss funds. The government would undoubtedly expect her to pay taxes on the amount, but even so she would still be wealthy.

Life was exceedingly wonderful right now, she told herself as she hired an airport limousine to take her home. How pleasant to be able to do things without worrying about where each penny was coming from. How delightful to be able to afford limousine rides and first class air line tickets. Paying the driver, she got out of the car.

With her over night bag over her shoulder, she walked across the short forecourt and went to open the lobby door.

Then something came down hard on the back of her head and she lost consciousness.

CHAPTER THIRTY-FIVE

"How do you feel?" a voice asked as she groggily opened her eyes.

"What happened?" she asked with an "ouch," as she tried to sit up.

"Lie back, dear," a nurse said. "We're going to take you for an x-ray. You had a nasty bump on the head. Have you any idea how it happened?"

The room seemed blinding white and she closed her eyes. "Someone slugged me, I suppose. I don't remember anything, apart from putting my key in the lock." Gail felt terrible and her eyes refused to focus.

Mr. Ludlow arrived in answer to her call, expressing dismay at the event. She told him about the man who followed her in England, and about her findings in the safety deposit box. Whoever hit her, she said, had stolen her over night bag containing the document copies. How relieved she was that she'd had the foresight to leave the originals in Switzerland.

The mugger had not taken her small shoulder bag, which she wore strap crossed over her chest, as did all good travelers, in which was the safety deposit box key and the bank books.

Mr. Ludlow's expression cleared when she told him that. "I will have a courier sent to Switzerland to obtain the original documents.

You must sign a letter of authorization, of course, but I can assure you that this time we'll soon have the originals in our possession. Mr. Rejistan must do more than sanitize his files once we have this proof."

"This is all so terrible and I don't feel safe. Do I get protection?" Gail felt scared, thinking the man might be aiming to kill her.

He nodded. "Yes. I've already arranged it with the police. They'll be questioning you about the incident. We have a police officer sitting outside your door right now, and he'll stay until you leave. I'll get you a body guard until we bring Mr. Rejistan to justice. Have no fear, Mrs. Haslett, you are quite safe." Mr. Ludlow squeezed her hand and left humming merrily.

Gail thanked her lucky stars someone was looking after her interests.

Two days later, when she could go home, Mr. Ludlow introduced her to Arthur Hodson, the body guard. He was tall and broad, and looked like an ex-boxer, though strangely his looks belied his gentle nature. Gail liked him immediately. He steered her through the hospital in a wheel chair and out onto the steps where a limousine waited.

Things were serene enough once she settled back home. Arthur stayed with her, sleeping on the convertible couch in the small bedroom she had assigned as her office. He accompanied her everywhere and she found him good company. Arthur was good at his job, kept her amused even as his eyes never stopped searching for anyone who might harm her. At odd moments he told her astounding stories about the movie stars he had guarded, and the politicians for whom he often worked.

One evening they had arrived at the O'Keefe Centre, when he roughly shoved her back into the limo and slammed the door. His bang on the side of the car was enough for the driver to pull away immediately.

This stunned Gail, who, gasping with fright, crouched below the windows as Arthur had instructed. Was Mr. Rejistan having all her movements watched? For a week nothing had happened and, convinced nothing could happen to her in a crowd, she purchased the tickets for an opening night. With cameras and reporters all around the O'Keefe entrance, Mr. Rejistan must be a stupid man if he thought he could get away with harming anyone in the full glare of publicity.

Arthur later told her he had spotted a nasty character that the police wanted for killing a police officer in broad daylight on a busy Toronto street.

"So if he's capable of that," Gail said, "He could kill me in a crowd, and crafty enough that no one would see him perform the act."

"True. Sorry, Gail, but you should stay at home until they catch him. It's too dangerous."

Two days later she felt bored. "I'm like a prisoner here, Arthur. I can't go down to the mall, can't go to the library and I want to get my hair done. How long is this going to last?"

"I couldn't say, but you can't go out."

She spent her time writing long letters to the children and Geoffrey, reading, playing cards with Arthur and watching television.

After four days, she started griping to the police. "This is not a good way to live. I want to walk in the park, to go to the mall."

The inspector soothed her nerves, Arthur made her tea, joked and laughed until she felt better. Nevertheless, it was still hard to take, this confinement.

Mr. Ludlow came to see her.

"Good news at long last. Mr. Rejistan is in jail. Apparently he managed to get back into the country without detection and was hiding in Montreal. The papers from Switzerland prove without a doubt his theft of the company from John. Your husband was indeed in the process of buying the company from Rejistan, since the man wanted to return to the middle east. You were right that insurance money went into his own coffers. Monterey Enterprises owes you a great deal, and we have an intensive audit underway."

"Does this mean I can go out?"

"I don't see why not, although I think you must keep Arthur until we are quite sure Rejistan didn't leave orders with an underling."

When Elie was picked up by the police, a fact reported both on television and in papers, several of his henchmen at Monterey suddenly vanished. Auditors started combing the office records, and soon papers they had thought destroyed came to light.

Mr. Ludlow called her. "Would you like to come over to the office? I've got more news for you."

It was a revelation. "Through our investigation I think I know the reason for John's secrecy, implausible though it appears. John was dealing with Iraq and Iran for the American company that employed him, so he obviously could not have any dealings with Israel. However, Monterey Enterprises was dealing with Israel through a branch office plus Saudi Arabia through another autonomous branch."

Gail nodded. That made sense. "John was a definite asset to his company since he carried two passports: the British one he never relinquished and a Canadian passport he took out when he became a Canadian citizen. His duality allowed him to use the appropriate passport, depending on which country he was doing business."

Mr. Ludlow nodded. "I suppose he used his British passport for business in Israel. It had stamps from no other Middle Eastern country. He also used it for trips to Australia, parts of Europe and England. His Canadian passport, we discovered, he used exclusively for the Middle Eastern countries. Checking the dates, we discovered that before the end of Monterey's first year of operation, the United States put certain embargoes into effect. Whereas Israel would deal with anyone, Saudi Arabia, Iran and Iraq refused to trade with anyone who dealt with Israel. It made dealing with Middle Eastern countries difficult, but John had the problem licked. He was a valuable contact man."

"Yes, I can see that. His bosses operated to strict rules and, knowing that, he never let either of his passports lapse."

"It appears now that Monterey, under Mr. Rejistan, ignored all trade sanctions and political trade barriers. Through various nefarious contacts, Rejistan discovered devious methods of smuggling goods to anyone via a base in Germany, and another in Greece. Once Canadian trade sanctions went into effect, an agreement was drawn up under which Rejistan would operate the company, while John kept a low profile. He became a silent partner, not visibly connected with the business. Rejistan was to pay John's money and profits into a Swiss bank account, and that much he did, as we now know. Any profits were to be split equally between the partners. Of course, when Rejistan returned to his home, the company became property of your husband. It is obvious that appears Rejistan kept the last few profit payments, along with the insurance money."

"Son of a bi… Sorry, I felt like letting off steam." Gail grinned. "I still wish John had confided in me, though."

"I think he was trying to protect you, sort of 'what you didn't know couldn't harm you'. Mind you, I think you should have brought up the subject of your finances." Gail nodded. He was right about that much. "The police have discovered Elie actively dealt with many countries against which trade sanctions exist. Ethics meant nothing to him once he found a way around the trade barriers, so he dealt with anyone who approached him. Records of a personal nature, not connected with Monterey, and hidden at Elie's rented home, show him acting as a go-between on arms sales of missiles and guidance systems to Israel, made via Germany. He was also dealing with Saudi Arabia, having won a six milliondollar contract and, if they should ever connect this contract to his operations in Iran or Iraq, they would have assassinated him as a traitor."

"Too bad!" Gail said, "His death might have solved a whole lot of problems. Knowing something of the way the ignominious way the Middle Eastern chauvinistic mind works, I have no doubt that on Rejistan's death his underlings would expunge all trace of John or his heirs. I imagine John was unaware of Rejistan's underhanded methods, because, for all his faults, John was an honorable man."

Mr. Ludlow ordered coffee and they sat chatting.

"Well, where does this leave us now?" Gail asked.

"Once the authorities have deported Mr. Rejistan back to the Middle East, you can resume your life without worry. It amazed me when I heard that, for some reason, probably diplomatic, the courts allowed bail of a million dollars, and he quickly took advantage of it. He has friends with lots of ready cash."

But during this period, Elie disappeared. Reports came in from various Middle Eastern countries where eye witnesses had seen him, not that anyone could provide proof. Then, two months later, a headless body was found near Beirut. The sole identification was a birthmark on the shoulder. Everyone knew this mark, as Mr. Rejistan had told everyone who had seen it that it was the sign of Allah's blessing - it was in the shape of an angel. They identified the body as Elie Rejistan and closed the case. This left Gail wondering how she was going to claim her inheritance and relied again on Mr. Ludlow.

CHAPTER THIRTY-SIX

It took another six months before everything was settled and then Gail began to life a new life. The rapid acquisition of vast wealth was a kick, but she adjusted to the new lifestyle admirably and quickly. Each day she thanked John for his proficiency in business, rueful that both could not share this fortune. She supposed he was aware of his partner's imperfections and taken steps to safeguard his investment, although, if so, that would remain a mystery.

She had, with guidance from Mr. Ludlow, taken over Monterey Enterprises as CEO and was steering the company toward less shark infested waters. Since its inception, the company dealt in telephone systems, control systems and high efficiency commercial data processing. While under Mr. Rejistan's influence, its dealings had been primarily with the middle eastern countries, Gail moved it away from this area and concentrated on Canada, the USA and Europe. She hired four bright young sales representatives with university degrees, technical backgrounds, practical hands-on experience, all possessing great personalities.

Within twelve months the company had expanded considerably and was manufacturing technical controls for various processes, along with computer network installations for large schools, industrial plants and offices. Her new staff included experts in robotics (the wave of the future), who were currently introducing a new line of robots for assembly line work for auto manufacturers.

It was not an easy life. No sudden happiness descended on her. It was, however, challenging and energizing. Each day she woke to new challenges, new problems, and thanked her lucky stars she had enough money to hire the best and brightest. Maybe it was because she was a woman, a woman who was out of her depth, that the staff rallied round, applied themselves and performed brilliantly. She spent most of her spare time sleeping, long days of problems had her exhausted. Nevertheless, she felt happy.

Each month she wrote to the children. Told them of the company and her role in it, said that this was all because their father had made a good investment. Their replies were non-committal, never mentioned the company, never asked how she was. Vincent and Patricia were running true to form. Robby was the only one who asked how she was and was she happy in Canada? He said he was looking forward to visiting her and buying a hamburger and milkshake. She smiled at that, Robby had not changed much at all.

Robert, now seventeen and a half, came to Canada for his summer holidays with Geoffrey's permission. Gail delighted in the change in him. He had become a personable young man, his height now close to six feet, and now had a deep voice. It was dark brown, Gail thought, listening to him relate some school story. John's voice had that same rich tone, his singing voice being bass baritone.

Since Robert considered himself too old to call her Mummy, he now called her Mater, a word she found amusing, whereas with Vincent she found it annoying. Robbie was well mannered and caring and, although his sense of humor had also matured, he was still extremely funny.

Twice she traveled to England to visit Geoffrey and Jill. Sadly, Jill had become a shriveled old lady, having suffered another massive stroke. Confined to bed, they did not expect her to survive another winter. Looking at the once vital lady in her present condition was hard, but steeling her heart, she could not show much sympathy for Jill who had been such a harridan, sure Jill would interpret any expression of caring as weakness. She did, however, feel it privately. How sad to see this once vibrant domineering woman as a mere shell of her former self.

Geoffrey, it amazed her to discover, was living in the west wing with Alan who had taken up residence at River's End, ostensibly as a house guest. Gail realized Jill knew nothing of Geoffrey's living arrangements. The shame of it would probably have finished her.

Sadly her eldest children were lost to her. They would never come back to Canada to live after they had been out in the world on their own, that much she understood. Knowing they had gone to Geoffrey and Jill for financial assistance was hard. They bypassed her as a poor relation, not realizing she her wealth. They wrote few letters in answer to her own, but were not concerned about how she fared. Obviously they never read any of her letters. Annoyed, she wrote to both of them again about Monterey Enterprises, wanting them to know their mother was now a major force on the stock market. As she expected, their letters became more frequent, though quite impersonal, and requests for money were the norm.

Her older children were not nice adults, she thought, sensing the underlying hostility in their words. What a shame they were both mercenary and aloof. Never mind, she often told herself, they would find it difficult to adjust to a life of work and worry after having had riches heaped upon them in their formative years. Nevertheless, stranger things happened. Look at her, for example.

When Vincent dropped out of university at the age of twenty two, and married an older woman, Geoffrey immediately disowned him. This did not worry who Vincent who wrote to his mother with details of a lavish wedding, telling her his wife's family considered him the ideal son-in-law. After looking at the few photographs he enclosed, Gail thought this familial admiration was probably because of his wife. Marjory, at the age of thirty-five was a professional wallflower, had the face of a prune, a figure like a plank, and looked excessively dominating. She looked the type who resorted to out and out rudeness. Vincent presumably saw only the green of her money and none of her faults. He presently worked in the family's stock brokerage in London, political ambitions forgotten.

When she finally met Vincent and his wife on one of her visits, she discovered the new even snobbier Vincent appraised her in a noticeably scornful and condescending manner. Hurt to the quick, she left him to his ugly, domineering wife in their ancient, cold and damp, manor house without a backward glance. Wasn't it strange, she thought, he was her first born, yet she felt relief when leaving the man he had become?

It staggered her when she learned Patricia was living with a much older man, a wealthy Jewish widower, who treated her like a princess. Trish met him on the Gstaad ski slopes during a school winter break and never looked back. She refused to return home or to correspond with Geoffrey, who completely disowned her.

Her children were not turning out the way she had planned, Gail mused, but made the excuse she'd had no real time to exert her influence - that the schools, their chums and the Hasletts had brainwashed them. Maybe that was a rationalization, but Gail refused to take the blame this time.

She had no intentions of traveling to Zurich where the happy couple, now called Trish and Teddy, lived in splendor in a ritzy hotel as they planned the wedding of the century. She wondered how Teddy would fare if Patricia spent all his money. Would she run back to River's End, or to Canada and her mother? The only explanation Gail could find for this mismatch was that passion had blinded the poor man. Wasn't there an old saying, something about 'more to be pitied than censured?' After all, an older man with a much younger woman was usually so grateful that he gave her everything. Deciding, she wrote to Patricia saying she would attend the wedding if invited. Also, Patricia and her husband were welcome to visit her in Canada at anytime.

That left her with Robert, his completely unspoiled and sunny self. Giving her word to Geoffrey that she would not sue him for divorce until Robert inherited Jill's bequest, they made a verbal agreement and amicable arrangements for Robert to spend every other summer in Canada.

Gail could have cared less about a divorce, for no longer did she need Geoffrey's financial support. Anyway, all kinds of people were living openly together these days without benefit of marriage, and was an option open to her. Until she found someone who loved her, she decided to live alone.

Her social life was wonderful because she had become ultra glamorous and dressed in the height of style. Visits to the health spa and cosmetician, masseuse and gym shaped and reformed her slim body. She suddenly became very attractive to men who would never have given her a glance before she took over the company. Gail perceived it was her money that attracted these would be suitors, but she used them. Their flattery and attention made her blossom. How proud John would be, how proud of her looks and accomplishments. She had no debts, no financial worries, she had found John's money and business, taken it over and was now self-supporting.

Business and busyness completely changed her life. At times she mused on how far she had come in the years since John's death, how different a person she was. Monterey Enterprises, through her efforts diversified widely. It was profitable and working toward a first billion-dollar year. The press and the business world feted her as a shining example of female entrepreneurship. She had her choice of lovers, and was very discreet.

Gail entertained Toronto's finest citizens at her large country home, amazed how easily she fit into their social strata. The tricks she learned in entertaining while married to John, and later to Geoffrey, proved their use. She hired caterers and agencies to do the actual work. It went to show what money could do, especially when you had lots of it, she thought. Not only was she a friend to the nouveau riche like herself, but she now gained entrance to some of the finest homes in the city.

Yes, she told herself often, she was content, not happy but content. She would be happier still when Robert came into his entire inheritance, when she knew he had settled in a profession, or took over River's End.

When Jill died in the spring, Gail blew a sigh of relief, but her death clearly devastated Geoffrey. He spent several weeks in a clinic suffering from depression, or so his letter told her. But then Gail learned Geoffrey was suffering from advanced illness aggravated by AIDS and very frail. Now he wrote that in a week he was to enter a hospice. She felt a great sorrow when she read his letter. Geoffrey was a good sort and had treated her well, no matter how much they disagreed. He even sounded pleased when she phoned and told him of her intentions to return to England. On her arrival, she said, she would take over River's End for Robert until he finished his higher education. He was studying hard to become a physicist.

She hired a new Chief Operating Officer and arranged her sabbatical. Soon everything was in place. The company did not require her daily attendance and even her weekly update calls were already unnecessary.

Gail settled back at River's End in her old rooms. Tomorrow was another day, but it would be as bright and cheerful as this one. She knew it, just like Scarlet O'Hara.

- E N D -